I0544055

Villainy in Vienna

- or -

Scull-duggery in Sanditon

WORKS BY THIS AUTHOR

Writing as S.M. Klassen

What Really Happened Before Mr. Darcy's Wedding
    A prequel to *Mary, Mary, Not So Ordinary*

The Adventures of Miss Mary Bennet, Continuing the tale of Jane Austen's *Pride and Prejudice*:

    Volume I: *Mary, Mary, Not So Ordinary*

    Volume II: *Mary, Mary, Oh So Contrary*

    Volume III: *Mary, Mary, How Extraordinary*

Above-Stairs/Below-Stairs Regency Era Mysteries,
keeping alive the characters from Jane Austen's *Pride and Prejudice*
and continuing *The Adventures of Miss Mary Bennet*:

    Volume I: *Mayhem at the Minster*

    Volume II: *Parlance at Pemberley*

    Volume III: *Villainy in Vienna*
                –or– *Scull-duggery in Sanditon*

Writing as Shelly McDunn

City of Dread (2nd edition 2025)
    A 1919 New Orleans Mystery

A Superior Menace
    A South Shore Mystery, continuing the story of Detective Jimmy
    O'Connor and Lillette Montague from *City of Dread*

Spies, Lies, & Shoo-Fly Pie
    A Jamey Knight Mystery

~ The characters of Jane Austen's Pride and Prejudice
live on in this series, continuing S.M. Klassen's
The Adventures of Miss Mary Bennet *~*

Villainy in Vienna

- or -

Scull-duggery in Sanditon

A Regency Era Above-stairs/Below-stairs Mystery
Volume III

S.M. Klassen

2nd edition
HOBBINS & DONAVON PRESS

Villainy in Vienna is a work of fiction, and the views expressed herein are the sole responsibility of the author. Likewise, certain characters, places, and incidents are the product of the author's imagination, and any resemblance to actual persons, living or dead, or actual events, is entirely coincidental.

Second edition published 2025
First edition published 2022

ISBN Paperback: 978-1-967523-06-1

SELECTED SOURCES

Austen, Jane. *Pride and Prejudice, a novel in three volumes by the author of "Sense and Sensibility."* London: Printed for T. Egerton, Military Library, Whitehall, 1813. www.gutenberg.org/ebooks/1342

Austen, Jane, "and Another Lady." *Sanditon*. Boston: Houghton Mifflin Company, 1975.

Jane Austen Collection: 18 Works, Pride and Prejudice, Emma, Love and Friendship, Northanger Abbey, Persuasion, Lady Susan, Mansfield Park & more! [Illustrated] Kindle Edition: Doma Publishing House, 2014.

Beresford, James. *The Miseries of Human Life; or the Groans of Samuel Sensitive, and Timothy Testy, with a Few Supplementary sighs from Mrs. Testy*. In Twelve Dialogues. London: Printed for William Miller, Albemarle-Street, by W. Bulmer and Co. Cleveland-Row, 1806. https://archive.org/details/miseriesofhumanl00bere/page/n9/mode/2up

Evelyn, John. William Bray, ed. *The Diary of John Evelyn, in two volumes*. Washington and London: M. Walter Dunne, 1901. www.gutenberg.org/ebooks/41218

Hutton, William. *The History of the Roman Wall, Which Crosses the Island of Britain, From the German Ocean to the Irish Sea. Describing Its Antient* [sic] *State, and Its Appearance in the Year 1801*. 2d ed. London: Nichols, Son, and Bentley, 1813.

Raffald, Elizabeth. *The Experienced English Housekeeper, For the Use and Ease of Ladies, House-keepers, Cooks, etc. Wrote* [sic] *Purely from Practice, And dedicated to the Hon. Lady Elizabeth Warburton*. Manchester: Printed by J. Harrop, for the author, 1769. https://archive.org/details/experiencedengl01raffgoog/page/n7/mode/2up

King, David. *Vienna 1814: How the Conquerors of Napoleon Made Love, War, and Peace at the Congress of Vienna*. New York: Harmony Books, 2008.

Scott, Sir Arthur. *Lady of the Lake*. Edinburgh: 1810. (E-book version: Boston, 1883.) https://www.gutenberg.org/files/3011/3011-h/3011-h.htm

SELECTED CHARACTERS

(P) From Jane Austen's *Pride and Prejudice,* begun in 1797, published anonymously in three volumes in 1813.

(S) From Jane Austen's *Sanditon*, an unfinished novel, begun in 1817.

(H) Taken from history.

All others created by S.M. Klassen.

(P) Annesley, Mrs: *former companion to Georgiana Darcy*

Ashton, Christopher: soon to retire from Col Fitzwilliam's regiment. (married Mary Bennet)

Beasely, Amelia: engaged to Lord Exeter

(P) Bennet, Mr & Mrs: of Longbourn in Hertfordshire.
   5 daughters: *Jane; Elizabeth (Lizzy); Mary; Catherine (Kitty); Lydia*

(P) Bingley, Mr (Charles): now of Beechwood Manor in Derbyshire (married Jane Bennet, daughter: Eliza)

(P) Bingley, Caroline: Mr Bingley's possibly betrothed sister

Bonnie Morgan (formerly Georgy): the Ashtons' spaniel puppy

(H) Castlereagh, Lord (Robert Stewart, (1769-1822)): British foreign secretary *1812-1822, married Amelia (Emily) Anne Stewart, Almack's patroness and arbiter of London respectability*

Chadwick, Mrs: the Ashtons' housekeeper in London

Chandler, Mr (James): *Fitzwilliam family acquaintance (married Anne de Bourgh of Rosings Park)*

(P) Collins, Mr: heir to Longbourn (married Charlotte Lucas)

Culpepper, Mr (Archibald): school chum of Mr. Bingley's

(P) Darcy, Mr (Fitzwilliam): of Pemberley (married Elizabeth Bennet, son: Gregory)

(P) Darcy, Georgiana: Mr Darcy's younger sister

(P) de Bourgh, Lady Catherine: Darcy/Col. Fitzwilliam's maternal aunt; from Rosings, in Kent; daughter: Anne (married James Chandler)

(S) Denham, Lady (of Sanditon House): Aunt to Sir Edward Denham

(H) Egerton, Thomas (c. 1784-1830): Mary Ashton's publisher

Exeter, Lord (Reggie): society gossip (unmarried)

(H) Evelyn, John (1620-1706): writer, diarist, gardener, etc.

(P) Fitzwilliam, Colonel (Richard): 1st cousin to Darcy, 2nd son of Lord and Lady Matlock of Devonham

Fletcher, Mr: butler at the Ashtons' house on Hertford-street, London

Hartleton, Mr (Perceval): Scholar/Bingley's school friend

(P) Hurst, Louisa, and Mr: Bingley's sister & brother-in-law

(H) Hutton, Catherine (1756-1846): English novelist/letter-writer

Lord Harold (Harry): colleague of Major Ashton & Col. Fitzwilliam
Lucy Pearl: lady's maid to Georgiana Darcy *Matlock, Lord & Lady*:
   (Earl & Countess of Devonham); Colonel Fitzwilliam's
   parents/maternal aunt & uncle to the Darcys
Molly Turner: lady's maid to Mary Ashton (née Bennet)
(S) Parker, Thomas: investor & promoter of Sanditon (wife: Mary)
(S) Parker, Arthur, Diana, Susan & Sidney: siblings of Thomas
(P) Reynolds, Mrs: housekeeper at Pemberley
Steele, Neville: from Audley Abbey in Kent, friend of Charles Bingley
(P) Wickham, George: son of the elder Darcy's steward (married
   Lydia Bennet)

SELECTED LOCATIONS:
(P) From *Pride and Prejudice*
(S) From *Sanditon*
All others from *The Adventures of Miss Mary Bennet* by S.M. Klassen.

Beechwood Manor: Charles/Jane Bingley home in Derbyshire
Devonham: Colonel Fitzwilliam's family estate in Derbyshire
(P) Longbourn: Bennet family home in Hertfordshire
(P) Meryton: town near Longbourn in Hertfordshire
(P) Pemberley: Darcy family estate in Derbyshire
(P) Rosings: de Bourgh estate in Kent
(S) Sanditon: seaside town on the Sussex coast
(S) Sanditon House: residence of Lady Denham

Friendship is certainly the finest balm
for the pangs of disappointed love.
— Jane Austen, *Northanger Abbey*

'My idea of good company...is the company of clever,
well-informed people, who have a great deal of conversation;
that is what I call good company.'
'You are mistaken,' said he gently,
'that is not good company; that is the best.'
— Jane Austen, *Persuasion*

Chapter 1

~~~~

~a letter from Georgiana Darcy to her former companion~

Sanditon House
October 1814

Dear Mrs. Annesley,

As you are aware, my cousin Anne de Bourgh left Lord Wickford at the alter last June and eloped to Scotland with Mr. James Chandler. At the time, Lady Catherine refused to acknowledge the union and arranged to disinherit her daughter irrevocably.

Despite little reason to do so, Mrs. Darcy held fast to the hope of a reconciliation and devised a parlance of sorts at Pemberley, her scheme being to reunite mother and daughter by holding a second wedding in our chapel. It was some time before Lady

Catherine agreed to the plan, but only under certain conditions—one being that Mr. Collins would perform the ceremony. He obliged, of course, and, despite a bit of drama, Anne was eventually well and truly married.

After the wedding, Aunt Catherine agreed to travel with her daughter and son-in-law to his ancestral home in Scotland. Considering the length and difficulty of the journey, this must be considered an excellent sign of improved relations.

Almost as soon as the carriages were out of sight, Fitzwilliam suggested a visit to the seaside. Specifically to Sanditon, where Mr. and Mrs. Gardiner have recently taken to residing during the summer months.

Given the fine weather we were soon on our way, in company with the Ashtons and the Bingleys. We stopped frequently, and after several nights at coaching inns we are now settled at Sanditon House, the grand home of Lady Denham. It is a fine place, to be sure, but set in the countryside. The Gardiners live in town and can walk along the seashore on a whim. (Fitzwilliam says we were lucky to find a house with so little notice and we are determined to be content.)

Miss Bingley and the Hursts claimed Sanditon is not fashionable enough, despite handsome assembly rooms and a long promenade beside the strand. They have gone to Bath instead, where they believe Mr. Hurst's gout will benefit from the healing powers of the water there. The distance from Pemberley is considerable, so they will probably not be returning to Derbyshire for some time.

The residents of Sanditon say the weather is unusually warm for so late in the year, which allows us to experience sea-bathing. Mrs. Ashton does not care for the shock of cold water (or changing out of a wet swimming costume in the bathing-machines) and therefore observes us from under cover of a tent on the sandy beach.

This is a place where nature is yet unspoiled and we take great pleasure in walking. As for society, the Gardiners introduced us to Mr. Thomas Parker and his family (it was he who convinced Aunt and Uncle Gardiner to purchase a house here). There is to be a gathering this evening at the Parkers' home, including his sisters, Susan and Diana Parker, and one of his brothers, *Mr. Arthur Parker, a gentleman obsessed with his health. He consults physicians frequently but without fail acts contrarily to their advice, instead relying on his sisters' recommendations for treating what may in fact be imaginary ills.*

In your last letter you asked after Lord Harold, who has been ordered to Vienna for the congress. You know I once entertained feelings for him but that has all come to an end. It is not only due to persistent rumours regarding his disinheritance, but recently Mrs. Ashton and I viewed his former home in London, which is for sale, and what we saw there has unfortunately led to further speculation.

Mrs. Darcy asked Mr. Bingley's school friend, Mr. Hartleton, to join us here. In the past weeks he has been using the Pemberley library for his research and chose to remain in Derbyshire to continue his work. He has with him his English Mastiff, a sweet, but fierce-looking animal. Recently, certain residents at the Albany complained about the size of the dog and as a result the two are quite homeless. He plans to return to London soon, for he is considering the purchase of one of the houses Mrs. Ashton and I viewed in his company, along with Lord Exeter. It is a beautiful place, though perhaps too large for an unmarried gentleman.

After viewing several houses, the Ashtons decided to remain in the house on Hertford-street. Christopher let us believe the house was owned by his Aunt Hermione, not by him, so Mary would not feel obliged to stay there, but she truly prefers it to all others. It is ideally situated and perfect in every way for them, especially now one of the larger rooms is to be converted into a library.

We are so pleased you and your sister will be with us for Christmas. My little nephew is an affectionate, cheerful infant, who has just begun to laugh and to grab his toes.[1]

Yours affectionately,
Georgiana

---

[1] Mrs. Annesley's sister is Mrs. Halifax, a midwife, who presided at Gregory Darcy's birth in June.

~~~~~

~a letter from Molly Turner to Mrs. Turner~

October 1814

Dear Mrs. Perkins,

Thank you for kindly reading my letters to my mother. I hope you and your family are well and that you enjoy hearing our news.

Dear Mum,

Harriet and Lucy asked me to send their greetings, as have Mrs. Ashton and Miss Darcy, who still help us with our letter writing.

Did the mustard paste help your cold? I copied the receipt from a book in the stillroom at Pemberley. There is a little footnote saying it can also take away the pain of a bee sting.

The grand lady whose house we are in has gone to visit cousins and left only a shy maid and an unhappy cook behind. It's a big house, and if Mr. and Mrs. Darcy hadn't brought some of their own servants from Pemberley the work would never get done.

On the way here the road was often little more than a narrow path. At times it was very rocky and on one of the days a carriage wheel got stuck on top of a boulder. Lucy and I were leaning so far to the side we thought it would topple over and be the end of us. After that, the road (you would call it a path) was covered by grass and the coachman could hardly make it out. We were so near the edge of a steep cliff that we held on to each other for dear life.

This house is not far from the town, which is right next to the water, and Mrs. Ashton and Miss Darcy said we should try sea-bathing. Yesterday, Lucy and I walked across the sand to what looked like a gypsy vardo (Mrs. Ashton says they call it a caravan). It was like those we've seen at the fair, but smaller. Inside there were plain benches and hooks for our clothes, with a door on either end. After we changed into our bathing-dresses, the horse pulled the whole thing into the water, and we had to sit down fast or we would have fallen. The dipper, as the bathing *helpers are called, was strong as a man. She helped me down the steps into the waves and tied a rope round my waist before pulling me away from the shore (you can be sure I held tight to her rope). She stopped when the water was just below her shoulders and lifted me up and told me to stretch out, flat on my back.*

Would you believe I was floating on top of the waves? I was thinking how lucky I was, looking up at the blue sky and puffy clouds, when I saw Lucy standing at the top of the vardo steps. She looked as scared as I've ever seen her, and the other dipper had to force her out.

Lucy says she'll never go again. If I do, I will alter the bathing costume. The one I wore blew up like a balloon in the water.

I must tell you about poor Harriet. The cook here complained about having to serve so many, being used to only the grand lady and her young companion, and never any guests for dinner. Harriet, being the kind person she is, offered to help and she's been in the kitchen ever since. Yesterday the cook gave her full charge of the apple butter, which she calls black butter because there's licorice in the receipt, which she said comes from Jersey Island, where she was raised.

Lucy and I helped peel and cut the apples, but later Harriet had to tend the fire and stir the mixture constantly, so we took on her regular duties. When I went to arrange Mrs. Bingley's hair, she said to do it in any style I liked. She is the oldest of the three sisters who have much in common but are still very different. One thing for certain is they are all kind mistresses.

The cook doesn't like talking at mealtimes and gives us fierce looks if we so much as whisper to each other, very different from Pemberley, where we are encouraged to talk during meals. I thought about offering to read some stories to them but don't think I will. There are some, I've found, who won't be pleased no matter what.

Bonnie, the Ashtons' spaniel puppy, has just come in to tell me it's time for her walk. I'll write with more news next week, and Harriet says she'll send a letter just as soon as she gets the black butter jars sealed with wax.

Your daughter,
Molly

Chapter 2

Fitzwilliam Darcy, his hair damp from a recent immersion in the bracing water of the Channel, found his wife Elizabeth in the front sitting room. The windows were opened wide to allow for a pleasant breeze and a view of the expansive lawn, with Lady Denham's milch asses in the distance.

"Why are you frowning, Lizzy?" he asked, coming to sit next to her.

"I was comparing the view from this room to Aunt and Uncle Gardiner's view of the sea."

"You would prefer to reside in town?"

"Perhaps." She smiled softly. "But I am very happy to be here, no matter the house or location."

"There's no harm in making comparisons. Mr. Parker tells me that a number of new terrace houses along the promenade are nearing completion and offered to show them to us."

She lifted a single brow. "I'm sure we would all enjoy a tour."

"He did say those houses may not accommodate us all."

"Should we ever decide to lease one, could we not squeeze together? After all, this is Sanditon, not Mayfair."

Darcy laughed. "There is something about being so near the sea...I begin to understand why Charles and Jane wish to venture out again aboard one of his ships."

Elizabeth frowned. "With Napoleon on Elba, surely travel must be safer?"

"Charles would never go while there was risk of that kind." Darcy looked round the room. "This house is not the style I like, but we were lucky to lease it."

Elizabeth laid a hand on his arm. "It was not purely luck. Uncle Gardiner says Lady Denham only decided to let Sanditon House when she learned that Mr. Darcy of Pemberley in Derbyshire was to make a long visit."

"Given what we've heard about her, he may be right," said Darcy. "But, for all our good fortune, I can't help thinking it would be pleasanter near the sea. It would certainly be easier on the horses." He ran a hand through his hair. "I wonder if the lady would have been so keen had she seen me in this state—even my valet is growing less strict."

"Apparently so," teased their brother-in-law, Charles Bingley, who had entered quietly, his own curled locks evidence of a recent plunge. He collapsed into one of the few comfortable chairs in the house. "I feel extraordinarily hungry. Do you think the cook would oblige us with a cold luncheon?"

Darcy was about to ring the bell, but Elizabeth motioned for him to stop. "There is no need. Aunt and Uncle Gardiner have asked us to come to them."

"They will no doubt offer sustenance, along with a view of the sea," said Darcy.

"A perfect combination," responded Bingley happily as they followed Elizabeth from the room.

* * *

In the breakfast room the next morning, Mary Ashton was spreading red marmalade made from Lady Denham's quinces on a crumpet when Georgiana Darcy gasped from behind a recent copy of the *Morning Post*.

"There has been a dreadful accident in St. Giles! An explosion at a brewery, resulting in a great cascade of beer."

Mary set the crumpet down. "Beer?"

"Incredibly, yes." Georgiana lowered the paper. "A huge vat burst, and the beer smashed through a wall twenty-two inches thick! The devastation is said to be equal to a great fire or earthquake." She ran a finger down the page. "The victims were women and children...one perished along with her three-year-old daughter...another drowned in the basement of her home. According to the writer, her son had died days before and she was with the body."[2]

Mary was looking at the illustration, horrified. "What is being done to help the people there?"

Georgiana read further. "There is to be a special meeting of parliament."

"Which means those in need of immediate attention may not get help soon...there must be something we can do."

Just then, the Darcys, Bingleys, and Christopher Ashton entered the breakfast room with glowing, telltale complexions.

Georgiana quickly told them about the flood and the newspaper was handed round. Once seated at the table they discussed their options and Jane suggested they each send instructions to their London housekeepers to bring food, clothing, and any other useful household goods to the affected area as soon as may be. "Those who bring the supplies can learn what more is needed."

Her plan was unanimously approved, and Elizabeth went to fetch writing materials.

A short time later, after Darcy instructed one of their footmen to send the letters by special messenger, they left the breakfast room together. Bonnie, the Ashtons' six-month-old spaniel, at the other end of the hall, gave a short bark and pulled hard on the lead, surprising Molly, who lost hold of it.

The pink-cheeked maid rushed forward, but Mary already had the lead in hand. "I'll take her—she knows this is the time for our morning walk."

Meanwhile, Christopher caught the puppy's eye and bent his arm up to his chest. Bonnie sat without hesitation, and he turned

---

[2] According to later reports of the event, which occurred on 17 October 1814 at the Horse Shoe Brewery at Great Russell Street and Tottenham Court Road, huge iron rings surrounding a 22-foot-high fermentation tank snapped and the tank ruptured, causing other tanks to fail, ultimately releasing more than 320,000 gallons of hot ale in a 15-foot wave filled with debris into the London slum.

to Mary in wonder. "Apparently, she chooses which elements of her training to exhibit."[3]

Elizabeth eyed her sister and brother-in-law. "Before you go out, Uncle Gardiner has engaged a boat for this afternoon, it being, as he said, a perfect day to enjoy being *atop* the waves."

Georgiana was clearly delighted at the prospect. "I have wanted to go sailing ever since Jane and Charles' voyage."

"This boat will be a bit smaller," said Bingley with a grin. "But I never turn down an offer to go sailing."

"Uncle Gardiner says it's a beauty," said Darcy.

"And referred to it as a yacht," said Bingley.

Elizabeth could not help laughing. "No matter its appearance or type, he wants us at the breakwater no later than two o'clock."

At the jetty, a crewman in nautical attire stood ready to see them safely across a platform to board the excursion boat. Formerly a fishing vessel, it was freshly painted in green and white and more than large enough to accommodate the Gardiners and their guests.

Once they were under way, with sails raised, the captain followed a course parallel to the shore at Mr. Gardiner's suggestion, who thought the ladies might grow fearful if they went too far out. It was not long before they changed course, however, for the weather was fine, the crew adept at trimming sails, the captain well-weathered, and the boom high enough so there was little chance of being knocked into the water when a tack was ordered.

Upon their return, Mrs. Gardiner took firm hold of her husband's arm. "This is the third time we've been boating since coming to Sanditon, yet I still feel unsteady when back on land."

Mr. Gardiner nodded. "The captain told me it helps to stay near the water at first."

---

[3] One of the Pemberley footmen knew a good deal about dogs and had been assisting Molly with Bonnie's training.

As the group sauntered along the shoreline, Mr. Bingley suggested a rock-skipping contest to his brothers-in-law and Mr. Gardiner.

Seated on a large rock nearby, Georgiana adjusted her parasol. "It is too bad Mr. Hartleton is not here, for I know he likes to sail."

"Does he?" Elizabeth, to her left, leaned back slightly to catch Jane's eye.

Georgiana nodded, her eyes on the horizon. "He said he would like to go with Charles and Jane on their next voyage."

"I think he would find it hard to leave his dog behind," said Mary.

Jane, sitting at the other end, turned to face them. "On our wedding-trip, the captain and his wife had their three small dogs with them. They were delightful and seemed unaffected by the movement of the ship." She sighed happily. "I look back on the entire experience with great pleasure and hope we might all go together one day."

Elizabeth examined a flat stone before tossing it into the water. "I may be brave enough to go with you, for I am becoming quite good at sea-bathing."

The sideboard in the Gardiners' dining room supported enough tempting morsels to satisfy any appetite enhanced by the sea. It was a casual affair, and they eventually separated into small groups.

Mrs. Gardiner came to stand with Elizabeth at the window. "I think you understand why your uncle purchased this house, and why he never wants to leave Sanditon."

"I do," said her niece, watching a group of seagulls take flight when a strolling couple approached. "And I think Fitzwilliam does as well." She glanced across the room, where her husband was conversing with Uncle Gardiner, Charles, and Christopher.

Aunt Gardiner said quietly, "The corner house on the terrace—the one nearest the cliff—has recently been vacated and is available for sale, so I understand. Mr. Parker does not like to see houses stand empty; I'm certain he would be pleased to arrange a viewing."

Georgiana had joined them in time to hear. "The pale pink house with green shutters? It is charming."

Elizabeth nodded. "I thought the same when we passed by it the other day. I will speak to Fitzwilliam."

She went to say a few words to him, returning with a light step. "He will see Mr. Parker as soon as may be. Imagine walking into town or along the promenade at any time of day!"

"The smallest house from which one could step outdoors without fuss would be preferable to a grand one set amidst the hills," said Georgiana, unconsciously echoing Mary, as she watched her dear friend play a clapping game with the children.[4]

"Even if it meant no orangery, orchard, or field of milch-asses?" teased Aunt Gardiner, for all three were the pride of Lady Denham.

"Certainly." Georgiana's eyes were dancing. "Speaking of those animals, I happened upon a treatise in the Sanditon House library, which extolled the extraordinary effects of asses' milk on various illnesses—including gout."[5]

"Perhaps we should transcribe pertinent information for Mr. Hurst," mused Elizabeth, half seriously. "One can only hope the consumption of the milk has *some* benefit, given that the daily purchase of it whilst we are in residence was a singular provision set by the lady herself."

"Something has amused you, I see," said Darcy. "I've been sent as an envoy to ask if you would care to walk along the promenade. It is too fine a day to remain indoors, and I should like to stop at Trafalgar House to speak with Mr. Parker."

---

[4] Prior to her marriage, Miss Mary Bennet was determined to remain a spinster, envisioning a tiny cottage as the perfect abode.

[5] Georgiana refers to a tome by Friedrich Hoffmann (1660-1742): *A Treatise of the Extraordinary Virtues and Effects of Asses Milk, In the Cure of Various Diseases, Particularly the Gout, Scurvy and Nervous Disorders; And of its Peculiar Nourishing and Restorative Qualities in all Consumptive Disorders, and Even the Decays of Old Age.* (Illustrated with Several Remarkable Cases.) Published by John Whiston, 1754.

~later the same day, Sanditon House

Jane Bingley turned her back to her husband. "Charles, will you please do the buttons? Harriet is needed in the kitchen again, and I do not like to bother the other maids." She wore an uncharacteristic frown. "Lizzy says the cook treats Harriet as if she were an under-servant."

Bingley was unusually quiet as he finished the buttoning. "Do you ever find yourself missing home?"

"I do." She turned to face him. "What with the Chandlers' wedding and afterwards coming here, we have been away far longer than I thought we would be. In the past couple days I've begun to think that with his sisters and Mr. Hurst in Bath—"[6]

"—we would have Beechwood to ourselves!" He took her hands in his. "You wouldn't mind leaving earlier than planned, or the long journey after so short a stay?"

Jane's half-smile appeared. "At this moment the thought of being at home—just us and little Eliza—is most attractive."

As they approached the door, Bingley whispered, "If Darcy and Elizabeth have no objection, we could leave tomorrow."

Jane held him back when he would have left the room, leaning quite close to the gentleman Mrs. Bennet had once despaired of securing as a son-in-law. "Sometimes I have to remind myself that we are no longer courting, but married."

Dinner that evening was a hodgepodge affair and they did not prolong the meal.

On their way to get warm shawls, Jane stopped Elizabeth on the landing to say she and Charles had spoken about returning to Beechwood.

"It is this oppressive house." Elizabeth eyed the painted ceiling depicting fanciful sea creatures with distaste.

"We must still be grateful Lady Denham was willing to lease it." Jane waited a moment, then spoke more softly. "The truth is,

---

[6] Caroline Bingley was as yet unmarried and often resided with her brother and sister-in-law at Beechwood, or in their house in London. Louisa Hurst (née Bingley) and her husband were also frequent guests of Charles Bingley before, and after, his marriage to Jane Bennet.

without Caroline, Louisa, or Mr. Hurst and his gout in residence, the thought of being in my own home is most appealing."

Elizabeth arched a brow. "And who knows how soon they will return?"

"Just so."

"If we have no choice but to remain here, Fitzwilliam may want to follow your example. After all, Aunt Catherine is no longer at Pemberley." Elizabeth's face lit up. "He may even suggest we leave tonight!"

The two sisters were smiling as they went to meet the others in the courtyard, for Darcy had proposed an evening ride. An earlier debate had ended with the unanimous decision to travel in a single open barouche, from which they could view the stars. "If I act as coachman and one of you sits on the box beside me—" Darcy made an elegant bow to his wife "—there will be ample room."

When everyone was settled, he lifted the reins and made a clicking sound. The horses proceeded at a modest pace down the tree-covered lane, two footmen with torches and a waxing moon lighting the way.

The Bingleys' departure was the first topic of conversation, which led to idle speculation about how long Caroline and the Hursts would remain in Bath.

"Louisa sent a single line informing me they were agreeably settled. Nothing more since then." Bingley made a long face. "When Jane and I saw Caroline and Exeter dancing together at the wedding, we thought there might be a reconciliation."[7]

Elizabeth turned her head round. "From our point of view it did seem likely. But if so, should we not have heard something?"

"Not long after the set with Lord Exeter, I believe she sought the attention of another," said Mary.

"You mean Hartleton, I suppose." Bingley shook his head. "I thought she was doing her best to catch his eye. If so, she's a fool. He has time only for his research." His shoulders sagged. "I must face the truth. She is destined for spinsterhood."

---

[7] Lord Exeter had allegedly proposed to (and been accepted by) Miss Bingley, who had recently—and inexplicably—changed her mind.

"Never mind, Charles," said Jane softly, pointing upwards, for they had reached the clearing. "The stars are lovely."

Nothing further was said of Miss Bingley that night, but there were one or two—possibly more—in the Darcy party who very much wished she would finally 'catch a husband' and secure a home of her own.

Chapter 3

Little did the Darcy party know, the concerns raised in the open barouche were at the same time uppermost in the thoughts of their subject, Miss Caroline Bingley.

Miss Bingley's previous—disastrous—attempts at reaching the altar were never openly discussed in her presence, and therefore it would not be unreasonable for her to assume those affairs had been of little interest to society (although they were). But now, given the stature of Lord Exeter, the affair was known by a much wider circle and she fully realized if she lost *that* gentleman's interest her matrimonial options would greatly diminish.

Louisa and Mr. Hurst had retired for the evening, leaving her alone in the opulent drawing room to pace from one end to the other while contemplating her future. She stopped to stare into the looking-glass above the mantel, the reflection showing studiously relaxed facial features and perfect deportment. Idly pinching her cheeks, she recalled the evening Lord E had taken her by the elbows and dared to admonish her in full view of several guests at Almack's. (She had been speaking her mind about the faults of Darcy's wife, and about those of the Bennet family in general.)

Immediately following the elbow incident, Miss Bingley adopted a methodical coolness towards him and meant to continue the treatment until he apologized and begged forgiveness. Neither was offered, however, and months passed before there was even a glimmer of hope...when Lord E accepted Elizabeth Darcy's invitation to the harvest ball at Pemberley.

In anticipation of the event, Caroline had perused the latest editions of ladies' magazines for wedding clothes. During the ball, Lord E was his usual charming self during their two dances but made no apology or reference to marriage and her multiple attempts to lure him to a secluded spot on the expansive lawn proved fruitless.

Never one to give up easily, Miss Bingley rubbed the lines from her forehead, set her chin determinedly, and sat down at the elegant writing desk to assemble quill pen, ink, and paper.

~~~

~a letter from Caroline Bingley to Lady Emily Biscat)~

Dearest Emily,

You must find it terribly dull in town, with all society gone to Vienna. One wonders at the attraction of travelling so far to attend a political conference. I would far rather stay in England, where the language is the same and one knows the best places.

Recently, I was again invited to Pemberley, the Darcy estate in Derbyshire, in company with Lady Catherine de Bourgh. I know her property borders your father's estate in Kent so this may be of great interest to you. The event that brought us together was her daughter's official wedding, which was held in Pemberley Chapel. This past June, Miss de Bourgh fled with Mr. James Chandler to Gretna Green, in complete defiance of her mother's wishes, leaving her fiancé, Lord Wickford—also of Kent—standing at the altar. You may have heard rumours, though the affair was quickly hushed up.

Rather than return to a sparsely populated London after the wedding, Louisa and I journeyed to Bath with Mr. Hurst. I searched for your name in the Pump Room guest book first thing but was disappointed. Do let me know if you intend to come here, for I would be pleased to describe in person recent events.

Mr. Hurst claims the steaming water immersion is highly beneficial to his health. Following my first experience, however, I chose not to bathe, but to observe instead the 'treatment for all ills' from the overlooking windows. I find the sulphureous air, combined with excessively hot water, wholly unpleasant.

It is not unusual to see brazen young misses exit the steaming water to parade along the colonnade in wet, clinging linen. No doubt they do so in naïve imitation of a particularly infamous lady whose name I need not mention here.[8] One wonders at this lack of decorum. An exhibition of this kind, especially when witnessed by our friends, would be reason enough for a cut-direct, would it not?

At the Pemberley Harvest Ball—held directly after the wedding—Lord E told me he may be going to Bath. I fear I may have been neglectful in my attentions towards him, for it fell upon me to entertain one of my brother's dearest friends, a great scholar who is shy when in company.

Unfortunately, Lord E was forced to leave Pemberley before we had the opportunity to speak privately. If you see him, do say I will be at home to him here.

Yours,
Caroline Bingley

n.b. Have you any news of Lord Wickford? One might assume he will come to Bath in search of another bride.

---

[8] Miss Bingley refers to Lady Caroline Lamb's infamous habit of dampening her muslin gowns—in all weathers—an affectation mimicked by many, sometimes causing pneumonia or worse (referred to as 'muslin disease').

Chapter 4

The next morning Elizabeth and Jane were sitting on their favorite bench at the edge of the promenade, from where they could observe the change in tide. Georgiana and Mary had gone to fetch Mrs. Gardiner for a walk designed to culminate in a visit to Mrs. Whitby's circulating library.

With a bit of time at their disposal, Elizabeth opened her reticule. "A letter from Mamma was delivered just before we left the house. Would you like me to read it aloud?"

"Please," responded Jane. "I would very much like to know how Kitty and Lydia are faring." (Mr. and Mrs. Bennet's fourth daughter, now Kitty Darnell, was expecting her first child and Lydia Wickham, their youngest, was with her, following a harrowing adventure at sea.)[9]

"We can only hope Mamma thought to include something about them," said Elizabeth as she unfolded the cross-written piece of foolscap.

> *My dear daughters,*
> *I write to the three of you at once to save both time and coins for the penny post. You will be happy to know Mr. Bennet and I miraculously arrived in York without*

---

[9] The ship Lydia had taken from the West Indies to England was captured by an American frigate (as mentioned in *Parlance at Pemberley*). All passengers were taken prisoner. Fortunately, the situation had not escalated and an exchange of prisoners was made with no harm to anyone.

misfortune, save a singularly unpleasant night at one of the coaching inns, about which I will say no more although I must strongly advise against stopping there. You would be given thin stew with stale bread, and no fire in the dining room.

The journey from Pemberley was exhausting. All the while I was convinced we would be waylaid by highwaymen, just as in the scene from one of Mary's books. You can well imagine how I longed to reach our destination. Although Mr. Bennet and I are pleased to be here, the distance is too great for us to attempt again. I am determined to convince Kitty and Mr. Darnell to move to Hertfordshire.

Our carriage was too wide for Grape-street, so the coachman took us to the back of Mary and Christopher's house, where there is a pleasant little garden. Imagine our surprise when we learned that the front door opens directly onto the street, with only the narrowest of pavements!

Additionally, I was shocked to find how small this house is, for I never quite believed Mary's description. Our dear Longbourn must be ten times its size, and I daresay the entire thing could fit inside the Pemberley ballroom!

The house is in a lively location and no matter the weather we can hear the noise of hawkers all day long, amidst the incessant chiming of church bells. Mr. Bennet says we will grow accustomed to it, but I have little hope.

Elizabeth used the page to shield her eyes from the sun. "I wonder if we should keep this part from Mary."

Jane thought for a moment. "She may find it amusing."

"I would not." Elizabeth read on.

Mr. Bennet enjoys the novelty of going out without troubling anyone and does so frequently. He has discovered a bookshop next door. When he first stopped there he came back to fetch me, for on one of the tables was a display of Mary's books! Ever since I told the bookseller Mr. Bennet was the father of the 'lady' who wrote them, the two talk about books and such each morning.

Your father has taken a liking to daily exercise and has walked from here to Kitty's house several times already. He says I must accompany him on foot when the weather allows and the pavements are clear. He thinks by doing so, and by choosing a different route each time, we will grow familiar with this confusing city.

As I think of it, sitting here at Mary's little desk, there is one benefit to smaller rooms, for we stay quite warm and cozy inside despite the breezes, which can be very sharp indeed.

Happily, Mary's housekeeper and two other servants know their duties well, for it is nearly impossible to make sense of what they say (though they insist they are speaking English). My poor abigail says she must ask them to repeat their words slowly every time they speak to her. Mr. Bennet, on the other hand, seems to understand them perfectly.

Jane leaned over to see the page. "Does Mamma say anything about Kitty or Lydia?"

Elizabeth looked ahead until she found a reference to their younger sisters. She read:

Our dear Lydia has grown thin and pale, with deep shadows beneath her eyes, but who would not suffer the same, given her recent, terrifying experience, fearing for her life when in the hands of those traitors? A defenseless female travelling alone—

Elizabeth turned to Jane. "I still cannot believe Lydia was so foolish as to be aboard a ship without proper escort." She frowned deeply. "Nor how Wickham could allow it, no matter how uncaring he is."

"There must have been a good reason," said Jane.

"Who can ever tell with those two?" Elizabeth shook her head and turned the page to the side, squinting at her mother's cross-writing. "There is a bit more." She read on.

...A defenseless female travelling alone, dependent upon the kindness of strangers. Even now, the thought of it brings palpitations to my heart. From this day on I shall

carry smelling salts in my reticule and advise you to do the same!

Again, Jane peeked at the letter. "Is Lydia staying with Kitty and Edward, or with Mamma and Papa?"

"You know Mamma—" Elizabeth made a face "—we may have to ask Papa for details and clarification." She scanned the page. "Ah, here is a clue."

We visit Kitty and Lydia each day.

Jane sighed. "So, she has written nothing about Kitty's lying-in."

"No, but you must know she would have, had there been concerns." Elizabeth refolded the paper. "At least we know Papa is happy."

"Walking along the cobbled streets of an ancient city does sound pleasant, but I hope he doesn't catch a chill."

Just then, Elizabeth caught sight of Aunt Gardiner, Mary, and Georgiana approaching and tucked the letter away. "Lydia's solo appearance could mean Wickham does not intend to return to England."

Jane rose from the bench. "There is nothing to prevent him coming on another ship."

"Except a very reasonable fear of being incarcerated for kidnapping and worse."[10]

Sanditon, October 1814

Lady Denham's milch asses had just been released onto the dewy grass when the Bingley carriage was driven into the courtyard of Sanditon House.

About an hour later, Charles Bingley inhaled the crisp early-morning air with pleasure as he handed his bundled infant daughter, Eliza Bingley, to Jane, who had quickly settled herself inside their landeau. He then waved gaily before stepping inside to join his family.

---

[10] Some of Mr. Wickham's evil deeds are described in the first two volumes of *The Adventures of Miss Mary Bennet*.

Having already said their goodbyes, the five remaining tenants of the grand house waved in return, waiting until the carriage was out of sight before returning indoors.

"We are a sorry bunch, with these long faces," remarked Christopher. "It is a beautiful morning...why not take advantage of our early rising?"

"And look for seashells?" suggested Georgiana.

Mary and Elizabeth were about to second the scheme when a horse and rider came galloping up the stone drive.

"It's the messenger boy," said Darcy, stepping out again onto the terrace, the others following with more concern than curiosity.

Upon reaching the house, the rider pulled hard on the reins, dismounted, and raced up the wide stone steps.

"Major Ashton?" he inquired, his glance going from one gentleman to the other as he reached inside his haversack.

"I am he." Christopher stepped forward.

The messenger handed him a packet with a diplomatic seal. "I was told to wait for a reply, if you please, sir."

"One moment." Christopher went back inside, entering the nearest sitting room, which was also the smallest, least comfortable in the house, presumably reserved for visitors Lady Denham did not care to encourage.

Elizabeth addressed the messenger. "May I offer you refreshment? Something for your horse?"

"Thank you, ma'am—" the messenger removed his cap "—but there's little time." He made a slight bow and returned to the courtyard, where he replaced his cap, reached into his pack, and took out an apple for his horse.

Moments later, Darcy, Elizabeth, Mary, and Georgiana stepped into the small room where Christopher had just begun to write a response.

"Is it bad news?" asked Mary.

"Not, perhaps, in the way you might imagine." Christopher re-dipped his quill. "Richard has been ordered to Vienna and will not be available for the trial of Miss Carlyle—er, Miss LeBlanc,[11] and

---

[11] Miss LeBlanc, a false name, was one of those who helped smuggle escaped enemy officers back to France, as reported in *Parlance at Pemberley*.

he has asked me to go in his place." He hesitated. "I would not care to shorten your holiday—"

Without pause, his wife of four months went to the door. "I will speak with Molly about the packing now." She turned back as Georgiana followed her out. "Would you like to come with us to London?"

Her dear friend was shaking her head. "You understand, do you not?" Her words were spoken so softly no one else could hear.

Mary, with only a hint of disappointment, whispered, "I believe I do."

Before anything more could be said, Darcy and Elizabeth stepped into the corridor and Georgiana turned to them with a determined smile.

"You know," said Elizabeth, "one might easily take offense at this sudden flight of so many of our guests."

Darcy looked fondly at his wife and his sister. "Shall we take advantage of the morning, as Christopher suggested, and prepare for an excursion?"

Elizabeth returned his glance before taking Georgiana by the hand and pulling her towards the stairway.

Moments later, Christopher stepped outside to hand his response to the messenger, then went to find Mary in their chamber, where she had already given instructions to Molly.

"The journey back to London must be completed without delay and will not be very pleasant, I'm afraid. Also, it would be best if we could leave tomorrow morning. Are you sure you want to come?"

Mary nodded firmly. "We could leave *this* morning if necessary." She stepped closer to him and took his hand. "I assume you would like to speak with your valet, but afterwards, might we go to the seaside one last time?"

He lifted her hand to his lips. "I will meet you directly."

"I have news," announced Darcy once they were underway, this time with the coachman in the driver's box. "Mr. Parker contacted the agent regarding the house by the cliff. We may see it this afternoon if convenient." His announcement brought immediate, affirmative responses, followed by pleasant speculation.

Once they stepped down from the carriage Georgiana took Mary's arm. "It seems you and I are destined to view houses together."

"And what a pleasure it will be, even without Lord Exeter, or Mr. Hartleton, to advise and entertain us."

Suddenly, Elizabeth waved to a couple strolling towards them. "It's Aunt and Uncle Gardiner!"

Once met, the two parties moved on together, the Gardiner children waiting only until their father cheerfully waved them away to begin hunting for seashells, baskets in hand. The adults followed in a stop-and-start fashion, for the waves had to be watched frequently, and careful examination made of each shell found either by the children or by themselves.

Later in the day, after the Gardiners returned home, the Darcy party met Mr. Parker at the seaside house, which he proudly referred to as a detached villa.

Stepping into the modest vestibule, they saw through to the sitting room at the end of the main corridor, where the view from a bank of windows included the gazebo they often chose as a meeting place, the cheerfully-painted bathing machines standing near the water, and the sea beyond.

In the distance they could also see white-capped waves and ominous clouds. Christopher turned to Darcy. "It looks like a storm could be moving in."

"Sanditon boasts the finest weather on the coast," insisted Mr. Parker. "We have our share of rain and wind, of course, but these newer houses have been built to withstand anything nature sends our way. Sturdy shutters can be closed at a moment's notice, and with only two stories the structure is better able to withstand strong winds—though the occurrence is rare." He leaned forward, gesturing to the right. "You cannot see from this angle, but the house is protected from the north and west by the cliff."

Elizabeth caught Darcy's playful glance as they followed Mr. Parker back down the corridor to view the remaining rooms on the ground floor.

Upstairs, in one of the bedchambers, Darcy and Christopher counted their strides across the room, much to Mr. Parker's confusion.

"We made a small wager about the size," explained Darcy. "Though relatively small, it does not feel confining."

Mr. Parker was nodding. "The unusual number of windows gives one a feeling of openness." He had of course brought their attention to the windows in every room they entered.

"I would prefer this house to Lady Denham's," said Mary quietly.

Georgiana nodded, turning away from what appeared to be a ship's porthole. "And, just as with your house in York, one can step outdoors without ceremony."

Mr. Parker had one more thing to show them. "Each of the bedchambers has a specially built wardrobe, which Mrs. Parker has adopted in our own house, being most particular about how clothing is stored." He opened the doors for their benefit.

After expressing honest admiration for the clever design, they returned to the sitting room where Darcy went to stand at the window facing the sea. "If we go now, we may miss the rain."

Mr. Parker was viewing the dark, low clouds with some concern as well, and after promising to come to his house for tea soon the Darcy party made haste to the waiting carriage.

Once underway, Christopher caught his brother-in-law's eye. "Well?"

Darcy's response was to turn to Elizabeth, whose dimples were showing as she said, "It is a lovely house, with a fine view of the sea."

Chapter 5

Sanditon House
October 1814

Dear Mum,

We leave for London tomorrow, so Lucy and I went to ask the cook if she would share the receipt for her black butter (Mrs. Ashton and the major like it on their toast at breakfast).

On the best of days the cook has a bad temper and today was no different. She turned red in the face and said she never wrote anything down (I think the truth is she wasn't taught how to read or write and didn't want to admit it). Still, I thought if Lucy and I offered to chop the onions she would tell us, but she said she didn't need the help of uppity so-and-so's and ordered us out of her kitchen.

I may try again later, but I just wrote a note to Harriet, who will soon be back at Beechwood Manor, to ask if she could write down all she can remember. After all, she did most of the work to put up this year's jars and I bet she could make it from memory just as well as the Sanditon House cook. Or better.

Mrs. Ashton has so little for me to do that I'll have plenty of time in London for sewing. There is so much fabric left from Mrs.

Chandler's gift[12] that I can make pinafores for every day of the week for you, with special pockets, which I can add to any of your dresses. Lucy and I have sewn them into a number of those worn by our mistresses, and also those of Mrs. Darcy and Mrs. Bingley, which they like very well.

We're supposed to return to Pemberley for Christmas, so when Harriet and I visit you, I will bring your new things!

Your daughter,
Molly

Sanditon, next day

Christopher Ashton was accustomed to early morning departures but did not fully believe his wife would have completed her toilette in time to join the Darcys for a light breakfast. Standing with her at the top of the stairs, he admitted as much. "And you are so beautifully dressed."

Mary laughed. "Molly can be something of a taskmaster."

They entered the candlelit breakfast room smiling, to find Elizabeth, Darcy, and Georgiana already assembled there. Most likely by design, conversation during the simple meal centered on the villa rather than on the Ashtons' departure.

Darcy waited patiently to speak until after nearly seven minutes, when there was a lull. "As it is reasonable to assume we will be frequent visitors to Sanditon, I would like to speak with Uncle Gardiner about making an offer on the villa." He motioned to the inadequate fire. "I think we would all appreciate the comforts of a modern building. And, if Mr. Parker is to be believed, the house would make a good investment." He smiled then, and amidst excited talk the rising sun appeared over the top of Lady Denham's prized stone pines, indicating it was time for them to assemble in the courtyard.

For the second time in two days Elizabeth was saying good-bye to one of her sisters, sounding very much like Mrs. Bennet as she warned against drafty rooms and smoky fires at coaching

---

[12] Molly refers to Mrs. Chandler's generous gift of several rolls of fabric, as a way to thank Molly and Lucy for making her wedding-gown (described in *Parlance at Pemberley*).

inns. "Take care, and please send word as soon as you are safely in London."

Mary promised, then turned to Georgiana, who smiled mistily. "I imagine I will be writing to you about the advantages of residing within walking distance of the sea and hope my letters will have you back here just as soon as the trial is over."

Mary blinked rapidly as she hugged her friend, then took Christopher's hand to help her into the waiting carriage, the two of them waving through the open windows until they could no longer see the Darcys.

Shortly before the carriage passed through the gates, he was using his handkerchief to dab the tears from his wife's face, for hers had been rendered useless. Soon, he handed her another. "I'm afraid your tears are dampening Bonnie's coat, my dear."

A few miles later he eyed yet another inadequate embroidered square of fabric in her hands. "When we're back at home we can look for a concert or lecture that will entice Georgiana to join us in town."

His diversion tactic worked. "Did I ever tell you about the lecture we attended on static electricity?" asked his wife. "It was at the Royal Institute—Aunt and Uncle Gardiner took us. Afterwards, Georgiana and I spent a good deal of time shuffling along carpets to create the phenomenon ourselves."

"Laughing all the while, I imagine." Before he could say more, the carriage abruptly leaned far to one side.

"Christopher!" Mary cried out in terror.[13]

Instantly, he leaned toward the other side, covering his wife and spaniel with his body. A breathless interval passed, then all at once the carriage was upright, proceeding at a much slower pace.

"All is well!" cried the coachman from his box, his next words—something about hidden boulders—only half understood by his passengers. "We'll soon be out of it!"

The two sat up, Mary pushing the front of her cap back from her face as she comforted Bonnie, whose nose was tucked into the folds of her travelling cape.

---

[13] Mary's fear was understandable, for she and Georgiana had experienced a serious carriage accident in *Mary, Mary, How Extraordinary*.

Christopher pulled at the lapels of his jacket and cleared his throat. "I do wonder why Georgiana remained behind, especially since Hartleton intends to return to London." He eyed his wife conspiratorially. "She seemed singularly interested in his research and very much at ease in his company when we were at Pemberley."

Mary looked doubtful. "Directly after the harvest ball, when Miss Bingley tried so hard to keep Mr. Hartleton's attention, Georgiana spoke about the joys of spinsterhood and of playing auntie to our children."

"An enticing picture." He reached for her free hand. "I did see Georgiana leading Hartleton *away* from Miss Bingley...a proprietary tactic, I should say."

Mary shook her head in wonder. "I never thought you were interested in romantic intrigues."

"As regards the man Georgiana Darcy chooses to wed, I am a *very* interested party. I would not wish her to choose a husband who would take her far away from you."

"She would never allow it."

"Still," pondered Christopher, "it is highly possible Caroline will attempt to capture Hartleton whilst Georgiana is deciding whether she likes him or not. He is an innocent, unlikely to suspect Miss Bingley's motives, or to withstand her machinations."

"Ah—" Mary nodded thoughtfully "—I begin to see why Elizabeth invited him to return to Pemberley at any time to continue his research. As added incentive, she told him about discovering the secret room where Darcy's ancestors hid supporters of Charles the Second during the reign of Cromwell."

He leaned back. "I'm not sure I ever heard that story."

"I will tell you later, at the coaching in. It will help you sleep." The danger of toppling over apparently at an end, she rested her head against his shoulder. "I wish we knew if Lord Exeter has any intention of marrying Caroline. Could you not invite him to your club, ply him with spirits, and ask him the question outright?"

"So—" he opened his eyes "—you are not completely taken in by Georgiana's proclaimed inclination for spinsterhood."

"Indeed, I am not."

Chapter 6

Darcy had suggested going into Sanditon so he could speak with Uncle Gardiner about the villa. When the two of them were closeted in the study, Aunt Gardiner suggested Elizabeth and Georgiana join her for a bracing walk.

Dressed in wool shawls, leather gloves, and sturdy walking boots the three went directly to the promenade, from where they could see a few young men braving the water regardless of the wind and absence of bathing-machines.

Continuing on their way, they talked about the previous day's tour. "I can imagine being quite comfortable in a villa by the cliff," said Elizabeth, her eyes dancing. "And Mary said it is at least three times as large as their house in York."

Aunt Gardiner nodded. "The design is more suitable for this area than Sanditon House, which is too imposing for my taste." A gust of wind almost took their bonnets, and they each tightened their ribbons. "Though prior to your residency I had only been inside it twice as Lady Denham does not often entertain."

"So we have heard," said Elizabeth with an arched brow. "However, according to Miss Susan Parker, Lady Denham's niece and nephew are frequent guests."

"You refer to Sir Edward Denham and his sister, Esther," said Aunt Gardiner. "Lady Denham claims they visit her only in hopes of being remembered in her will. The relation is on her first husband's side (the late Lord Denham) who was an impoverished baronet. The only property Sir Edward inherited is Denham Park, said to be in a low-lying area and a trifle derelict." She paused. "It was Lady Denham's first husband, Mr. Hollis, who left her Sanditon House, along with complete control of his fortune."

"Are the niece and nephew at Denham Park now?" asked Georgiana, raising her voice above the waves.

"They are currently away, I understand," replied Mrs. Gardiner. "But last month we often saw them in company with their aunt."

"It almost sounds like the plot to a novel," said Georgiana.

"Impoverished relatives and a wealthy aunt who lives in a dark mansion with only two servants," mused Elizabeth. "Mr. Walpole could do something with it for certain."

Another sharp gust of wind had them turning back. When they reached the house they found Mr. Parker in the sitting room, who had come at Darcy's request.

"But where is Mrs. Parker?" asked Mrs. Gardiner.

"My sister Diana believes my dear Mary suffers from a cold and said she must remain in her chamber or it will fester." Mr. Parker wore an uncharacteristic frown.

"I am sorry to hear it," said Mrs. Gardiner. "May I send something from the kitchen? I know she is fond of our cook's fairy cakes."

"Mary would appreciate the kindness, I'm sure. She said she would enjoy a bit of time with a novel recently acquired from Mrs. Whitby's library. But—" he leaned forward conspiratorially "—she is determined to join me in our regular walk along the cliff path tomorrow."

"Your sisters are ever mindful of the health of others," noted Mr. Gardiner with a discernible twinkle.

"Too much so." Mr. Parker sighed. "But one cannot argue with Diana."

No one contradicted the statement, for each had received advice on all matters of health from both Miss Diana and Miss Susan Parker, who sometimes embraced ridiculous treatments for their own ever-changing, mysterious illnesses.

"Will your brother and sisters remain in Sanditon over the winter?" inquired Elizabeth.

Mr. Parker shook his head. "Arthur claims the windows at the inn are too drafty, even in warm weather, and my sisters always miss the comfort of their own home." His countenance brightened. "It is my brother Sidney who I hope will join us, and whom I particularly wish you to meet. *He* is a model of excellent health and never misses an opportunity to go sea-bathing, even during the winter months."

Mr. Gardiner laughed. "I imagine your sisters have something to say about that!"

"They do," admitted Mr. Parker. "But Sidney only teases them when they try to order him about." He turned to Elizabeth and Darcy, together on a settee. "I am pleased to hear you liked the villa." His eyes went to Georgiana. "Here in Sanditon there is much to offer those who care to enjoy what nature provides, as well as a select society, and the occasional assembly to entertain us in the evenings." He unconsciously repeated what he had told them upon first acquaintance. "Mrs. Parker and I gave up our old house in the country when the new one was finished and have not once regretted the decision.[14] And now, I must see how Mary gets on." He rose with alacrity. "I may be able to convince her to go out walking yet this afternoon, if Diana is no longer with her. Sea air is extremely beneficial to the health."

Darcy followed Mr. Parker to the door, where the latter donned his coat, scarf, and gloves. "If there is any way I can assist you, please let me know. The agent assures me the owner is eager to sell."

Once Darcy returned to the warmth of the sitting room, Mr. Gardiner said thoughtfully, "The price is reasonable...lower than I might have expected." He tapped his lips. "Perhaps because the house is vacant and winter looms."

*   *   *

Back at Sanditon House, a footman brought a message for Darcy, who with a great sigh handed the small square of paper to Elizabeth. "Lady Denham is returning earlier than planned."

Elizabeth's eyes narrowed as she read what appeared to be a hastily written note. "Today, sennight! How can she do this?"

---

[14] Unbeknownst to Mr. Parker, his wife had told Elizabeth that she sometimes regretted the sale of their former home.

"Never fear, Lizzy. It may in the end be to our benefit." Darcy calmly went to the bellpull, the summons quickly answered by their footman. "John, I will be returning to Sanditon."

"Very good, sir." The footman bowed smartly and left.

"What are you planning?" asked Elizabeth, though given her expression she had already guessed.

"I know of a charming house near the sea, currently empty, and available for purchase or lease." He bent down to kiss her cheek. "I will return after the business is completed."

Georgiana, a silent witness in the room, came to stand near Elizabeth, who was looking about with a critical eye as she said, "I will not miss this house and doubt we need be concerned about ever returning...an invitation to tea from Lady Denham is highly unlikely."

There was mischief in Georgiana's eyes. "I understand her visits to the Parkers are generally during their teatime."

Elizabeth laughed as they began to ascend the stairs, stopping for a moment on the landing. "What if there is another interested party?"

"Mr. Parker made no mention of the possibility."

"And yet I am nervous," admitted Elizabeth with a sigh.

The two Darcy ladies repaired to their cavernous chambers, where their maids were waiting to help them change. Elizabeth, in no mood for dallying, was soon ready and went to fetch Georgiana, who she found sitting at the dressing table while Lucy rearranged her hair.

Elizabeth perched on the edge of the enormous four-poster bed. "Shall we wait for Fitzwilliam in the library? It is warmer and the light is better."

Georgiana nodded and soon they descended to the ground floor via the grand staircase, then proceeded at a decorous pace along the lengthy corridor to the library, the shelves of which were filled with handsomely bound books requiring a paper knife to separate the pages. As Lady Denham had not invited her guests to enjoy them, none had been taken from the shelves, the current residents relying on Mrs. Whitby's limited collection instead.[15]

Too impatient to sit, Elizabeth stood at the hearth studying the large portrait above the mantel. "This is curious. Lady Denham's second husband, Sir Henry Denham, is given prominence—" she swept her arm towards an inconspicuous group of miniatures to her right "—whilst her first husband, Mr. Hollis, the one with the great fortune who left her this house, hangs in obscurity."

"Mr. Hollis had no title." Georgiana went to the window seat, idly taking up a well-thumbed volume of Goldsmith's *The Vicar of Wakefield*.

"Of course." Elizabeth tipped her head to the side. "Sir Henry must have been many years older than Lady Denham."

"Much, much older." Georgiana set aside the book and took out a folded packet, waving it in the air. "Here is something to keep our attention—a letter from Aunt Matlock."

"News at last!" Elizabeth left off the study of portraits and joined her sister-in-law at the window.

Georgiana did not immediately refer to the cross-written page, having previously read the letter she was able to recount some from memory. "My aunt and uncle are in good health and well-pleased with their accommodations in Vienna, located near handsome monuments and city parks. She says they were fortunate, for housing is scarce with so many people swarming to the city for the conference. They are calling it the largest social gathering in history."

"Lord Harold must have arrived by now," mused Elizabeth. "Does she say anything about him?"

Georgiana's lips thinned slightly at the mention of the man with whom she had mistakenly thought herself in love. "My aunt says he is already a favourite amongst the rich and titled ladies, married and unmarried alike. Apparently, entertaining them falls within his diplomatic duties, and he is obliged to be charming." She went on, seemingly unaware of her companion's scrutiny. "My aunt also says Vienna is teaming with spies. Lady Castlereagh

---

[15] The treatise on milch asses had been left on a side-table, presumably for their edification.

no longer trusts her own abigail, who came with her from England, and my uncle has twice replaced his coachman."

"One begins to wonder if some form of intrigue is practiced by all governments," said Elizabeth. "If so, we may have judged Harry unfairly—his superiors could have ordered him to entertain certain people in his London house so he could spy on them."

At her sister-in-law's dubious look she said pointedly, "We know that Lord Castlereagh ordered Christopher to court Miss Bingley when Mr. Petersham showed interest in her."

At the mention of that gentleman's name, Georgiana's cheeks grew slightly pink. "We also know how relieved he was when the assignment finally came to an end."[16] She shook her head firmly. "If Harry did not wish his friends to think poorly of him, he could have given us some hint about his assignments."

At this somewhat unreasonable statement, Elizabeth smiled and pointed to the letter. "There must be more to tell."

"There is." Georgiana turned her attention to her aunt's elegant script.

Vienna is crowded with political leaders, nobles, and society from every country on the continent, each intent upon swaying the opinions of the delegations' members and willing to go to any lengths to accomplish their goal.

"I would not care to be there, amongst false friends and schemers." Georgiana was shaking her head as her eyes moved to the next paragraph. "I think you will find this part interesting."

Upon their arrival in mid-September, the Castlereaghs were assigned incommodious lodgings. They have since been moved to an appropriately large, impressive suite of rooms near the Hofburg palace, but I thought you would be interested to know that their first small apartment was at one time occupied by Wolfgang Mozart, who eventually married one of his landlady's daughters (much to his father's displeasure). The lodgings are in a narrow street called the Milchgasse, where the composer wrote the comic opera, Die Entführung aus dem Serail.

---

[16] At the time, Mr. Petersham was suspected of treason. And rightly so.

She looked up. "According to Signor Clementi, the work is more accurately called a singspiel, which is essentially a play with music. We know it as *The Abduction from the Seraglio*. The libretto is in German instead of the customary Italian, possibly an attempt by Herr Mozart to gain the Austrian emperor's approval."

Elizabeth was frowning. "Remind me, if you please. What is a seraglio?"

"Molly and Lucy recently asked the same question of Mary and me, strangely enough. Seraglio is Italian for harem—serail is the German term." Georgiana glanced at the closed door before continuing in a lower voice, "They were reading a magazine story about a recently-wed young lady who was taken prisoner by pirates and sold into a seraglio."

"And what did you tell them?"

"Mary said a seraglio is a very large house."

"I would not have thought gently bred ladies knew about these things," said Elizabeth, half-seriously.

Georgiana leaned forward. "My German tutor had me translate the libretto to the opera as practice—but you need not say anything to Fitzwilliam."

"Say anything to Fitzwilliam about what?"

The two had not heard Darcy enter the library, and Elizabeth greeted him with a cheeky smile. "I would prefer to ask *you* a question...were you successful?"

Going to stand near the fireplace, Darcy repositioned a porcelain figurine to align it with the edge of the mantel while his wife and sister waited to hear his answer, but not patiently.

Finally, he turned to face them. "I have signed a lease for the house."

"Oh, Fitzwilliam!" Elizabeth was at his side in an instant, embracing him. "When do we go?"

"It can be furnished by the end of the week." He paused. "But why are you frowning, Lizzy?"

"Only because Lady Denham has already proved whimsical and may return earlier than stated."

He thought for a moment. "I can request immediate occupancy, but, as you saw, the house is only partially furnished, and there is very little to be had in Sanditon."

Elizabeth was not deterred. "If necessary, I'm sure Aunt and Uncle Gardiner would be happy to loan us anything we are unable to live without."

"You said you signed a lease, Fitzwilliam," said Georgiana. "But Mr. Parker led us to believe the house was for sale."

"He did, but the owner has also proved whimsical and will only consider selling in the spring."

"At least we have a place to stay," said Elizabeth. "I am not quite ready to leave the seaside."

"I feel the same," admitted Darcy, "but sincerely hope capriciousness is not the prevailing characteristic of the Sanditon inhabitants."

Chapter 7

Bath
October 1814

Miss Caroline Bingley, three times disappointed in the getting of a husband despite her fortune of £20,000, had finally acknowledged—at least to herself—that her presumed match with Lord Exeter was in danger of becoming genuine fiction. And food for the gossips.

Having suffered the great humiliation of being taken by the elbows (and shaken) at a public assembly months earlier, she had considered it vital to show Exeter in no uncertain terms that actions of this kind were not to be tolerated and deliberately treated him with cool disdain when given the opportunity. Sadly, such opportunities had been infrequent.

Now in Bath, her fear of yet another failed engagement heightened considerably when she and Louisa, out shopping, had sought refuge from the wind in the Grand Pump Room.

Across the crowded space, Miss Bingley was vexed to see her supposed fiancé in the company of a woman she had never met, but knew was Mrs. Amelia Beasely, a widow with a fortune greater than her own, an acclaimed beauty universally praised for her charm and wit, and a prized guest amongst society hosts.

Caroline Bingley was no fool and recognized the woman as a serious rival. She therefore quickly sought the attention of one of the few unattached gentlemen in the Pump Room: Mr. Archibald Culpepper, a school chum of her brother's she had formerly scorned.

With a brilliant smile she complimented his blue coat, then took his arm and directed him towards her objective. Nodding politely to several people along the way, each holding a glass of the healing water, she suddenly came to a stop as if taken by surprise.

"My dear Exeter!" Miss Bingley was at her most charming. "I am surprised to see you here. At Pemberley, you mentioned your plan to join all of society in Vienna." With an elegant lift of a single brow she glanced significantly at Mrs. Beasely.

If Lord Exeter felt uncomfortable, he hid it well as he introduced the two women.

"So pleased," said Miss Bingley, introducing her own companion, still with a possessive hold upon him. She looked about with apparent perplexity. "But where is *Mr.* Beasely?"

With the slightest lift of a hand, Mrs. Beasely prevented Lord Exeter from responding on her behalf. "Sadly, my husband was taken from me a number of years ago."

"I am so sorry." Miss Bingley appeared not to have heard of his demise as she made a deliberate study of her opponent's face. "You must have enjoyed many years together."

"Scarcely five," responded Mr. Beasely's widow quietly. "But I have precious memories as comfort." She opened her reticule to remove a beautifully embroidered handkerchief. "Only the kindness of my friends kept me from becoming a complete recluse after my period of mourning."

"I am sure you have many acquaintances," said Miss Bingley. "Your children are grown, I assume?"

Mrs. Beasely blinked, then replied calmly, "We were not so fortunate." She turned to Mr. Culpepper, who was by then standing upright after having freed himself from Miss Bingley's hold to remove a mark on his shining Hessians. "Will we see you at the assembly this evening?"

At this, Miss Bingley regained firm hold of Mr. Culpepper. "I believe so. Archibald watches over me when I am without my usual escort." She looked pointedly at Lord Exeter.

"I am happy to hear it," responded Mrs. Beasely. "I must go now, for it is the time I walk my comforter spaniel each day." She dipped her head, and Lord Exeter made a swift bow before leading her away.

Miss Bingley watched the two exit the room before releasing Mr. Culpepper. "What time should Louisa and I expect you to arrive at our lodgings?"

"You were serious about attending the assembly?" He looked confused. "I thought you found them tedious and dull."

"It is the country dancing at a dress ball I abhor. Tonight is the fancy ball, with cotillions, which are far superior." She tapped his shoulder with her fan. "I assume you have a subscription?"

"Of course."

"Good. What time shall we expect you?"

"Er...nine o'clock?"

"Very well." She smiled flirtatiously and tapped him again. "Do be prompt."

*   *   *

Perhaps one of the most attractive ladies attending the fancy ball that evening was Miss Bingley, which was no small accomplishment.

She was accustomed to being noticed, and that night was no exception. Behind exotically painted fans, matrons and their daughters whispered about her £20,000, and about two (possibly more) betrothals with mysterious terminations. Therefore, regardless of her evident charms, there was some hesitation amongst the gentlemen to approach the master of ceremonies for an introduction and the privilege of requesting a dance.

Happily for Miss Bingley, Mr. Culpepper was fond of dancing and, prior to stepping inside the Upper Rooms, had thought to engage her for the first set.

It was later in the evening, in the tearoom, when Miss Bingley overheard an animated conversation between a group of older women. Their subject was Lord Exeter's recent engagement to Mrs. Beasely.

Caroline Bingley had too much pride to lose countenance, and without sign of disturbance sipped the weak tea (without sugar or cream). To her sister, she unnecessarily announced her intention to return to the ballroom. "I promised the next set to dear Archie. He will be looking for me."

Louisa Hurst, ostensibly her chaperone, followed her, but slowly, due to the pinching of her new dance slippers. The assembly held little pleasure for her, as Mr. Hurst could not be bothered to come, and she had found scarcely any acquaintances amongst the guests.

Mr. Culpepper was not actively seeking Miss Bingley when she appeared at his side, but managed to seem pleased. "You're in good time. They're beginning to line up."

During the dance, Miss Bingley inquired after Mr. Culpepper's school friends, especially those she knew were acquaintances of her brother as well. "I have not seen a single one since my arrival."

"Now you mention it, neither have I, and Bath is their usual stomping ground this time of year."

"Perhaps most have gone to Vienna—though I know at least one who has remained in England. I saw him recently at Pemberley...but what was his name?" She pretended to think. "Harrington?"

As dictated by the dance, Mr. Culpepper followed the other gentlemen, completed the figure with grace, and returned to her. "I don't know of a Harrington, but you may be thinking of Hartleton—a nice enough chap, if a tad scholarly. Always has his head in one book or another. I did see him occasionally at parties put on by a lady whose name I can't recall at the moment, but it is of little matter for I heard she is no longer hosting." They joined another couple in a circle, and he returned to the topic when they were once more in the line. "I haven't seen him lately, but he and Charles often went about together." He glanced down at her and said with decision, "You must be thinking of Hartleton, Miss Bingley."

She smiled at him. "Mr. Hartleton, of course! How silly of me. He recently visited Beechwood, Charles' new estate in Derbyshire—quite close to Pemberley."

"I've never been to visit but have heard it is quite the thing." He stepped forward to complete a turn with a different young lady, then returned. "What was Hartleton up to? He would never venture so far from town unless it had something to do with dusty old books."

"I believe he was reading dusty old letters."

The two laughed companionably, and once the set was over Mr. Culpepper surrendered Miss Bingley to her next partner, Mr. Steele from Kent.

Mr. Steele had ignored the whispers and in the interval between the second and third sets requested an introduction, after which Miss Bingley granted the sixth set to him. He was the perfect match for her, being extremely well-dressed and nearly as pleasant to look at as herself.

She remained strategically cool in his presence, and it was he who opened the conversation once the dancing commenced.

"I come from Kent, Miss Bingley, where Audley Abbey is my ancestral home." Mr. Steele made a face. "Unfortunate nomenclature, but there you have it. The ancestral pile is just outside Tunbridge Wells." He waited until she caught his glance before saying more. "It is a charming village. You must visit once you have tired of the pleasures in Bath."

This presumption might normally have led to censure, but having seen Lord Exeter and Mrs. Beasely pass down the line together she asked Mr. Steele to describe his abbey in detail, and to tell her all there was to see in the fashionable resort town. After listening to his descriptions of various points of interest with what appeared to be genuine surprise (she had been to Tunbridge Wells on two occasions), she said, "I must ask my brother-in-law, Mr. Hurst, to take us there for my sister and I have never been."

At the end of the evening Miss Bingley was able to greet Lord Exeter and Mrs. Beasely with perfect equanimity, strengthened by the knowledge that she had her hand on the arm of a very handsome—reportedly very wealthy—gentleman, who had asked for the final set of the evening and restated the invitation to visit his abbey.

After Mr. Culpepper had seen Miss Bingley and Mrs. Hurst home, the former wished him a curt good night. Minutes later she rebuked her sleepy maid for yawning, complained about the low-burning fire, and once in bed had lain awake, plotting.

She awoke with unkind thoughts about Mrs. Beasely still in her head when the maid brought tea, plain toast, and the latest edition of the *Bath Chronicle*.

When it was time to dress, Miss Bingley was more demanding than usual about her coiffure, and also refused to wear the morning gown so carefully pressed hours earlier.

Her maid, who regularly told tales about her mistress below-stairs, always performed her duties well, so when Miss Bingley finally stepped outside her chamber she was looking her best and ordered the servants to say she was 'in' to callers.

In the morning room reserved for her own use, Miss Bingley inspected the fire to make certain it had been laid properly, patted the pillows to see if they had been plumped as instructed, and saw that each of the curtains were hanging at precisely the same distance from the windows. She then sat down at the dainty desk, and, with pen in hand, a cat-like smile appeared.

~ a letter from Caroline Bingley to Belinda Thacker ~

Bath, October 1814

My Dear Belinda,

The last time we spoke I believe you mentioned a newcomer to society—a Mrs. Beasely. If you would, please write to me with all you know about her, because a mutual friend of ours has sadly succumbed to her charms. It seems all our friends in Bath have been fooled as well. For myself, I see nothing in her. She is too tall, laughs too much, and has an unfortunate habit of looking elsewhere when one is addressing her. I have no doubt she simply covets our dear friend's title and fortune, with no genuine affection for him. If we are to prevent an alliance, we must act quickly.

Louisa and I will remain in Bath at present, but once our credulous friend is set free, we may leave for London. The quality of people at the assemblies here is inferior to what we have come to expect—undoubtedly a result of that horrid conference!

As the purpose of this letter is urgent, I will close here. Rest assured, when next I am in town I will make a point of visiting you first of anyone.

Yours,
Caroline Bingley

n.b. Each passing moment adds to the seriousness of our dear friend's entanglement.

Chapter 8

Leaning back in the soft leather chair, feet upon the desk in his study, Christopher Ashton was studying the report Colonel Fitzwilliam had submitted before departing for Vienna. Included was new testimony from Miss LeBlanc, whose connections with France kept her stubbornly silent when questioned.[17] That is, until she was given a very realistic idea of her future if she did not cooperate.

Mary stood at the open door, smiling. "I'm sorry to disturb you, but the architect is not here and the workmen are unsure about the window seats." She indicated the report sitting open on his desk. "Has Richard arrived in Vienna already?"

"I doubt even he could make the journey in so little time." Christopher rose and motioned for her to lead the way. As they walked down the corridor he added, "Although, riding horseback and attended only by his batman, it could take half the time as in a coach."

"Going so far on horseback seems risky."

"You needn't worry about those two. They have seen many campaigns together and have traveled through more dangerous territory in far less comfort."

They entered the former, scarcely used, sitting room, the most prominent elements being dust, loose boards, and ladders. The architect had been confident about a timely completion, but the work had not progressed as quickly as expected. It was of little

---

[17] As told in *Parlance at Pemberley*.

matter to Mary, however, who was simply pleased to see the project underway.

After deciding upon the ideal height for the window seats, Christopher suggested they take Bonnie for a walk. "The rain stopped nearly two hours ago, so the pavements should be dry."

Mary, who had never cared for walking in the countryside, enjoyed it very much in London. "I'll fetch a pelisse and meet you in the vestibule."

"Vestibule?"

"I've seen the term often enough in Mrs. Radcliffe's novels, and used it in a chapter this morning." She looked up at him. "It sounds grand, does it not?"

"It does." Christopher made a formal bow. "I shall see you momentarily...in the vestibule."

A little later they were walking along Piccadilly-street, with Bonnie heeling nicely at Mary's side.

"What did Molly have to say about their visit to St. Giles?" asked Christopher, for he knew Mary's maid and one of the footmen had taken a cart filled with clothing and household goods to the devastated area the day before.

"She is impressed by the residents' fortitude, and also with Jimmy's sincere concern for their welfare." Mary sighed. "He will be missed."

Christopher patted her hand, which she had tucked beneath his arm. "He will not leave service for some time, mind you, as he is in the early stages of his training."[18] He waited to speak again until two gentlemen, immersed in a good-natured debate about a recent play, tipped their hats and walked on. "I thought you might be interested to hear that an upper servant is amongst those awaiting trial for aiding in the escape of French prisoners. This servant was privy to many of his master's activities and was able to point out sheltered bays on a map, with access to hidden caves along our shoreline. The waterguard has typically focused on the narrowest part of the Channel in Kent—" he paused as they acknowledged another passing couple "—but this man was able to

---

[18] Major Ashton and Colonel Fitzwilliam had recruited Jimmy for various assignments on behalf of the foreign office. Those in charge were suitably impressed, and Jimmy had begun official training to become an agent.

identify points along the Sussex coast that are also smugglers' havens."

"Sussex?" Mary tilted her head back to see him properly. "Sanditon is in Sussex...might it be dangerous there?"

"I doubt any more so now than it ever was, but I will inform Darcy and Uncle Gardiner."

By then they had reached The Green Park, and as they strolled down the wide pavement alongside it, Christopher asked, "Would you like to stop at Hatchards? We may want to start thinking about how we are to fill all those shelves."

Surprisingly, Mary shook her head. "Not today, thank you."

"Would you care to turn back? I understand our cook is making oysters in batter for our afternoon repast." (The couple had started their own tradition of a light midday meal when they first moved into the house on Hertford-street.)

"Oysters?" With a pleased look, Mary gave him Bonnie's lead. "I believe it is time." As they turned their steps for home, she was thoughtful. "I would like to have books of interest to ourselves and to our guests, rather than acquire a collection of volumes meant to impress that no one dares open."

"You're thinking of the library at Sanditon House, I presume?" Christopher's tone was playful. "I agree with you. Also, one might consider choosing books for the edification of our children."

A blush filled her cheeks. "One certainly might...it is a serious undertaking, which I hope we will enjoy immensely."

"Given the state of the room we have plenty of time."

"I had hoped we could visit the Temple of the Muses one day. Mr. Hartleton says they stock over one hundred thousand books at any given time—both old and new collections."

"Then we shall go."

Once at the house they sat down for the informal meal, after which Christopher returned to his study and Mary went to the garden room, where she patted the settee cushion to invite Bonnie up before opening Georgiana's letter, apparently written with some haste.

~~~~~

~a letter from Georgiana Darcy to Mary Ashton) ~

Sanditon, October 1814

Dear Mary,

We are leaving Sanditon House! Like one of those characters in novels who like to cause trouble, Lady D sent a note informing us that she will return in a sennight, when she expects to take up residence in her home. As a result of this, Fitzwilliam decided to lease the villa.

A seasonable chill has ousted the warm weather so we cannot expect to bathe in the sea any longer, but from the villa we can visit Aunt and Uncle Gardiner each day, and watch the waves from indoors, in perfect comfort.

I had a letter from Aunt Matlock, who has seen the exterior of Herr Mozart's former home (she used the word inauspicious). Lady Castlereagh, who resided there upon first coming to Vienna, described the rooms as humble. (Of note: the Castlereaghs' new residence includes two entire floors in one of the grandest buildings in the city.)

There is to be a much-anticipated concert given by Herr Beethoven, despite rumours about his ill health and exceptional irascibility. He has ever been ill-tempered, according to the Viennese, making one wonder at the cause. I would consider a life in music entirely satisfying.

This evening we will have our last formal dinner in Sanditon House. With the aid of Elizabeth's purse, Lady Denham's mercurial cook agreed to prepare a meal for a large party. This includes the Gardiners, Mr. and Mrs. Thomas Parker, and Arthur, Diana, and Mary Parker, who have returned for a brief visit. There are two others joining us: Sir Edward and Miss Esther Denham, brother and sister, who are nephew and niece to Lady D's second husband.

I will write again once we are settled, and in the meantime look forward to hearing your news, especially about the flood victims.

Most affectionately,
Georgiana

Chapter 9

Sanditon
October 1814

Four days prior to Lady Denham's expected return most of the servants had already gone to the villa, along with the trunks, when the Darcys stepped out upon the front terrace, their carriage only feet away.

At that moment a coach and four came up the lane and a few moments later Lady Denham descended from her landau with determined pomp, giving her tenants the briefest nod. "Mr. and Mrs. Darcy, I presume?" She eyed Georgiana coolly. "Do come inside."

They had little choice but to follow her into the least comfortable sitting room, where she took possession of the most comfortable chair. Unbidden, the cook appeared with tea and pastries, curtseyed, and said a little breathlessly, "Welcome back, m'lady."

Lady Denham eyed the tray, was apparently satisfied, and dismissed the cook with a wave of a hand. She then offered tea, which Georgiana and Elizabeth took plain in hopes of shortening the interview. Darcy, who had stopped to say a few words to his footman, remained standing in the doorway. He had just refused refreshment when that same footman brought an urgent message.

Darcy thanked him and caught his wife's eye before unfolding the (blank) note then abruptly interrupted their hostess, who was extolling the virtues of being in one's own home. "You must excuse us, Lady Denham, but we can no longer delay our departure." He made a formal bow, reminiscent of the one offered when introduced to Mrs. Bennet and her daughters at the Meryton assembly (on the same night he infamously refused to ask Miss Elizabeth Bennet to dance). "We will inconvenience you no further."

Before their hostess could swallow a rather large ball of fried dough, the Darcy ladies had set their cups down and moved to the door, Elizabeth pausing to say, "Good day, Lady Denham. I imagine we will see you in Sanditon at some time or other." There was a distinct flush in her cheeks as she stepped outside.

Upon reaching the villa, they found Mr. and Mrs. Gardiner waiting to welcome them to their new home.

When told about Lady Denham's unannounced return, Mrs. Gardiner shook her head in disbelief while Mr. Gardiner muttered something about the follies of the very rich.

"Never mind her," said Aunt Gardiner. "Shall we look over the house?"

"It would be a pleasure," replied her smiling niece and the five went together to view each room on the two floors, save those in the servants' wing.

Back in the sitting room Elizabeth said to Darcy, "Everything has been arranged so comfortably, we need nothing more by way of furnishings."

Nodding in agreement, he went to the window. "I recall one of us saying how easily we could step outside. Would anyone care to join me in a brisk walk?"

Only Mr. Gardiner said he was willing to face the sharp wind and Darcy turned to Elizabeth. "You will not mind if we leave you?"

"Not at all." Her eyes were dancing. "We can watch your progress from here."

While the two men were forced to hold onto their hats as they approached the promenade, the three ladies sat in comfortable chairs facing out to sea. Leaning back, Mrs. Gardiner sighed. "Only two weeks ago your uncle was suggesting we sell our house in Cheapside and become permanent residents in Sanditon, but with the onset of colder weather his resolve to stay through the winter has begun to wane." She gave them a sly look. "I wonder if now he will wish to remain for the duration."

"I think it would be exciting to experience the change in weather here," said Georgiana.

"Perhaps not every day." Elizabeth shivered. "Charles has described waves the size of Betsom's Hill."

"Those would be far out to sea, my dear," assured Mrs. Gardiner with a twinkle in her eyes. "And as you know, Mr. Parker promises that Sanditon is well protected from such things."

~a letter from Lucy Pearl to Molly Turner~

Sanditon, October 1814

Dear Molly,

We're in the new house now and it stays a lot warmer inside than in the last one. I share with the new chambermaid, and we each have our own cupboard. Everyone calls her Millie, but she told me she likes Mildred best. She lived on a farm before this, and says she never saw so much sand on shoes, even after the shortest walk. We're constantly sweeping it from the floors. I even found a small pile under Miss Darcy's gloves after I had shaken them. You know how much we found stuck to the hems of dresses after only one walk, but Miss Darcy was out four times today! The new cook has always lived near the sea and says to let everything dry before brushing the sand off.

Miss Darcy asked if I could make a scent for her like those you do for Mrs. Ashton, but not too sweet. Can you suggest something? Millie said she would help me (her mum was a stillroom maid before she married the farmer).

I miss our talks at night. Please write soon.

Your friend,
Lucy

Chapter 10

Overnight, rain fell in sheets and had not abated when Elizabeth and Georgiana entered the dining room for breakfast.

Darcy was standing at the window. "There is no sign of clearing yet, so if you two don't mind I would like to take advantage of the weather and see to neglected matters of business this morning."

"Not at all," said Elizabeth, pouring tea. "We thought it would be fun to explore the house thoroughly this morning."

Darcy joined them at the table and took a hot scone from the basket, the three having agreed that such meals would be a casual affair. "You might bring a lantern—it is a dark day."

It was still raining when the two explorers set out with a notebook, graphite pencil, lantern, and a set of keys. They viewed each room in the main house first, before going to the servants' wing by way of a connecting passage.

After taking a cup of tea with their recently acquired cook/housekeeper, a local woman with a cheerful disposition, they meant to return to the main house but found the way blocked by a wooden door arrayed in iron, completely out of character with the rest of the building.

Elizabeth tried the handle, but it did not budge.

"We must have taken a wrong turn." Georgiana's eyes widened as her sister-in-law tried to fit one of the house keys into the lock.

Seeing this, dimples appeared in Elizabeth's cheeks. "We did say we were going to explore the entire house, did we not?"

"We did," answered Georgiana. "We might find the key above the door. Mary often places them there in her novels." She glanced behind her before whispering, "But what if the owner does not wish us to go beyond this point?"

"Fitzwilliam did say we might explore anything on the property." Elizabeth tipped her head back. "Since you are taller than me, would you mind?"

"Not at all." Standing on tiptoe, Georgiana gingerly ran her fingers along the ledge, ducking her head just in time as a heavy metal key fell to the floor.

They stood as if frozen for a few seconds, then Elizabeth picked up the key and slid it into the lock. Unlike in novels, there was no jarring sound of metal against metal, only the slightest click as the lock was released. Nor did the hinges creak ominously when she opened the door. She slipped the key into the pocket of her dress. "Shall we proceed?"

Absently wiping her hands on the skirt of her morning dress, Georgiana nodded. But, given past experiences shared with Mary, she made certain the door would open again before closing it behind them.

The lantern proved useful, though it barely illuminated the winding, narrow passage that terminated at another locked door.

"If we gain access to whatever is behind this, and we see thick cobwebs or hear a ghostly voice," whispered Elizabeth, "we are turning back immediately."

"Agreed," said Georgiana.

"Since the two doors are much the same, maybe this will work." Elizabeth removed the key from her pocket and slipped it into the lock. Following a distinct click the handle turned easily and the door swung noiselessly inward.

The two stood staring into the darkness until Elizabeth took a breath, lifted the lantern, and stepped across the threshold into what was evidently a cavern.

Following her, Georgiana blocked the door open with a brick presumably left aside for that purpose. "Unsuspecting heroines are forever getting trapped inside places like this," she explained.

"Well, if we are trapped, at least Mary can benefit from our experience by using it in one of her novels." With a twinkle in her eye, Elizabeth lifted the lantern and approached a line of crates stacked high beside the stone wall. "Do you think this is the seaside version of a cellar?"

"It could well be." Georgiana leaned closer to the crates. "Most of the labelling has been blacked out on these; what is readable is in French."

"Can you translate it?" Elizabeth held the lantern closer.

"It appears the contents are—or at one time were—bottles of cognac and other French wines."

Elizabeth's brows went up. "How interesting. I find news about tariffs and smuggling tedious. Is there still an embargo?"

Georgiana shrugged. "Fitzwilliam will know, but it is possible these have been here for some time."

Elizabeth moved on to a shorter stack of crates, on top of which she found a small package wrapped in burlap. "All this may be the private hoard of the owner. If so, no wonder we were not given keys. Perhaps we should leave."

Georgiana nodded and the two moved quickly to the door, but just as she bent down to move the brick they heard the undeniable sound of footsteps approaching. In a moment of panic they returned to their place by the crates, each striking a pose of confidence.

As the footsteps came closer, Elizabeth gave Georgiana an encouraging smile. Just then a distant male voice hissed, "George!"

The footsteps ceased.

"She's coming! Get back here now!"

There was a grunt followed by more footsteps. This time in the opposite direction.

Once the sound faded away, the Darcy ladies waited a full minute before exiting the cave, locking the door, and making their way back up the tunnel.

This time they found the correct way back to the main house and managed to get there without meeting another soul. When they finally stopped to catch their breath, Georgiana asked, "Who is George, and why was someone telling him to turn back?"

Elizabeth shook her head. "I cannot say, but I think we should speak with Fitzwilliam first thing."

* * *

Darcy pressed his signet ring into the final wax seal, then stretched his arms wide and yawned, having been up for much of the night with his son and heir, little Gregory, who was experiencing something called teething.

Leaning back in the chair, the first-time father closed his eyes, the sound of rain against the windows lulling him to sleep. At the sound of a knock followed by someone entering he opened his eyes, which widened at the sight of disarranged hair and sooty smudges on the face and clothes of his wife and sister.

Before he could give voice to any of his questions, Elizabeth asked, "Fitzwilliam, did you send a servant to find us?"

"No. Were you in the attic? You show signs of—" he sought the right word "—exploration."

"I think it was something on the walls of the tunnel," said Georgiana, who followed Elizabeth's example and sat down near the fire.

He joined them there, the pelting rain accompanying the somewhat confused tale given alternately by the two young women. When they finished, he rubbed his face. "You're certain the name you heard was George?"

The two nodded.

"I don't recall anyone by that name amongst the new servants."

"Nor do I," said Elizabeth. "Is there reason for concern?"

Darcy thought for a moment. "There may be nothing sinister about it. George—which could be a nickname—might only have been going to the cellar as part of his duties and was called back to perform some task or other. Wine cellars are generally kept locked, and as we have no butler here a spare key makes sense."

Elizabeth shifted in her chair and with a look of surprise reached into one of her pockets, removing the burlap package from the cellar. "I was still holding this when we heard that voice."

She handed it to Darcy, her face flushed. "My only excuse for this thievery is lack of sleep."

He smiled back at her and untied the string holding the burlap in place to reveal a round wood container, the name and place of origin stamped on top. "This is Époisses de Bourgogne, a cheese no loyal Englishman would have in his cellar now, or in recent years." He placed it on the low table between them. "There may be nothing in this, but given Richard and Christopher's recent investigation into the smuggling of French prisoners, along with the unsettled state of affairs with France, it might be best if we say nothing about this for now."

"Very well." Elizabeth stood up. "I must change before looking in on Gregory."

Darcy promised to meet her in the nursery soon, returning to his desk to compose a message to his brother-in-law in London. After the sealed packet had been taken by a trusted footman, he went to find his wife and child.

Later that afternoon, Elizabeth's uncle came in response to a note from Darcy, who led him directly to the study. "Will you take something against the chill?"

Mr. Gardiner was standing near the fire, hands outstretched. "Port, if you please."

Darcy poured two glasses and once they were comfortably seated relayed Elizabeth and Georgiana's tale. "If the crates contain illegally obtained French goods, they could have been purchased by a procurer. Still not legal, but less sinister than smuggling."

"And you're right—George could simply be a nickname for one of the servants." Mr. Gardiner rotated his cigar as he held a taper to its foot. "One thing we know for certain is the owner of this house is elusive. All his business is done through an agent—even Mr. Parker has never met him."

"The desire for privacy, or anonymity, is not unusual amongst property owners, especially those with trusted agents," suggested Darcy as he lit his own cigar.

"I agree. What I find curious is why he didn't have those crates moved elsewhere prior to your tenancy."

Darcy sat straighter. "We changed the day of possession, and that was done through the agent. It's possible he didn't think it necessary to inform the owner."

"But why store valuable goods in a place where he might not return for an extended period? This house has been unoccupied since Mrs. Gardiner and I came to Sanditon. Surely any activity in or around it would have been noticed."

"If the cellar is indeed a natural cave there could be another entrance on the water, or with easy access to it."

"It will be interesting to hear what Christopher has to say." Mr. Gardiner took time to think. "You know, this man George could be one of the *owner's* servants, one familiar with the house, who might still have certain keys."

"And he risked being seen because...?"

"He may have been sent to move the goods deeper into the cave, or to another entrance, perhaps with access to the water." Mr. Gardiner used his cigar to point outdoors. "Although choosing a rainy day when all would likely remain indoors does seem short-sighted."

Darcy sipped his port. "There is another possibility. The owner may be unaware of the cave and its contents. It wouldn't be the first time an absentee was abused in this manner."

"A very good point. But there's still the man who told George to come back. Who is he?"

"A good question." Darcy looked directly at Elizabeth's uncle. "Do you think there is any danger to us?"

"What I understand from talking to Christopher is that until the countries so badly wounded by Napoleon are given reparations by the French, embargoes will remain in place and smuggling will still be a highly profitable, if dangerous, occupation." Mr. Gardiner thought for a moment. "I would not care to be wrong about this, but I cannot see reason enough for you to change your plans." He reached for his glass. "At least until you can get Christopher's opinion."

Darcy sat back with a sigh. "In the meantime, I will speak with my own footmen about increased vigilance."

Chapter 11

Mary Ashton was thinking—not about the pages on the desk before her—but about something Christopher said recently, which, upon reflection, made her feel there was something important she had forgotten to tell him in return. And so, instead of attending to the changes to her latest novel as suggested by Miss Paige, the publisher's assistant, she sat staring out the French windows into the back garden, where Bonnie was chasing her tail.

Suddenly, she rose and rang for Molly, for she had finally remembered what had been plaguing her.

However, when asked, Molly could not say where her new friend Annie had gone to live after her master and mistress were arrested.[19] "I'm sorry, madam, but she never even said where she's from originally."

Mary folded her arms. "Most likely, with her master in prison, she would either have returned to her family or taken a new position."

"I remember her talking about her uncle, but she never said where he lived, other than at the seaside." Molly removed a loose thread from her sleeve. "She *did* say she has a sister in service in a fine house, who hoped to get her a position there."

---

[19] Annie was one of the maids who worked in the smuggler's house prior to his arrest by Colonel Fitzwilliam and Major Ashton. She told Molly her uncle used to smuggle goods across the Channel (as mentioned in *Parlance at Pemberley*).

"Did Annie say where this house was, by any chance?"

"No." Molly's shoulders drooped. "We didn't have much time to talk. Her mistress was in a foul temper, and she had to hurry back."

Mary opened one of the French windows and her young spaniel came running inside. "Do you suppose any of the servants might still be in that house?"

"There is one way to find out, madam. Would you like me to go? They might remember me and be more willing to say if they know where Annie went."

Mary bent down to pet Bonnie. "Do take one of the footmen with you...Jimmy, if he is here today."

Molly's cheeks were tinged with pink. "He's out most afternoons lately. We know he's been training with the Major and Colonel Fitzwilliam, but he refuses to say for what, which is surprising because he likes to talk."

Mary did not satisfy her maid's obvious curiosity, but crossed the room to give the bellpull a tug. "It is probably best not to delay, but you should not go empty-handed. I'll ask Mrs. Chadwick to prepare a basket."

"I'll go as soon as you like," said Molly, unconsciously tucking a stray hair into her cap. "Strike while the iron is hot, as my uncle likes to say."

"Your uncle?"

"On my mum's side. He's a blacksmith."

"This is your first mention of him, I believe."

"Yes." Molly hesitated. "He's something of a black sheep. My mum says it's best not to talk about him too much."

Mary could not help laughing.

*　　*　　*

Later, on her way to speak to Christopher, Mary came across one of the footmen who had a special delivery letter for Major Ashton in hand. She offered to take it and went first to the study, it being his usual time for correspondence. The various papers littering his desk indicated recent activity, but he was not there. In the library she found only workmen, and in the dressing-room she was told by his valet that the master was undoubtedly in the study.

With the letter still in hand, she returned to the ground floor. Near the music room she heard a violin and tiptoed to the door, leaning her head against it until the last note faded away.

When it was clear Christopher was not going to continue, she opened the door and stepped inside. "That was lovely."

"Mary!" He eyed her suspiciously. "How long have you been listening?"

"Only a short while." She drew closer, glancing at the manuscript on the rosewood stand. "What were you playing?"

"A work by Telemann—the third of twelve fantasias assigned by my music master when I was younger." He closed the book. "I'm out of practice."

"It was enchanting...even melancholy at times." Her expression grew quizzical. "I hope it does not reflect your state of mind?"

"Not at all." He carefully placed the violin in its case and closed the lid. "The first section is more energetic."

"I hope I can hear you more often, now your duties have lessened."[20]

He bowed his head. "Perhaps you and I can play duets?"

"For Christmas at Pemberley?"

"Yes, but also for our own pleasure."

"I have been shamefully negligent of the keyboard, but will remedy the situation." Mary held out the letter with the familiar Darcy seal. "This arrived not long ago—it took me a while to find you." She waited impatiently as he unfolded it. "I hope the news from Sanditon is good?"

Christopher scanned the page. "It's partially encrypted, but it seems Elizabeth and Georgiana discovered something unusual at the new house."

"Another mystery?" Mary glanced at the page. "I imagine you would like to see to this now, but the reason I came looking for you was to say we've been invited to another of Mrs. Penrose's

---

[20] Major Ashton had recently requested fewer assignments with his regiment, preparatory to resigning his commission.

literary evenings. She expects Walter Scott to be amongst her guests."[21]

"Some say Scott has taken to writing prose, and that it is a great secret."[22] Christopher pocketed Darcy's letter and lifted her hand to his lips. "I would happily be your escort."

"I must warn you: Miss Hutton is to attend."

"Then we shall brave the fierce authoress together, as well as pay obeisance to the great poet."

*   *   *

An hour or so later, Christopher found Mary at her writing desk in the room adjoining their bedchamber. He waited until she had set aside the quill pen before regaling her with the tale of the Darcy ladies' recent adventure.

"Is it safe for them to remain in that house, or even in Sanditon?" Having begun to pace at the onset of his tale, Mary stopped, hands on hips. "Lady Denham has put them in an intolerable position. She has behaved abominably!"

"I agree about the grand lady, who I am certain would make an interesting character in a book. As to the safety of the new house, Darcy will not hesitate to leave if he has any reason for concern, or to encourage the Gardiners to do the same. I've sent an urgent message to the shore guard, whose attention is already focused on Sussex due to the recent testimony of Miss Carlyle." He took her hands in his. "I came to you before responding to Darcy but shouldn't delay any longer."

With that, he excused himself and Mary returned to the onerous task of working through the long list of changes for her book.

---

[21] Walter Scott did not become Sir Walter Scott until 1820, when he was granted the title of 1st Baronet by the Prince Regent. This was due to Scott's involvement in the 1818 recovery of the Honours of Scotland, also known as the Scottish Crown Jewels.

[22] The rumours were correct. Walter Scott's first novel, *Waverly*, was published (anonymously) in the summer of 1814.

~a letter from Molly Turner to Lucy Pearl~

London, October 1814

Dear Lucy,

The new house sounds nice, but the best part is you don't have a grouchy cook below-stairs! It's chilly here and the leaves are turning. My mum always says autumn begins when the apples start to fall (we had apple tart yesterday). The day after we got here I went to St. Giles with Jimmy and Alice, the maid with red curls. We took a great many baskets of food and clothes. I wouldn't have liked to live there even before the beer flood, and pity those who must stay. Jimmy says seven were killed, all women and children.[23] But there are so many others badly hurt. Mrs. Ashton came with us the second time, along with as many crates of bedding, kitchen things, lanterns, and food as could be gathered, and there is still more needed. Tomorrow I'm going with her to a servant registry office to engage maids strong enough to help injured people, and willing to go to St. Giles by day. She wants me along so I can describe Annie, who we met at that smuggler's house, because she might know something important that could help the major. I went to the house on the south part of Grosvenor-street today, hoping to find her, but the servants were all gone and the caretaker didn't know where anybody went.

Mrs. Ashton is already talking about Christmas at Pemberley when we will be together again, which makes me happy. There are workers in the library every day here, and Bonnie hides under the furniture when they start hammering.

Miss Darcy might like the scent of bergamot orange (citrus bergamia). Any well stocked stillroom should have it, but I'm including a packet of dried peelings if you can't find the oil.

Your friend,
Molly

---

[23] Jimmy had read a slightly incorrect report in the newspaper. In fact, eight deaths were reported following the flood; all were women and children.

Chapter 12

Bath
October 1814

Alone in the drawing room, save for the presence of a footman, Caroline Bingley grabbed the letter from the polished salver.

Once the door was closed behind the impatiently dismissed servant, she broke the seal and began to read. Her look of pleasant anticipation quickly disappeared, however, and had any of Miss Bingley's acquaintances seen her they would have been surprised—shocked, perhaps—to see an unflattering ruddiness flood her countenance.

With no witness to her actions, she dropped the missive to the floor and stamped her elegantly-shod feet upon it before taking it up again, squeezing it into a ball, and tossing it into the fire with such a cry of rage that the maid bringing fresh tea turned on her heels and retraced her steps to the kitchen.

~a letter from Belinda Thacker to Miss Bingley~

London
October 1814

Dear Caroline,

Do you not recall the day we vowed never to attend another assembly in Bath? Such a lovely town that has sadly become a place for young hopefuls of little fortune and failed seasons, so desperate to catch a husband they will risk Muslin Disease in their quest. The gentlemen are no better, as wealth and position are all they seek in marriage. I cannot help but reflect upon how fortunate I am to have met Mr. Thacker.

I was shocked to hear you and Louisa are there now, but I suppose you went in hopes of meeting Lord E, who has always taken great pleasure in watching a parade of fools and later entertaining us with his accounts.

As for your apparent rival, Mrs. Beasely, I cannot write anything against her. Those who truly know her must feel only sympathy for all she suffered when tied by marriage to a tyrannical beast, whose temper was so bad he more than once nearly strangled her. From the very first, Miss Crimson—as she was known to me prior to this unfortunate marriage—not only abhorred, but feared him. Her father had died the year before, and she begged her stepmother not to force her into a loveless marriage.

It is enough to say Mrs. B was a very lucky woman the day this monster of a husband died. Once free of him she was independent and cut all ties with her stepmother, who had, she has since learned, accepted a large sum from the prospective groom to approve the marriage.

Your picture of Lord E as the victim of a fortune hunter is inaccurate, for Mrs. B is a wealthy widow and has no need to marry. Should she choose to do so, it would be only for true, reciprocated affection, something I believe she has found with him. I must also inform you that Mr. Thacker and I enjoy their company and they are frequent guests at our house.

Perhaps at one of the assemblies you will be fortunate enough to meet a gentleman at your level, who can match you in wit. But take care, after hearing tales of multiple unfortunate alliances, the type of man willing to court you now may not be acceptable to your friends.

Sincerely,
B. Thacker

At the time her sister was reading the vexing words in the much-anticipated letter, Louisa Hurst was enjoying the benefits of having laced her husband's tea with a tall measure of spirits. As he lay sprawled in an easy chair, snoring, she reveled in the privacy of the window seat, a new novel in one hand, an iced biscuit in the other, and a glass of sherry on the sill.

The sharp click of heels warned her of an interloper. She swallowed the last of the biscuit and peaked round the drapery to see her very upset sister. Raising a finger to her lips, she swung her legs to the floor and wordlessly tiptoed out, leading the way to her own small sitting room. Once there, she was given an abridged version of Belinda Thacker's letter.

"It is over! I am not to be Lady Exeter!" Miss Bingley stamped her foot. "We must leave, Louisa. Today. I will not endure further humiliation at his hands!"

"Caroline, you know it is not possible in so little time. Mr. Hurst must be awakened, his valet alerted, and our maids cannot be rushed or our gowns will be ruined." She rubbed her brow. "And frankly, I doubt Mr. Hurst would agree to go, as he has paid for the month in full."

"Very well." Miss Bingley's lips were dangerously thin. "I will go alone, with only my maid. You need not send any of your own servants." She stomped to the door. "One of Charles' grooms can return your carriage after I reach Beechwood. You and Mr. Hurst will not be inconvenienced, for if you must go out a sedan chair will do."

"Yes, Caroline." Louisa seemed ready to say more but was too long about it and her sister swept from the room.

Within the hour, Miss Bingley entered her brother-in-law's carriage with the shades pulled down, her angry maid perched outside on the coachman's box.

In the dining room that evening, Mr. Hurst looked up from his plate of roast duck and boiled potatoes. "Where is Caroline? I suppose she is out chasing after Exeter again."

"She is not, I can assure you." His wife informed him of her sister's sudden departure, but not the reason for it, and said nothing about her taking his carriage.

Mr. Hurst harrumphed and drank from his goblet of fortified wine. "So, she met the competition and for once in her life realizes she cannot win." He then applied his silver vigorously to his meal, his wife staring into the fire burning in the hearth.

Chapter 13

Beechwood Manor
Derbyshire
November 1814

On a lovely autumn afternoon, Jane and Charles Bingley were reclining on the south lawn after an impromptu meal of hard cheese, bread, apples, and wine.

Idly watching his daughter Eliza, Bingley was prepared to rise in an instant, if need be, for she was a fast crawler.

"Mrs. Bingley?"

"Yes, Charles?"

"When you were Miss Bennet of Longbourn and I was Mr. Bingley from Netherfield Hall, did you ever once imagine us doing this together?"

Jane leaned her head back to view the clouds, the formation they had recently deemed a rabbit still visible. "I do not think I could have imagined this, Charles, no matter how many novels I might have read."

Suddenly, Bingley was running after Eliza and was just returning her to the blanket when a servant came to announce the appearance of Mr. Hurst's carriage at the gatehouse.

Mr. and Mrs. Bingley stared at one another for a moment, not entirely able to disguise their alarm. Then, with resignation, Jane rose to her feet and shook the fallen leaves off her velvet pelisse.

~~~~~

~a letter from Jane Bingley to Elizabeth Darcy~

Beechwood
November 1814

Dear Lizzy,

Here is a surprise for you: we have a return visitor! It is Caroline, who arrived yesterday, having travelled on her own (save her maid) all the way from Bath.

You must wonder what could possibly lead her to take this risk, as did we. She refused to speak of it until Charles threatened to send a letter of inquiry to Bath with the Hursts' coachman. I must admit the reason is cause for great disappointment. Lord E is engaged! Not to Caroline, as we hoped, but to Mrs. Beasely, who Mary and Georgiana met at an assembly in York, and who you suspected was more than Lord E's 'acquaintance'. The engagement is a certainty for the announcement was in this morning's Times.

We can only hope Caroline's temper will improve when Mr. Hartleton returns. He has not yet decided upon a house in town, but is considering one he saw in company with Mary and Georgiana. In his last letter he mentioned certain documents in the Pemberley library he would like to study further (related to Charles II and Cromwell), but he will not visit while you are away.

Meanwhile, we have heard nothing from Mary since we left Sanditon. And she a writer! She must take after Mamma, who has not responded to my last, written a sennight past.

Affectionately yours,
Jane

n.b. You may be interested to know that Eliza has been standing upright with the aid of an ottoman in my dressing room. Earlier today she stood for a full five counts and Charles expects to see her walking any moment now.

*   *   *

Sanditon
November 1814

Two riding officers, all that could be spared from the limited number of men responsible for patrolling the entire British coastline, quickly ascertained from Darcy all that was necessary to begin their investigation. He led them to the cavern, where they were to take stock of its contents and afterwards seek another way out, presumably leading to the sea.

"It's best we keep the reason for our presence quiet," said the senior officer before they parted ways.

Darcy, well pleased with their competence, returned to the house, intent upon speaking with Elizabeth and Georgiana. However, as he approached the sitting room, he might have chosen to retrace his steps had their visitor not spied him from her place near the door.

"Mr. Darcy!" Lady Denham motioned imperiously for him to enter.

Darcy stepped inside the room, coolly greeting their former landlady before dipping his head to a young woman in a faded, ill-fitting dress.

"You must meet my new companion, Miss Hollis." Lady Denham poked her companion's back to make her sit straighter. "A distant cousin on my dear first husband's side. The fog and smoke of London have had a dreadful effect upon her health—only observe her pallid complexion!"

Darcy greeted the newcomer properly and Lady Denham resumed the topic she had raised prior to his entry. "The situation is most vexing! In fact, I thought you might have taken her with you."

"One of Lady Denham's maids has gone missing," explained Elizabeth for Darcy's benefit, setting her cup down with exaggerated care before addressing their elderly guest. "At Sanditon House, we were served only by those we brought with us from Pemberley, and the agency sent no one who was in your service to *this* house. You might speak with our housekeeper, who is from the village. Or perhaps your own cook may have a notion of where the maid has gone." She offered more tea, pouring for

Lady Denham and Georgiana, but not Miss Hollis, who had declined after the look given her by her patroness.

"My cook would only say the shameless girl took to flirting with the messenger boy." Lady Denham whipped open her fan and waved it near her face. "The disappearance of a mere serving girl would normally be of little matter to me, but as you seem to have engaged any who might be suitable for Sanditon House, it will be difficult to replace her."

"Perhaps it might be wise to learn the whereabouts of the young man," suggested Darcy, who had taken his tea to the window. "Mr. Parker may be helpful in that regard, for he appears to be familiar with nearly all the inhabitants in this area."

Lady Denham snapped her wrist to close the fan. "It is time I paid my respects to the Gardiners—your relatives, I understand." This statement was addressed to Elizabeth. "Afterwards I will do as you suggest and see the Parkers at Trafalgar House. No doubt the messenger boy and the maid have run off together, and by now have realized their folly. But no matter how she begs, I will *not* take her back!" She rose and glared at Miss Hollis. "Say thank you to Mr. and Mrs. Darcy, child."

Blushing, Miss Hollis rose, her head lowered as she whispered her gratitude.

"I do hope we will meet on the promenade," said Georgiana kindly to the unfortunate cousin.

After their guests were gone, she turned to Elizabeth. "I sometimes wonder about her ladyship's nature—to openly accuse you of stealing one of her maids!"

"Never mind her," said Darcy. "If you would ready yourselves for a walk, I will tell you about my meeting with the riding officers as we take advantage of the sun's warmth."

~~~

~a letter from Elizabeth Darcy to Jane Bingley~

Sanditon
November 1814

Dearest Jane,

Recently, Georgiana and I came across a tunnel leading to a cave at the cliff side of the house, where there were numerous crates that we later learned were filled with French cheeses, Champagne, Cognac, and fine lace. The riding officers who routinely scour the shoreline for signs of smuggling came to investigate and discovered an entrance to that very cave on the sea, accessible only by boat. (Notably, the Riders have been discreet, as have we, yet it seems everyone in Sanditon has heard about this.)

One would think that illegal trade between our country and France would have come to an end with the armistice, the crowning of a new French king, and Napoleon exiled on a distant island, but the Riders say it will probably continue while high customs duties exist. Meanwhile, we are enjoying a variety of French cheeses, as are the Riders, the Gardiners, the Parkers, and several others—despite wondering if it is unpatriotic to do so—for the colonel in charge said they would spoil en route to London, where confiscated goods are kept.

Your news about Caroline's engagement is disappointing, though I still wonder if there was ever an official understanding between her and Lord E. Perhaps Charles has other unattached school friends you could invite for a prolonged visit.

Gregory remains content to crawl despite Fitzwilliam's efforts to teach him to walk (which have greatly increased since hearing about Eliza's achievements).

Affly,
Lizzy

n.b. Mamma has not responded to my last letter, in which I particularly asked for advice regarding Gregory's teething. One wonders how you and I ever became good correspondents!

~~~~~~

~a letter from Jane Bingley to Elizabeth Darcy~

Beechwood
November 1814

Dearest Lizzy,

I found your tale about the cave a bit worrying, but Charles insists Fitzwilliam would never allow you to remain in the house if he thought there was any danger. I suppose we must be grateful it was primarily comestibles and spirits you found, and not French officers waiting for a smuggler's boat to take them back to France. Still, please take care.

Eliza has begun to crawl so fast that we must block the stairs. Mamma warned me about this. When Gregory begins to do the same you will never be able to let him out of your sight.

Our nursemaid suggested her own mother's remedy for teething, chewing on licorice root, which Eliza absolutely refuses. Needless to say, I would very much like to know what Mamma did for the five of us.

As for another matter, due to your excellent suggestion we invited another of Charles' friends to Beechwood: Mr. Neville Steele. We have also asked Archie Culpepper, a school chum. This was Caroline's idea, for she saw him in Bath and he is no longer 'irritating or lacking in taste' (her words). We expect them this week, along with Mr. Hartleton and his dog.

Dare I say it would please us very much to have you back in Derbyshire?

Affly,
Jane

n.b. I had a letter from Lydia, who claims Papa is restricting her movements in York. Apparently, despite her being a married woman (or because of it?) he objects to her being escorted to social events by a certain person who protected her when they were taken prisoner by the Americans. Additionally, Kitty does not leave the house anymore, which lessens Lydia's freedom considerably.

Sanditon
November 1814

After reading Jane's letter, Elizabeth found Darcy at the sitting room windows, staring out to sea. "Is the water patrol boat here?" She was only half teasing.

His answer was to put an arm around her shoulders. "I can't help thinking how the discovery in the cave has changed things."

She leaned her head back. "You feel the pull of home, perhaps?"

"Ever since the day I brought you to Pemberley as my bride it is where I most like to be, but I would not care to go until it is *your* wish to do so."

"Jane and Charles have invited three of his friends to help entertain Caroline." She reached up to rearrange a stray lock of his hair. "Mr. Hartleton is one of them."

"You think Caroline will do her best to ensnare him?"

Elizabeth glanced over her shoulder to make certain they could not be overheard. "It wouldn't be the first time she has turned the attention of a gentleman away from Georgiana to herself. Her attempts to do so at the harvest ball were not subtle." She reached for a large shell on the sill, a memento of one of their early-morning walks. "Mr. H is a good match for your sister— anyone can see how she lights up in his company."

"He's a better choice than Harry ever could be. I think I'll have him investigated."

"Should we decide to return home, my only concern is disappointing Aunt and Uncle Gardiner by leaving before our stated time."

"Given how seriously the Riders are taking the possibility of smuggling activities here, your uncle has expressed some doubt as to the wisdom of remaining."

"Truly? And Georgiana?"

"There is but one way to know how she feels. Shall we go speak with her now?"

Elizabeth smiled and took his hand.

*   *   *

Mr. and Mrs. Darcy need not have worried about Georgiana, for she too thought it was time to return to Derbyshire, and was especially keen upon hearing that not only was Caroline at Beechwood, but Mr. Hartleton was expected there as well.

The decision made, they walked the short distance to the Gardiners' house, where their hostess asked if they might consider delaying until the following week. "Given the success of the beach bonfire on Guy Fawkes night, Mr. Parker is planning another to be held in the next few days." She tapped her lip. "There is also the assembly, and we must have a dinner party before you go."

The next day Mrs. Gardiner walked to Trafalgar House to issue an invitation to the Parkers for the Darcys' farewell dinner.

Mr. Parker accepted straightaway, then asked if Lady Denham and Miss Hollis might be included.

Mrs. Gardiner looked surprised but was gracious. "Miss Hollis is a relative of her ladyship, I understand."

"On the side of Lady Denham's first husband, Mr. Hollis," said Mr. Parker. "I'm afraid Lady D offers very little opportunity for the entertainment of her companions."

"I'm certain they would not expect an invitation," said Mrs. Parker with a sharp look at her husband. "Besides, it would make three gentlemen and six ladies!"

Mr. Parker seemed completely unaware of her displeasure. "You are correct, my dear...I wonder if Arthur is available."

Mrs. Parker shook her head firmly. "Dearest, if Arthur comes, then so must Diana and Susan, which makes four gentlemen and eight ladies!" She looked apologetically at Mrs. Gardiner.

Just then Lady Denham was announced and she swept into the room, taking the open seat next to Mr. Parker and pointing to the one farthest away for Miss Hollis. "I heard laughter."

In the brief silence following this statement, Mrs. Gardiner apparently felt obliged to issue an invitation to the two newcomers.

"I do not care to make plans with so little notice," replied the great lady. "But in this case, I suppose I must make an exception. The Darcys were, after all, my tenants."

"Then we shall see you again soon." Mrs. Gardiner rose, said there was much to do, and slipped out before anything more could be said.

*   *   *

Mulled wine helped ease conversation at the Gardiners' dinner party, the first topic being the bonfire held the evening before. Unfortunately, just after the kindling started to burn, a sustained wind off the sea led to panic and the fire was doused before any hot ashes could travel to the rooftops in Sanditon.

"I can still feel the sand in my eyes." Lady Denham's tone was accusing as she faced Mr. Parker, who had planned the event.

Mrs. Gardiner quickly broached a second topic. "I wonder if the Riders have learned the identity of the villa's owner. It seems no one in Sanditon or in the nearby villages can name or even describe him."

"I understand the man has assumed more than one alias," said Lady Denham with more than a hint of superiority.

Mr. Parker rubbed his forehead. "Why did I not suspect something was amiss? The man was never available for an appointment. I simply accepted all the excuses given by his agent."

"The house agent must have corresponded with the owner at some point," said Elizabeth. "Where were the letters sent?"

Mrs. Parker, generally a quiet woman, answered for her husband. "The agent only recently admitted to Tom that he was instructed to leave any correspondence with Mrs. Whitby, which was then collected by a man who is a stranger in this area."

Mr. Gardiner leaned forward. "The Riders have a description of *him*: a plain man with dark hair and no livery."

"Which seems suspicious in itself," said Darcy.

"Never mind all that—there is still the matter of my missing maid!" exclaimed Lady Denham as she chose the most ornately frosted teacup cake from the proffered tray before turning to Mr.

Parker. "I thought you were privy to all that goes on in Sanditon. Surely you have heard something!"

"I believe I may know where your former maid has gone." Mr. Parker set his glass of wine down with care. "Yesterday, I spoke with young Stringer—our foreman for various building projects," he added for the Darcys' benefit. "He is a friend of John Horner, the local messenger boy who has been seen in company with your maid. Recently, Horner accepted an offer to partner with his uncle in Brighton, an innkeeper with no children of his own."

"What has this to do with my maid?" demanded Lady Denham. "Other than she probably made a fool of herself over this boy whilst taking advantage of my good nature." She took a large bite of cake.

Mr. Parker glanced at his wife, who responded for him. "It seems your maid and Mr. Horner have been secretly engaged for a year, and the uncle's offer enabled them to marry."

Lady Denham harrumphed. "She is but a child. And he hardly more so!"

"According to Stringer, the lad is twenty-five years of age, and your maid nearly twenty-two," responded Mr. Parker bravely.

"*Former* maid." Lady Denham sniffed. "Should she ever want her position back, she will be very much disappointed!"

"It was by all accounts a very merry occasion." Mr. Parker lifted his glass. "If the two were here now I would wish them joy, for nothing pleases me more than to see a young couple happily wed."

*   *   *

At about the same time those at the dinner party were discussing Lady Denham's missing maid, Lucy and her new friend Mildred (the local maid hired when the Darcys moved to the villa) were doing the same.

"Freya, I mean Mrs. John Horner—" Mildred giggled "—never liked working at Sanditon House." She lowered her voice to a near whisper. "She said Lady Denham was too stingy to keep enough servants for so big a place, and her duties were at least twice what ours are here. *And* she was expected to help the cook, who had a foul temper!"

"She still does," said Lucy. "My friend Harriet, lady's maid to Mrs. Bingley, offered to help in the kitchen every day and never once did the cook say thank you." Her brow crinkled. "Why would Freya stay as long as she did?"

"Positions in service are hard to come by in these parts." Mildred looked to the right and left, as if someone might overhear. "She saved every penny to keep her young man from taking extra work with those who go out in their boats under cover of night, if you take my meaning."

Momentarily confused, Lucy gasped. "Smugglers? Here?"

Mildred nodded. "Most of them have fallen on hard times or need money to fix their fishing boats. Freya didn't want John to have any part in it."

"But the war is over now. I don't understand why they need to smuggle at all."

"The boats will go back and forth until there's no profit in it, I suppose," said Mildred, wise beyond her years.

"But to risk so much!"

"Not many here are willing to do it." Mildred waved a hand dismissively. "My brother says the older fishermen plan to make changes to their boats so they can take passengers out when the weather is good. The whole town is talking about the one your mistress and the others sailed on."

Lucy shuddered. "I could never go out on a boat like that."

"You're afraid of the water? I was swimming before I could walk!"

"I went bathing with Molly once." Lucy lifted a single finger for emphasis. "I won't do it again."

"Never mind. The sea is not for everyone." Mildred pointed at a book on the table between the beds. "Would you read for a while? We've only a couple more nights to finish it."

Lucy's face brightened. "We're nearly to the part where Molly and I...but I won't spoil it." She took up the third volume of one of Mrs. Ashton's earlier novels, *The Wine Cellar*, opening to the page marked by a braid made of delicate ribbons, a gift from Miss Darcy.

Mildred puffed her pillow, leaned back, then pulled the quilt up to her chin. "Promise to tell me when something is based on what really happened to you and Molly."

"This part did." Lucy grinned. "I'm Lilly."

Lilly slunk to the slightly opened door and leaned flat against the wall to see through the narrow gap. Holding a finger to her lips, she grabbed Mae's hand and quickly pulled her down the hall and into an empty room on the opposite side. The door closed behind them with a bang. Mae waited ten counts before re-opening it, just wide enough to allow a narrow view of the doorway through which the valet had gone.

Chapter 14

Pemberley
November 1814

During breakfast, there was so much talk of horses that Elizabeth laughingly begged Darcy and Georgiana to go riding.

Airily, she dismissed their half-hearted objections. "I've been remiss about correspondence since coming home and can see to it while you're out, which I think had better be soon for the clouds are gathering."

She had her way and was soon in her cheerful morning room, watching her husband and sister-in-law race across the lawn. When she could see them no longer, she went to the desk Darcy had given her to mark their first anniversary. On it lay four letters—each in a familiar hand. With a sigh she chose one, then bent low to whisper into the cradle beside her, "Shall we begin with your Aunt Lydia?"

Gregory responded to her voice by kicking his legs, but did not wake.

~a letter from Lydia Wickham to Elizabeth Darcy~

Garden Place, York
October 1814

Dear Lizzy,

You must know by now that my ship from Jamaica was captured by those horrid Americans and I was taken prisoner with everyone else. You cannot fathom how frightened I was, without Wickham to protect me! Each hour I thought I would be killed, and, without the protection of a certain gentleman (Mr. Milton, who promised faithfully to visit me here in York), I believe I could have died from trembling! Worse still, once we were released, I was forced to suffer the long journey to York in a poky carriage with an older couple and their tiresome children, for I dared not spend very much from what little I had left of the money Wickham gave me when we parted.

Now I am in York and there is absolutely nothing to do! Kitty has grown too large to be seen by anyone outside the family, and rarely steps outside her own chamber. She is constantly asking for something special from the kitchen, then sending it back untouched, even by me, for she claims she cannot bear the smell of food in such close quarters. In the next instant she wants beef tea, and potatoes with pea gravy!

Some days I'm forced to wait until she is asleep to get what little food I can, for she begs me not to leave her alone. Oftentimes, there is only her to talk to and she grows less amiable each day. Mr. Darnell is always at his place of work, and Mamma and Papa only come for the afternoons when the weather allows. When they are here I finally get a proper meal, but Papa frowns at me if I ask for more than one glass of wine (and I know the servants have been told to cut it with water). No one seems to care how poorly I am treated. And I, a married woman!

One day last week, Mamma agreed to sit with Kitty while I went to visit Mrs. White (a friend of Edward's who has been kind to Kitty). Her pug is a little dear and I am determined to have one for myself, but Edward claims a puppy would disturb his household.

When Wickham comes to York we will have our own house, and I will do exactly as I please. Meanwhile, Mrs. White has promised to write to her breeder on my behalf.

Kitty is ringing her bell again, but before I go to her I must tell you how unfair Papa is being. He will give me no allowance, and refuses to pay for the two new gowns I ordered, even though Mamma agrees that nothing I have is suited to this climate. Kitty's house is so drafty, while Mary's house stays warm even *on windy days (the house is so small you could fit three of them in the ballroom at Pemberley). I need so many things: morning and afternoon dresses, bonnets, shawls, gloves, shoes, and at least one ball gown. And one must be prepared for invitations, for there is a cavalry barracks just outside the old wall. A few days ago I saw the most wonderful fur-lined mantle in a shop window.*

Time is of the essence, so please send my allowance now instead of on the usual date and instruct Jane and Mary to do the same. It would be best to send more than usual, for of course I cannot ask Wickham just now and you know how stubborn Papa can be.

Who has ever heard of Sanditon, and what does one do there? Brighton is a far better place, but even there the water is nothing compared to what we have in the West Indies, which is warm, soft on the skin, and so clear you can see the bottom. Wickham and I were very fond of sea bathing.

By-the-bye, Mr. Milton said I had good sea legs because I never once experienced what they called 'mal de mer' during the crossing, unlike so many others. He said it was because I had a good appetite, and never once frowned at me for taking more wine.

Your sister,
L.W.

n.b. Please send the money straightaway, for each day the wind grows sharper. Also, when Wickham is back in England he will probably look for me at Pemberley.

Elizabeth stared at the ceiling for a considerable time. Then, she bent to peek inside the cradle and her frown disappeared.

~a letter from Elizabeth Darcy to Lydia Wickham~

Pemberley
November 1814

Dear Lydia,

You must try to be more patient with Kitty. She is likely frightened about what is to come and confused by unpredictable emotions, just as you may be one day. Also, both Mamma and my midwife said fierce cravings are perfectly normal (Jane and I asked for many things we now find abhorrent). It may be helpful if Kitty's cook has a ready supply of plain biscuits on hand.

It is fortunate you made friends aboard the ship, but I must caution you against encouraging further acquaintance with Mr. Milton. Papa would certainly disapprove, and rightly so. A lady must always be guarded in her behaviour; it is the friendship of other married women you should develop.

Given the state of relations between our country and America, a letter from the West Indies could easily be confiscated, lost at sea, or purposely delayed. Perhaps you could write to your husband—

At this point she whispered to Gregory, "With any luck, you will never meet him."

His eyes still closed, he frowned, lifted his tiny fist to his mouth, and she wrote more quickly.

—in care of your friends in Jamaica. In the meantime, should a letter from him come here, you may rest assured it will be sent on to York post-haste.

I am enclosing two coins, after which I will send half a paper note in two separate letters, as Papa recommends. As to Jane and Mary, it would be best if you wrote to them personally, but this time I will ask them to send what they can. Meanwhile, I advise you to curb your spending where possible—at least until you hear from your husband.

Please tell Mamma and Papa we have returned to Pemberley, Jane and Charles to Beechwood, and Mary and Christopher to London. We hope to be together again at Christmas, when we will all look forward to hearing news of the safe delivery of Kitty's baby.

Your sister,
E. Darcy

Taking two guineas from a beautifully carved box she had discovered in one of the Pemberley attics, Elizabeth wrapped the coins in a scrap of muslin, hiding each inside the folds of the letter.

She was considering taking her sleeping child from the cradle when Darcy entered, followed by his prized spaniel, Samson. At that moment Gregory began to giggle.

Darcy, always pleased to see his son, lifted him up and took him to the window. "As you can see, my boy, we are no longer at the seaside, but at home once more." He sniffed, then turned to Elizabeth with an easily understood expression and she rang the bell.

While they waited for the nursemaid, Elizabeth told Darcy about Lydia's letter. "She has no idea of Wickham's whereabouts."

"Indeed?" Darcy carefully shifted Gregory to his other arm.

"She thinks he might seek her here."

"He knows full well he will never be welcome in Derbyshire."[24] Darcy kept his tone light for his son's sake.

"Not at Pemberley, certainly, but Jane is so soft-hearted—" Elizabeth left the unthinkable unspoken.

"Charles would never allow it. I'll write to warn him."

The nursemaid knocked at that moment and Darcy brought Gregory to her. She took her charge away forthwith, young Master Darcy looking none too happy.

---

[24] Wickham's evil doings that led to this lack of welcome are described in *Mary, Mary, Not So Ordinary*. His thwarted plan to elope with Georgiana years earlier is described in Jane Austen's *Pride and Prejudice*.

Elizabeth turned back to her desk. "I also have a letter from Jane. Would you like to hear the important parts?"

"Certainly." He settled into a chair next to the desk as she opened the letter and scanned the first paragraphs.

"Ah...this may interest you. Mr. Neville Steele has arrived. He is from Kent, and was junior to you and Charles at school."

"The name isn't familiar, but in those days I had little time to associate with students younger than myself."

"Mr. Hartleton arrives tomorrow."

Darcy narrowed his eyes. "You have that look about you, Lizzy. Am I right in supposing you think we must act now, to protect our somewhat absentminded friend?"

"Yes," she responded pertly. "And to do that we must either invite him here or go to Beechwood."

Darcy sighed, shaking his head. "Then I had best leave you to your plotting."

Chapter 15

Hertford-street, London
November 1814

Mary was in the small sitting room that Christopher's Aunt Hermione had filled with exotic plants and where each of the walls had been painted floor to ceiling with a scene from some faraway place. She had gladly relinquished the house keys directly after her nephew's marriage, had gone travelling, and was currently in Vienna.

Even if Aunt Hermione never returned, Mary did not wish to change a single thing about the room, and, having decided upon the perfect place for her writing desk, she turned her attention to the recently delivered model of the house on Grape-street in York.[25] Every detail had been meticulously recreated by the craftsman, even to the chimneys, mullioned windows, and the slate tiles on the roof, while the base included the narrow pavement in front and the garden in back.

There were telling sounds in the hall before Bonnie raced into the room, then Molly followed with the dog lead. The two had just been for a morning walk.

Mary bent down to pet her panting puppy before opening the hinged panels of the model to reveal the interior rooms, the tiny furniture modeled after those pieces included in the sale of the house. "My sisters used their replicas of Pemberley and Beechwood to help choose wallpaper, fabrics, and so on." She reached inside to take out a miniature desk. "This is not at all like

---

[25] The model was a gift from Christopher who had, unbeknownst to his wife, commissioned the work shortly after he purchased the house.

the one I used."

Molly hid a smile and pointed at the model.[26] "The curtains are the same as those hanging when you and the major were renting the house. Do you think new ones would be nice?"

Mary replaced the desk. "White muslin would lighten the room, as would a fresh coat of white paint on the walls, I believe, but the exposed timbers should be left as they are." She straightened up. "Aunt Hermione left a paintbox somewhere."

"In the cabinet, madam," said Molly, crossing the room to retrieve it.

Inside was an array of dried pigments in containers, ready to be mixed with oil or gum arabic, all carefully labeled. "Aunt Hermione was fond of blues, greens, and whites," noted Mary as she studied the walls of the sitting room in turn. "I wonder if she painted these?"

Just then, there was a knock and the butler entered. "A message for you, madam."

"Thank you, Mr. Fletcher," said Mary. "Is someone waiting for a response?"

"Yes, madam, if you please."

After reading the note she penned a response on the back. "I will require the carriage this afternoon."

"Very good, madam. What time shall I tell the coachman?"

She thought for a moment. "Two o'clock will do. There is a little shopping, which can easily be done prior to this appointment."

Mr. Fletcher hesitated. "Pardon me, madam, but I overheard your remark about the walls of this room. It was one of Miss Hermione's greatest pleasures to paint them." He bowed his head and departed silently.

"Aunt Hermione is a true artist," said Mary as she closed the paintbox, her eyes on a scene depicting charming white houses built on the side of a hill overlooking a large body of water. "The message was from Mrs. Stewart at the hiring agency. She has found the maid, Annie, and we have an appointment this afternoon."

---

[26] Molly knew the major had secretly ordered a (life-size) version of the desk to be made for his wife, as the owner of the Grape-street house had refused to sell the one Mary used when they were in residence.

*　*　*

The shopping was completed in good time, but the coachman was forced to take a longer route to the hiring agency due to an overturned cart, and they arrived at the office building five minutes later than the appointed time.

Mrs. Stewart's rooms were located on the second floor and Mary was a trifle breathless when entering the office. The woman at the front desk greeted her politely before instructing Molly to take a seat in the outer corridor. She then led Mary to the matron's office, a narrow space with a window facing the adjacent brick building.

"Mrs. Ashton! It is lovely to see you back here so soon." Mrs. Stewart, an open, friendly woman, greeted her without reservation. "I am pleased to say those you engaged to help the unfortunates in St. Giles are finally feeling welcomed there. It took time, as one might expect, for those poor souls are not accustomed to kindness the like of which you have shown."

"This is good news, thank you." Mary took a seat in the only available chair.

"I've prepared for you a schedule of when and where they will be working for the next fortnight." Mrs. Stewart slid the paper across the desk and sat back, fingers interlocked. "Annie Clarke is here, ready to meet with you."

"I was very pleased to get your note saying she is amongst your clients." Mary said nothing more, as Christopher advised, since Annie was technically a witness to the illegal goings-on at her former place of employment.

"I'm certain you will be pleased with her—she is well-mannered and a hard worker, if a bit shy in manner. Something I appreciate in young girls, to be honest." Mrs. Stewart rose with difficulty, leaning on a heavy walking stick as she indicated the bell on her desk. "I'll fetch her now; you need only ring when your business is complete."

Not two minutes later, Annie entered the room, head bowed. The hem of her ill-fitting dress was frayed, and the cuffs of her sleeves imperfectly sewn in a clear attempt to hide signs of wear. But her hair was neatly braided and her face and hands were clean. "You wished to see me, ma'am?"

Mary remained seated as she introduced herself. "My maid, Molly Turner, came to the house of your former employer recently, when I believe she told you the story about a young girl named Elvira?"

"I remember Molly very well," said the young maid, lifting her head slightly before lowering it again. "And the basket she brought for us. It was very kind of you."

"I am pleased it was well received." Mary considered the young maid silently for a few moments, then her expression grew resolute. "I have come to offer you a position in my house."

Annie looked up. "I was a kitchen maid in my last position, but I'm a hard worker and willing to learn new skills."

"I am glad to hear it," said Mary with a gentle smile. "A good deal of Molly's time is taken up in the sewing room of late and we are in need of someone to take on certain of her other duties. Do you think you would enjoy learning the skills of a ladies' maid?"

"I would, yes, very much. Thank you, ma'am." With barely suppressed elation Annie dipped a curtsey, then Mary rang the bell and Mrs. Stewart's light knock sounded moments later.

After hearing what had transpired, the matron suggested Annie sit with Molly in the corridor while the necessary documents were signed.

When Mary came out to meet the two maids, Molly shared what she had learned from the former kitchen maid: Annie had not been paid for her last three months at the smuggler's house, nor had she found a new position, and her current situation was bordering on desperate.

"Well then, why not come with us this very day?" suggested Mary, and once outside asked Annie to give the coachman the address to her lodgings near Holborn Bridge.

Upon reaching the house, Mary asked Jimmy, one of the two footmen accompanying them, to go inside with the maids. She held Molly back for a moment, her eyes on the dingy ramshackle building. "Do not tarry."

The landlady followed the three who had come in the fine carriage up to the garret and to the tiny closet where Annie had been resting her head at night. Then she stood watching from the doorway, arms folded across her chest.

"Ignore her," whispered Molly as she helped Annie gather her meagre possessions into a box.

The landlady made them stand in the narrow space outside the tiny room while she inspected it, then led them back down the stairs. Before they reached the door she turned round, pointing a crooked finger. "She's not leaving 'til she pays the rent due me."

Annie blanched, but Molly would not be intimidated. "What is the amount?"

"A bob." The old woman glared at them. "And a bender for interest."

Molly watched as Jimmy produced the shilling and sixpence without argument. However, he did not put the money in the landlady's outstretched hand, motioning instead for her to step away from the door. He then waited until the two maids were outside the building before dropping the coins into her open palm.

Mrs. Chadwick, the Ashtons' housekeeper, was familiar with the generosity of her young mistress, and not at all put out by the appearance of a poor young stray. When Annie joined the other servants for dinner (in one of Molly's dresses, quickly altered) the other servants welcomed her as kindly as Mary could have wished.

In such company, Annie overcame her shyness, and before the meal had ended all were aware of her preference to be called Anna. "Annie was what my former mistress thought I should be called."

"Then Anna it shall be," said Mrs. Chadwick.

Chapter 16

The next day Mary was standing upon a round pedestal. Molly was kneeling on the floor, pinning the hem of a new gown she had designed. "I made the back longer, madam. It's a new style I saw in one of the ladies' magazines."

Mary glanced over her shoulder. "Not so long that I might trip on it, if you please."

"The magazine calls it elegant, but I'll make sure it's safe." Molly pulled out the pins and remeasured, working silently for a time, then leaned back on her heels. "If you'd like to see, I've finished pinning."

Mary twisted back and forth to view her reflection in the looking glass. "I like this. It reminds me of the gown you made for Mrs. Chandler's wedding—but simpler."

Molly rose and tidied her skirt. "It's all in the cutting." She circled round her mistress, looking for stray threads and misaligned beads. "I will have this ready before Mrs. Penrose's party. There's only the hem to do."

As Molly helped remove the gown, Mary asked how Annie was adapting to her new home.

"She's less shy than she was at first, and asked if we would call her Anna because the mistress at the Farringdale house was the one who decided she should be called Annie."

"I prefer Anna myself. Do you think she will be happy here?"

Molly nodded. "Last night before we went to sleep, she talked a lot—Mrs. Chadwick gave her Lucy's bed."

Mary smiled. "Mrs. Chadwick is a kind, wise woman."

"Like Mrs. Reynolds at Pemberley." Molly put the pedestal in a corner and began to tidy the sewing table. "Anna says belowstairs at the other house was nothing like here, what with the temper of the mistress and master, and everyone afraid of being dismissed at any moment."

"I hope you find her a good student so she can relieve you of some duties in the near future."

Molly stuck a few loose pins into the cushion tied to her wrist. "But which would I give her?"

"What do you least like to do?"

"The ironing. I'll start training her today."

Mary laughed, then went to meet Christopher in the music room.

He was tuning his violin when she entered. "How do you like the new dress?"

"Very well. Molly is a fine seamstress."

"I know you don't like to think about her leaving us one day, but, if she should choose to, you will be her most valued client." He smiled and indicated the music on his stand. "I took the liberty of choosing the andante from Beethoven's second sonata."[27]

Mary sat down on the bench and turned the pages. "Thank you for not choosing the allegro vivace. Georgiana would have no trouble with it, but not I." She regarded him for a moment. "Perhaps we can alternate when we're at Pemberley...she can play the faster movements."

"You underestimate your ability, my dear, but we'll focus on the slow ones for now. More melody, less technique." He grinned, tucked the tailpiece of the violin beneath his chin, and Mary played the eight-bar introduction.

An hour or so later, after frequent stops to refine various passages, she rang for tea. "I hope the servants don't mind my requesting it at such odd times."

---

[27] Being a violinist, Christopher did not feel the need to specify that the sonata was written for piano and violin as opposed to a solo piano sonata.

"Mrs. Reynolds has told them to expect it, so you need not worry. She finds your refusal to be dictated to by tradition or societal rules a refreshing change."

"Does she?" Mary looked doubtful.

Christopher laughed. "It was your refusal to adhere to rules in general that attracted me."

"Mamma says I am lucky to have caught you, for no one else would have me."

At this, he wrapped his arms around her.

Those below-stairs were growing accustomed to various habits of their master and mistress. Therefore, the maid bringing the tea made certain her heels clicked against the polished floor as she approached the quiet music room.

By the time she entered, Mary was straightening a stack of music and Christopher was closing his violin case.

*   *   *

The next evening Mary appeared in her new gown, twirling for Christopher's benefit.

"You look nothing like a bluestocking, my dear."

"Is it too much? Molly made it longer in the back." Mary tried to see behind her. "She said it is the height of fashion."

"It is lovely. Mr. Scott may well be inspired to compose a quatrain in your name."

"What a pleasant thought. But it should be for Molly, not me."

Together they descended to the hall. Once there, he helped her into her cloak and adjusted the collar. "Shall we, my dear?"

They stepped out onto the pavement and into the waiting carriage. En route to the Penrose house, Mary spoke of their new maid. "Anna is fitting in well below-stairs, I understand, and is already proving helpful." She folded her hands in her lap. "As I said to you last night, it was an impulsive act to bring her home with me, but I could not bear to think what might happen if we didn't take her in."

"It was well-done, Mary." Christopher rested a hand upon hers. "Many months ago, you asked how I felt about your continuing as an authoress once we were married. You said you wished to use at least some of your earnings to help others. Your thoughtfulness and generosity are one of the many things I love about you, and I will always support your projects."

Mary squeezed his hand. "I doubt many men would care to hear you speak to your wife in this way."

He rested his head against the cushioned seat. "We must resign ourselves to being unusual, I suppose. I've always thought you were remarkable, and only wish I could have seen you dressed in plain, ill-fitting gowns, wearing your grandmamma's spectacles, with your hair pulled back so tightly no one could admire it."

"It is just as well you never saw me back then." She leaned back for a second then sat up again, mindful of her coiffure. "I wonder how we will find Miss Hutton this evening."

"She may be pleased to know that your publisher has sent your fourth novel to the printer."[28]

"Maybe so. But she will ask if I added social significance to the tale, and what will I say to her?"

Christopher was quiet for a moment. "Though subtle, I have found numerous instances of social significance in each of your books. Therefore, I think you could answer her with a single word: yes."

The sound of a lively string quartet wafted through the great hall as they followed other guests up the wide staircase to greet their hosts.[29]

"Mrs. Ashton! How wonderful to see you!" Mrs. Penrose took Mary's hands in her own. "Once I have greeted the last of my guests—you see them ascending now—you must allow me to introduce you to Mr. Scott." She used her lorgnette as a pointer. "You see him over there, behind the potted palm? He has been

[28] Mary had sent the revised manuscript of her latest novel, *The Bell Tower*, to her publisher the previous week. It included all but two of the changes suggested by Miss Paige, and a small number of those made by Lady Catherine. She had been both relieved and somewhat surprised to receive Mr. Egerton's announcement of its forthcoming publication.

[29] The music being performed when the Ashtons arrived was the first movement (allegro con spirito) of Haydn's String Quartet, Opus 76 No. 1.

hiding these last five minutes at least." She turned her head. "And over there...well, she must have moved on, but Miss Hutton is here as well and is most anxious to speak with you."

Mary managed to look pleased and moved on to greet Mr. Penrose, who was unfailingly polite but never appeared to be entirely comfortable at his wife's gatherings.

As promised, once all her guests were properly greeted, Mrs. Penrose led Mary and Christopher to Mr. Scott. Progress was slow, for their hostess stopped to introduce them to anyone who was not engaged in conversation.

When they found the great poet (behind a different potted palm) he greeted the Ashtons a bit distantly, but after hearing from Mrs. Penrose that Mrs. Ashton had published three novels under the guise of A Lady, he responded with geniality and asked for the titles.[30]

"I am delighted to meet you Mrs. Ashton," he responded, "for I have read your books, and enjoyed them enormously. You have a gift for subtlety, and humour, which any discerning reader can appreciate!"

Mary could not prevent a blush but thanked him properly.

Mrs. Penrose, clearly pleased with their meeting, moved on and Mr. Scott whispered, "I am a great enthusiast of pseudonyms. Keeping one's identity from the public allows an author, or authoress, to go about without fear of overhearing opinions regarding one's works, be they good or bad. Do you not agree, Mrs. Ashton?"

"I do indeed."

Mr. Scott leaned forward conspiratorially. "I also find great pleasure in being mysterious." He laughed and began to talk of other authors, most particularly Miss Edgeworth. "I am a great admirer of her works and find revisiting them most instructive."

"I hope we might meet her one day," said Mary. "Perhaps at a literary evening."

---

[30] Mary's novels in order of publication are *The Turret Room*, *The Count of Camalore*, and *The Wine Cellar*.

But Mr. Scott shook his head. "We have recently begun to correspond, and I believe she intends to remain on Irish soil, in Edgeworthstown, with her father and extended family."[31]

Mrs. Penrose, meanwhile, had found Miss Hutton, and returned with her in tow. That lady nodded to the Ashtons before addressing Mr. Scott. "Please say you agree with me about the responsibility of all writers to add something of social significance to each of their works."

Happily, there was no time for him to reply, for the gong was struck and the guests invited to take their seats at the long table.

Before Miss Hutton went to find her place, however, she insisted upon setting a date for tea with Mary so they might discuss the question. "Shall I come to your house?"

Ignoring the twitching of Christopher's lips, Mary answered in the affirmative and the appointment was set.

When all her guests were seated, Mrs. Penrose signaled the musicians to cease. From the podium, she proudly introduced Mr. Walter Scott. "He has kindly agreed to read to us from his phenomenally successful work, *The Lady of the Lake*."

There was prodigious applause, allowing the great writer to arrange his papers. In a deep, rich voice, he began the first canto:

The Chase.
Harp of the North! that mouldering long hast hung;
On the witch-elm that shades Saint Fillan's spring;
And down the fitful breeze thy numbers flung,
Till envious ivy did around thee cling,
Muffling with verdant ringlet every string,—
O Minstrel Harp, still must thine accents sleep?

---

[31] Scott had in fact received a long letter from Maria Edgeworth, dated 13 October 1814, who had just read (in company) *Waverly*. The book had been sent by Scott's publisher, at the author's request, which began a long correspondence and lasting friendship between the two writers.

*   *   *

Mary woke later than her usual time the next morning, looking round the empty room with confusion before ringing for Molly, who appeared in short order with a breakfast tray and a look of apology. "It would have taken too long for fresh coffee, madam, so I brought tea."

"It will suit me perfectly this morning." Mary sat up, fluffing the pillows behind her. "There was so much conversation at the table last night, I was unable to finish any course before the plates were taken away." She spooned quince marmalade onto a warm crumpet. "Has the major already taken breakfast?"

"Yes, madam." Molly was pulling back curtains and closing windows. "He left a note for you—it should be there, on the tray."

Mary lifted the folded napkin. "Here it is, and one from Miss Darcy as well, I see."

She read Christopher's note first, which informed her that he had gone to meet with his superiors about smuggling activity in Sanditon, as reported by the Riders.

After stirring two lumps of sugar into her tea, Mary unfolded Georgiana's letter and found a small packet from Elizabeth inside.

"I must say, it is quite pleasant to begin the day in this manner. Thank you, Molly."

Chapter 17

~ ᴗ ᴗ ᴗ ᴗ

~a letter from Georgiana Darcy to Mary Ashton~

Pemberley
November 1814

Dear Mary,

Christopher and Fitzwilliam have been exchanging letters, so you probably know we are back at Pemberley and Aunt and Uncle Gardiner will be returning to London. Although I miss the sea already, I am pleased to say all matters concerning the villa and attached cave are in the hands of those who patrol the coastline.

What you may not know is that Caroline has returned (alone) to Beechwood. I wonder if this sudden change in plans is related to the recent announcement in the Times *about Lord E's engagement to Mrs. B. Do you recall when he introduced her to us at the Race Ball in York? I suppose we should have guessed the outcome at the time, and I sincerely wish them joy.*

Elizabeth is making plans for Christmas and would like everyone to be prepared to play or sing. She asked if you and I could perform duets, and therefore I am enclosing a list of requested works so you will have a chance to practice them (I've marked one Mrs. Reynolds particularly likes). Jane and Charles will bring Mr. Hartleton with them, and Caroline too, I suppose. There is also Mr. Neville Steele and Mr. Archibald Culpepper, a friend from Charles' school days.

Cousin Anne wrote from Scotland with good news. Aunt Catherine has begun to recognize fine qualities in Miss Diana

Leigh, who is to remain with them through the winter season.[32] *The weather will prevent anyone from travelling for some time, allowing my aunt to see how very suitable a match would be between Miss Leigh and our cousin.*

I would like to visit Scotland and experience life in an old castle partially hidden by fog and mist. When I said as much to Elizabeth, she laughed and said the desire comes from reading The Castle of Otranto, *which Mr. Hartleton recommended to me.*

When you write again, add more details if you please. Your last was sadly lacking.

Affectionately,
Georgiana

Mary finished her breakfast and rang the bell.

"Only the simplest of hair styles this morning," she said to her fleet-footed maid. "I wish to make the next post."

"Very good, madam. There's a new style I've been wanting to try."

Once clad in a morning gown, Mary sat down at the dressing table, keeping still as Molly divided her hair into three sections. "Many ladies admired my gown last evening and asked if I would share the name of my modiste. When I told them you are responsible for the design and the sewing, Miss Hutton was so shocked that I had to insist you do it by choice. Had I failed to convince her, I think she would have openly compared your circumstances to those of the poor girl from the Grimm brothers' story—the one with the wicked stepmother."

"There are many wicked stepmothers in those stories, madam, but I think you might mean Cinderella."

"Yes, the poor girl who sleeps in the cinders. Anyway, it was necessary for me to say you have refused to surrender your duties as my personal maid. Only after Miss Hutton heard Anna was engaged to help you was she prepared to forgive my evil deeds."

"I'm sorry if they thought badly of you because of my stubbornness, madam."

---

[32] Georgiana's cousin Richard (Col. Fitzwilliam) has long held tender feelings for Miss Diana Leigh, but his lack of fortune has prevented him from taking steps.

"Not at all. And you are tenacious, not stubborn." Mary watched Molly work for a short time before asking if Anna's ironing skills had improved.

"If anything, she's gotten worse. Luckily, she's only been practicing on an old apron. It's covered with scorches and burn holes." Molly went silent as she wound a plain bandeau at the end of the single plait, covered it with a pretty ribbon, then took a step back. "Do you approve?"

Mary twisted round. "Yes, I do. And it took comparatively little time." She rose and stretched. "I nearly forgot. Four of the ladies asked if you might teach their abigails some of your techniques with hair and sewing, as you did in York with my sister's maid."

Molly huffed, straightening the items on the dressing table. "Agnes! She was far worse than any of Cinderella's stepsisters."

"Happily, Agnes may soon be in Botany Bay, paying the price for her crimes."[33]

"She'll be lucky if she doesn't have an appointment with the hangman." Before her mistress could admonish her, Molly added in a much sweeter tone, "I would be happy to show the other abigails how to do a few things."

~ ~ ~

~a letter from Mary Ashton to Georgiana Darcy~

Hertford-street, London
November 1814

Dear Georgiana,

It is a relief to know nothing untoward occurred in Sanditon, and I look forward to hearing the details of your adventure in person. One must wonder why anyone would leave precious goods behind in a leased house.

Last night Christopher and I went to another of Mrs. Penrose's literary meetings, where we met Mr. Walter Scott. She introduced him as 'the great poet' and teased him about recent

---

[33] Mary and Molly are referring to incidents in York, as recounted in *Mayhem at the Minster*.

projects but was unable to force an admission from him regarding the authorship of a recent novel, about which there is much talk. Interestingly, when he learned I wrote under a pseudonym, he had much to say about the desirability of not giving one's name for all the world to know. He was garrulous and entertaining, yet I wondered at times if the vivacity he showed others was forced, perhaps disguising a guarded and nervous man—the perfect temperament for a writer! He suffers from a pronounced limp, reportedly due to a childhood illness. Mrs. Penrose warned us not to remark upon it as he is extremely sensitive. Had she said nothing, we probably would not have noticed, for he moves about easily with the aid of a stout walking-stick. We spoke of novels for a good while, especially Miss Edgeworth's Patronage, *which Mr. Scott highly recommends, and the works of Milton and Shakespeare as they have been instrumental in his writing. I am determined to read* Paradise Lost, *for I was ashamed to admit I had not read it.*

Christopher found the conversation most entertaining and said he would escort me to any of Mrs. Penrose's soirees in the hopes of meeting Mr. Scott again. He suggested we read Waverly *together (you may recall he had hoped to discuss the work with Papa).*

Miss Hutton was also a guest, and spoke to me at great length about her father's history of Birmingham, which contains what she calls a 'particular account' of the riots in 1791. I did not admit my complete ignorance of the event and thankfully she asked me no questions. But I digress. She is assisting her father with his work while planning her next novel, which she believes will give her readers a better understanding of the negative effects of the rise in industry in our nation, especially to the supply of fresh air. Her inspiration comes from travel into North Wales many years ago. She recommended Madame d'Arblay's latest, The Wanderer *(you and I were unable to find a copy when it was first published and chose Lord Byron's* Lara *instead). Miss Hutton claims* The Wanderer *was fourteen years in the making and believes both I and my novels will benefit by it. Before the evening came to an end, she restated her wish to meet with me and I am duty-bound to read a five-volume novel—one hopes it is still available—and to research the riots of 1791 before she comes for tea next week!*

You may remember Molly befriending a young maid from the house where they kept the escaped French officers. The maid has an uncle who used to be a smuggler and I wanted Molly to meet with her in the hopes of learning something useful for Christopher and Richard's investigation. We were lucky to find this maid (Anna) through a servants' registry, for all from that house had scattered. Anna was in so perilous a state we brought her to Hertford-street and Molly is teaching her to be a lady's maid.

I would like to hear more about Mr. Neville Steele. Did Charles invite him to Beechwood solely for Caroline's benefit I wonder?

It is time for the post, so this much detail will have to do. I will only add how very much I miss seeing you each day.

Affly,

Mary

n.b. Please tell Elizabeth I will send all funds for Lydia to Papa, so he may issue them as he deems appropriate. Also, you never said how you found the company of Lady Denham's niece and nephew. And lastly, I received good news: Mr. Egerton approved The Bell Tower *for publication![34]*

---

[34] *The Bell Tower* is a work of fiction, with moderately embellished accounts of events described in *Mayhem at the Minster*.

Chapter 18

A burning log shifted in the fireplace and Elizabeth woke with a start. For a few moments she lay still, then rose up on one elbow, whispering, "Fitzwilliam, are you awake?"

"No, Lizzy." Despite his response, Darcy did not sound awake.

"I had a dream." She leaned back into her pillows, hands folded over her chest. "There was a celebration...the servants were dancing. When I woke just now, I thought it presaged a wedding—even Caroline's—but then the bonfire on the sand came to mind. It was a fine event, was it not? Until the wind started."

After a momentary silence, one of his eyes opened. "And?"

"Well, the dream makes me think how lucky we were to be party to even an abbreviated Guy Fawkes celebration in Sanditon, but the servants here had none. Must we wait until next year? Perhaps we could host a special event while the weather still allows. It could also be a source of entertainment for Jane, Charles, and their guests."

Darcy yawned and stretched his arms above his head. "If the servants desire it—considering they will do most of the work—then I see no reason not to."

Elizabeth kissed his cheek, pulled her pillow closer to his, then laid her head down.

Later, Mrs. Reynolds described to her young mistress the delighted reaction of those below-stairs, and, as the moon had been full the night before, the plan was set for the following day.

Invitations to Darcy's tenants and to those who lived close enough to Pemberley to attend with so little notice were quickly dispensed, and a groom was sent with a note to Beechwood.

Before noon on the following day the west lawn had been transformed. Tents were raised a safe distance from the pyramidal wood pile, with water buckets placed discreetly about the perimeter. Torches surrounded the area, to be lit with ceremony at dusk, and a platform had been constructed especially for the country dances. There were also shawls and blankets in each of the tents to prevent their guests catching a chill.

"Mrs. Reynolds and I decided to keep things as simple as possible for the meal," said Elizabeth as she and Georgiana strolled about the site, keeping out of the way of those who were hurrying between tents to prepare the table settings.

"No one, except perhaps Caroline, will object," said Georgiana.

"We will know her opinion by and by." Elizabeth's lips twitched as she turned to look at the house. "I thought Jane and Charles would be here by now, in company with Mr. Steele and Mr. Culpepper."

Georgiana tipped her head back, shielding her eyes to see the top of the wood pile. "And Mr. Hartleton."

"Oh yes." Elizabeth too looked up, then immediately back down. "That makes three gentlemen, and I feel quite dizzy."

Gaily, Georgiana took her sister-in-law's hand. "Come, we had better get dressed or we risk not being there to greet the guests, including the Bingley party." Upon reaching the side entrance to the house, she stopped at the threshold to say, "The Burnabys are generally early, and will certainly be so today if Deidre knows three unattached gentlemen are to be here."

"Georgiana!" Elizabeth feigned shock.

The Bingley party happened to arrive when their hosts were dressing, and all were escorted to their respective apartments or chambers to do the same.

An hour or so later Georgiana descended the staircase alone, adorned in a flattering long-sleeved gown with matching velvet pelisse, tendrils of hair peeking out from her stylish cap.

Lucy had learned much from Molly and studied the plates in ladies' magazines to copy both costume and hair, reading over and over again the accompanying description for clues as to how to achieve them. The result of her efforts could be seen in the admiring looks of the gentlemen assembled in the hall, and perhaps the less-than-pleased look Miss Bingley hid in an instant.

Mr. Bingley greeted her fondly, then began to introduce the newcomers. "Mr. Steele lives in an old abbey; he and Hartleton have been talking nonstop about the place."

"How delightful. Do you have resident ghosts?" Georgiana unconsciously imitated the outspoken heroine in the novel she was reading.

"One or two," answered Mr. Steele easily. "But they are benevolent."

Bingley laughed, his sense of fun and camaraderie always contagious. "And here is Mr. Culpepper, a fine chap, even if he did play for a rival cricket team."

Georgiana greeted Mr. Culpepper in the same gracious manner as she had Mr. Steele before turning to Mr. Hartleton to bid him welcome. "It is good to see you again."

There was a coolness in her tone and the slightest lift of the chin as she spoke, reminiscent of Lady Catherine, which may or may not have caused a look of confusion on the gentleman's part.

Darcy, coming down the stairs with Elizabeth, suggested they proceed outdoors. "The first carriage is coming up the drive as we speak."

The barouche came to a stop and a footman jumped from his post to lower the step. Elizabeth shared a glance with Georgiana when Deidre Burnaby exited first, full of breathless exuberance when greeting the Darcys. She dipped a saucy curtsey to Mr. Hartleton and Mr. Culpepper, but towards Mr. Steele she was inexplicably cool.

"Miss Burnaby and I were introduced at Almack's last season," said that gentleman with a slight bow. "It is a pleasure to see you again."

Mr. Burnaby was speaking to Darcy at the time, but Mrs. Burnaby observed the exchange. "Deidre is a delight to watch on the dance floor." Her tone might have been called frigid by some.

Bingley clasped his friend's shoulder. "I'm afraid Steele was never a great dancer, but I understand he is a fine scholar."

Mr. Steele laughed. "I cannot say I excel at either."

"But we squeaked by in the end, didn't we?" Bingley grinned.

More carriages were by then appearing on the drive, so Elizabeth suggested the others proceed to the lawn to partake of refreshments. "Fitzwilliam and I will join you shortly."

Mr. Steele offered his arm to Georgiana, after which Caroline Bingley took Mr. Hartleton's, leaving Mr. Culpepper to escort Deidre Burnaby, her parents maintaining an appropriate distance behind them.

~a letter from Lucy Pearl to Molly Turner~

Pemberley
November 1814

Dear Molly,

Since the Darcys were in Sanditon on Guy Fawkes night, they had a bonfire yesterday. It reminded me of when you were almost kidnapped by that French valet.[35] One of the under-gardeners said it couldn't happen again, but still I was nervous. Then, when the effigy was brought to the wood pile and everyone was chanting 'remember, remember, the fifth of November', I had a bad case of the shivers because of what happened in York![36] I think I'm only brave when you're with me. Except for the sea-bathing.

The Bingleys came for the bonfire, and Harriet has been making special dishes from receipts they brought back from the Italian states. M. Renault even gave her a worktable of her own,

---

[35] Molly's frightening experience is chronicled in *Mary, Mary, Oh So Contrary*.
[36] Lucy is recalling events described in *Mary, Mary, Oh So Contrary*, and *Mayhem at the Minster*.

but she says it's only because it means he won't have to work so hard. Today she's making lemon biscuits (she calls them something I can't spell), and a special kind of macaroni, shaped like little hats, and promises they'll be much easier to eat than those long noodles.

Miss Bingley is here again and so is her maid, who still pretends to be French (it's strange, when you think about the war). Our meals aren't as fun when she's around and every day we hope Miss Bingley will keep her working past our dinnertime, which she often does. There are also three valets with their gentlemen. They are friendly enough, but I avoid all valets after what happened to you.

Mrs. Reynolds said we can sit on the stairs and listen to the music tonight. I can't imagine anyone playing as well as Miss Darcy. Miss Bingley plays everything so fast it makes me nervous.

Now the dressing bell has rung, so I must go.

Your friend,
Lucy Pearl

~~~

~a letter from Georgiana Darcy to Mary Ashton~

Pemberley
November 1814

Dear Mary,

Last night we held a bonfire. Elizabeth thought it only fair to hold one for the servants and tenants, as we were in Sanditon for Guy Fawkes night. It was an ideal evening, with clear skies, glittering stars, and no wind. I cannot imagine a more perfect background for dancing.

Along with Charles and Jane came Caroline, Mr. Culpepper, Mr. Hartleton, and Mr. Steele. Mr. C is cheerful and talks a good deal of horses, while Mr. S is somewhat quiet and has an ancestral property in Kent (an abbey).

Mr. H hopes to spend time in the library, as expected, but promises to join our morning rides, and to go on the excursions

Deidre Burnaby is planning. All this is aside from Elizabeth's schemes, of course. One of her plans is for us to read aloud to one another, by turn, and my suggestion to read Patronage *was eagerly taken up. I believe sharing thoughts about a book is one of the best ways to get to know someone.*

I am to assist with Mr. H's research once again, but you need not fear for my reputation. Caroline has offered her services as well, claiming we must act as chaperones for one another.

You may already be matchmaking, so I will share what little I have observed. When Mr. C danced his two sets with Deidre last night he was always smiling or laughing (something I have never seen him do in Caroline's company). Deidre, in turn, seems to have taken a shine to him. Mr. S has excellent manners and is able to attend solely to whomever he is with at the moment, but I suspect his true character is not easily known.

Our little niece and nephew are constant sources of entertainment. Eliza took two steps yesterday without help, while Gregory refuses to do anything other than crawl, no matter how Fitzwilliam coaxes him. Elizabeth said she fully expected the two cousins to be in competition with one another, but not their fathers!

A letter from Richard came today. He and his batman reached Vienna without incident, but based on my brother's expression while reading the news from there, it was not all good.

Affectionately,
Georgiana

n.b. The situation in St. Giles makes me want to do more. I happened to speak with Mr. H about it this morning at breakfast and he had some very good ideas.

*   *   *

Darcy and Bingley were in the billiard room, awaiting the three other gentlemen, their conversation going quite naturally to Colonel Fitzwilliam's letter.

Darcy, cue in hand, leaned his shoulder against the wood panel while Bingley lined up his shot. "I didn't want to frighten our wives, but I'm afraid Richard's news was not all good." He paused. "An agent he was to meet was found in the River Wien."

Bingley's ball went wide. "I take it you don't mean he was bathing."

"Sadly, no. The agent had been observing customers at the café mentioned in the note tucked inside that French novel in Harry's library."[37] Darcy's expression was grim. "Do you mind if we hold off playing until the others join us?"

"Not at all." Bingley placed his cue in the rack. "Was it murder?"

"Vienna's chief of police, who reports directly to the emperor, is certain of it. Richard wrote that the police have agents everywhere, acting as coachmen, valets, maids, or customers at coffee shops." Darcy went to the sideboard to pour from a pitcher of porter-beer brewed in Lambton. "It sounds a mess. But not all are without aptitude. Recently there was a plot to assassinate the Austrian emperor, which the agents discovered in time."

"Does Richard think Lord Harold may be involved in some nefarious plot?"

Darcy shrugged. "There is evidence to indicate it."

~a letter from Lady Matlock to the Darcys~

Vienna
November 1814

Dear Fitzwilliam, Elizabeth, et alia,

You will be pleased to know that Richard has arrived safely. He is also in good health, thankfully, for there is a plague epidemic in areas of the Ottoman Empire, with guards at the Austrian border to prevent transmission of the disease.

Vienna is a lovely place, and with much to see and so many of our friends here I am never idle. As for your uncle, he has little time away from the business of this congress, for it migrates from locked rooms in the day to salons in the evening.

---

[37] As noted in *Parlance at Pemberley*.

Music is much prized here, as you can imagine. Lately, we were treated to a recital on a glass harmonium, an instrument said to be the invention of Mr. Franklin (the former American diplomat to France, but it is of no matter for the arts must be borderless). The most ethereal sounds emanate from this device, nothing like we have ever heard, though, as I told your uncle, it is a wonder the performer did not tear his hands to shreds, for the harmonium is made completely of glass. He sat as one would before a pianoforte, with hands resting upon the graded cylinder. Lady Castlereagh says Herr Mozart composed for this instrument, and Marie Antoinette learned to play it.

Given the success of this recital, Lady Castlereagh now hopes to present one with a panharmonicon, a mechanical instrument that reportedly imitates the sound of brass and woodwind instruments playing all at once. This was created by a Mr. Maelzel, who is said to have made ear trumpets for Herr Beethoven. However, as the two have since fallen out (regarding proprietary rights of a composition, so they say), there is some reluctance on the part of the performer to offend either the composer or the inventor by giving a public performance, so it appears we will have a private one.[38]

Every day we hear more about the spying here. The chief of police (Baron Franz von Hager, an interesting man) has placed agents inside every cupboard in every house, if we can believe the rumours. No new servant can be trusted, and we speak only of trivialities when we are not alone. Even when in our own carriage, or inside our chamber with the doors locked, we find ourselves whispering to one another. Your uncle disposes of all correspondence in the fire, stirs the ashes himself, and douses them with water. Apparently, this placement of agents throughout the city is in part due to an assassination plot against the emperor of Austria.

---

[38] The proprietary rights are regarding Beethoven's *Battle Symphony*, also known as *Wellington's Victory*, for which Maelzel convinced Beethoven to include a part for his panharmonicon. The work was so popular, Beethoven later published several different arrangements for various combinations of instruments. At one point, Maelzel claimed ownership of the work and Beethoven threatened legal action against him.

But let me return to the more pleasant topic of music. Last week we attended a recital of lieder (the German word for songs), including some by a very young composer who accompanied the singers on the pianoforte. His name is Franz Schubert, who, at seventeen years of age, has many works already to his credit. Your uncle says it would be fruitless to send any music to you at this time of upheaval, which is regretful, but I highly recommend the purchase if you can find manuscripts of his songs in London. This promising young man studies with Maestro Salieri (the Imperial Royal Kapellmeister), who counts Beethoven amongst his students.

I will write more about music in my next, for the list of upcoming concerts is delightfully long.

Your loving,
Aunt M

n.b. Jacob Grimm, one of the brothers who wrote the German folk tales Georgiana and Mary enjoy reading, is in Vienna, acting as secretary to a small delegation. Of particular interest to your uncle is that he was once private librarian to King Jérôme of Westphalia (Napoleon's youngest brother), though it appears Grimm's loyalty has always been with the Hessians. The cafés are popular with musicians and artists, so we may meet him by chance one day.

Chapter 19

London
November 1814

Mr. Gardiner, having returned to London with his family only the day before, called at Hertford-street when the Ashtons were still at breakfast. Having taken none himself, he was pleased to join them at the table.

"Your aunt sends her regards, along with an invitation to dine with us tomorrow," he said, waiting until the servant had gone to explain his errand. "I've been charged by the Riders to tell you in person about an incident that may be relevant to your recent investigation into escaped French officers." He leaned forward. "A former maid of Lady Denham's and the messenger boy from Sanditon were recently wed in Brighton, after which his uncle offered the use of his fishing cottage by way of a post-wedding holiday. However, the young couple did not return on the expected day and by late afternoon the uncle was so concerned that he rode on horseback to the cottage. Their belongings were there, but the couple was not, and his yawl was missing. He went to the local pub to ask after them, where he came across a member of the Riders who had seen them go out on the water a day or too earlier."

"Oh my," said Mary faintly.

"You need not worry, my dear," said her uncle kindly. "The couple survived. They had been out exploring, and the young man had rowed the boat far inside a large cavern when they were surprised by the sound of men arguing in what they thought was French. With the echo they could not tell just how far away they were, but knowing there were smugglers in the area the young man wisely rowed the boat to a length of sand near the cave wall where he hid it as best he could, and the two crept into a tunnel. Unfortunately, a sudden wave lifted the yawl from the sand and it slid back into the water. Needless to say, they were soon discovered by a ragged group armed with pistols. The young people were bound hand and foot, with filthy handkerchiefs drawn tightly over their mouths, then two of the men took the yawl and followed the other boat to the edge of the cave, slipping out as soon as it was dark."

He paused to sip his coffee, which the Ashtons habitually took with breakfast. "The couple managed to free themselves, but they dared not try to escape the cave until morning, when they saw the only way out was to scramble to a precipice and follow a narrow ledge to the mouth. It was slow going, and once they reached the edge they found the only way to get safely away from the water was to climb a steep cliff. Luckily, they were spotted by the Preventative Waterguard sailing close to shore in a revenue vessel. This was none too soon, for the pair had no food and their clothes were damp. Also, had it not been for water trickling from the rockface they would have had nothing to drink."

"Should those who left them ever be caught, the charge will be a serious one." Christopher shifted in his chair. "Did they understand anything those men were saying?"

"Only a few words, which are similar in English, but they cleverly mimicked the sounds of others, repeating what they heard to one another as they made their escape." Uncle Gardiner began to search his pockets. "I have it all written down...here it is." He took out a folded scrap of paper and handed it to Christopher.

"*Capitaine* and *commandant* are simple enough, and *sharpay*—" Christopher frowned "—could be *s'échapper*."

"Escape," whispered Mary, who had been listening intently.

Her husband nodded. "The next are like those on the message we found in the unfortunate courier's saddlebag. *Caporal La Violette* is a code name used by Napoleon's supporters in France, and what the captives heard as '*elbar*' or '*elbow*' could be the island of Elba, where he is exiled. The last—'*spray*' and '*pare*'— could be prepare." He looked at the other two. "If you will excuse me, I should report this to the foreign office at once."

When he had gone, Mary offered her uncle more coffee.

"Thank you, no. I must get back, but we shall see you tomorrow."

When Christopher returned, he found Mary in the garden room staring through the windows as she absently petted Bonnie. The two looked up only after he cleared his throat.

"Do you think the Corsican Fiend can escape Elba?" Mary's fear was written on her face.

"He does have ships under his command, along with a small army—supposedly for his protection and to maintain peace on the island." Christopher sat in the chair nearest to her, shaking his head in frustration. "Despite all this it is assumed he will not try to escape, and the foreign office may not take what that young couple heard seriously. In which case I've sent a coded message to Richard, who will share the information with someone who will listen. However, it will be many days before he gets it, and it could be intercepted."

"Might Darcy's uncle be sent the same message, in case yours fails?"

Christopher drummed his fingers on the arm of his chair. "Lord Matlock has for many years played a quiet role in politics— one might even say clandestine. It is a good idea, but if Darcy sent word to him it would have to be in code."

"It was Georgiana who deciphered the message we found tucked inside the French novel at Harry's house...perhaps she could assist."

Christopher leaned forward. "You are a remarkable wife."

*   *   *

Pemberley
November 1814

A cold rain having made her usual morning ride inadvisable, Georgiana was tucked inside the window seat in her room, reading a letter from Mary, when she slipped her feet back into her mules and went to her writing desk, took out a sheet of foolscap, and wrote down a series of characters before beginning to decipher the secret message her dear friend had sent. An hour or so later she went to Darcy's study to show him the message and to explain the cipher. Then, leaving him to his task, she went in search of Elizabeth and Jane, who she found descending the stairs from the nursery.

Elizabeth caught her eye and held a finger to her lips. "We've just managed to get Gregory and Eliza to sleep."

"There is something I need to tell you," whispered Georgiana. She silently led them to her private sitting room, waiting until they were comfortably seated near the fire to explain.

"I had a strange letter from Mary this morning. At first it was as usual, with a note about the cooler weather, a report that they are in good health, and a comment on how different London seems with so many gone to Vienna. But then she launched into a description of a literary meeting they recently attended. The funny thing is she had already written to me about it, and in great detail. In this recent letter she described things differently—even clumsily—and I was concerned about her state of mind. But then it struck me: she had written the letter using the cipher we worked out together recently, when in London!"[39]

"Was it done in jest?" asked Jane.

"I thought so at first, but no. She used the cipher to ask me to tell Fitzwilliam to expect one of a similar nature from Christopher, who wants him to send important information to Uncle Matlock in Vienna."

"How very interesting," said Elizabeth. "Was there a letter for Fitzwilliam this morning?"

Georgiana nodded. "I showed him the key to the cipher and he is currently working on Christopher's letter."

"I suppose we had better see that our guests are entertained," said Elizabeth with a little sigh.

"There is no need, Lizzy," insisted Jane. "Charles said he would ask Mr. Culpepper and Mr. Steele to join him in a game of billiards, and I understand Mr. Hartleton is in the library." A fine

---

[39] Georgiana refers to the message she had helped to decipher that had to do with a government agent, a certain street in Vienna, and a French novel, as described in *Parlance at Pemberley*.

line appeared on her forehead. "Caroline will remain in her room with a headache. She claims owls kept her awake last night."

"Owls?" Elizabeth shook her head in disbelief.

"It explains her absence from breakfast at least," said Jane, turning to Georgiana. "Did Mary give any indication of what Christopher was going to write to Fitzwilliam?"

"None at all, but I assumed it is a serious matter."

Elizabeth rested her feet on the ottoman between them. "Why is this family continually plagued by intrigue?"

"You used to complain that these things happened exclusively to Mary and Georgiana, or their maids," said Jane with a smile.

"I've decided I am much happier when nothing out of the ordinary occurs."

This made Georgiana smile. "Nothing untoward occurred on the day of the bonfire. Everyone seemed well-pleased, and we could not have had better weather."

"It did go well," admitted Elizabeth. "Aside from Deidre and Caroline's argument about diadems." She raised a hand to her forehead. "Those two will assuredly fix upon something else during tomorrow's fossil-hunting excursion. Unless it continues to rain...and if it does, what shall we do?"

"We will have tea, conversation, and cards, followed by dinner," said the ever-practical Jane.

"Restricted to indoors, listening to Deidre and Caroline's little barbs as they prance and pose." Elizabeth rolled her eyes. "I wish we could convince Mr. Steele to propose to one of them and be done with it!"

"Lizzy!" exclaimed Jane and Georgiana.

*　*　*

Fitzwilliam Darcy had never been a student of ciphers. Even with Georgiana's help the transcription was arduous. He worked without interruption and when the letter was finished took it to the stable himself to give strict instructions to Pemberley's fastest rider, a retired jockey.

Upon returning to the house, Darcy found Elizabeth waiting for him in his study.

"Fitzwilliam!" She came to his side. "I was about to go looking for you. I understand if you cannot divulge anything, but I do wonder at the reason behind Mary and Christopher's letters."

Darcy wrapped his arms around her. "It seems Christopher suspects Napoleon has a plan to escape Elba, and there are many in France who will support him in an attempt to regain power."

Chapter 20

Derbyshire
November 1814

Elizabeth's fears about the rain proved to be unfounded, and her guests were in good spirits as they stepped out into the sunny courtyard. Also, the fine weather allowed the gentlemen to ride horseback, which freed her from making challenging seat assignments.

Following a pleasant twenty minutes on the lane connecting the two properties, they arrived at the Burnaby estate. Before the Darcys' barouche came to a stop the lady of the house hurried to greet them, insisting they enjoy a respite before venturing out again.

As they entered the grand hall she pulled Elizabeth aside. "I am sorry to say Mr. Burnaby and I cannot join you in the search for ancient sea relics today. He has a slight indisposition—nothing serious, mind—but we had not the heart to disappoint Deidre. Would you be so kind as to keep watch over her in our stead? I would not wish her to scuttle about the hills or stumble over loose stones." She rested a hand on the younger woman's arm. "This excursion is all she has talked about for days."

Of course Elizabeth acquiesced. "Fitzwilliam and I will happily keep watch over her."

"Thank you, my dear." Mrs. Burnaby leaned forward to whisper, "Please don't say I asked you to do this...it might cause her to act out."

"We shall be discreet." Elizabeth's eyes were on their subject, who had taken Mr. Steele by the arm before going inside the house. Behind them was Caroline, firmly attached to Mr. Hartleton.

Since Deidre's parents were not joining the party, it was decided that Mr. Culpepper and Mr. Steele would leave their horses behind to travel in the Burnaby carriage, along with Miss Bingley who was quick to offer her services as chaperone.

Darcy and Bingley chose to continue on horseback, leaving the other carriage for Jane, Elizabeth, Georgiana, and Mr. Hartleton.

Their destination, Monsal Dale, did not disappoint. There was a walking path alongside the river for strolling, well-built bridges to go over it, and stepping-stones for those who dared cross in the shallow water. There were also uphill climbs for the more adventurous. Fossils of small sea animals were visible at nearly every turn, loose limestone rocks exhibited detailed outlines of ancient seashells, and, as Mr. Hartleton observed at the onset of their exploration, there was a ready supply of chert in the area, which was used by ancient peoples for tools and weapons.

This comment led to Deidre Burnaby bending down to pick up one rock after another, holding each out for them to see.

Whilst she was exclaiming over one thing and another, Georgiana leaned closer to study the surface of a boulder. "These *are* a little frightening."

The boulder was replete with fossils, and Mr. Hartleton bent to examine them himself. "These are crinoid echinoderms—a type of animal, like a starfish." He ran his fingers gently over the stone. "What amazing specimens—I have seen only illustrations before."

Elizabeth took one look and grimaced, as did Jane. Even Charles could not hide his aversion. "These are the things of nightmares, Hartleton." He pointed. "And what on earth are those? They look like fingers!"

Georgiana was closest and bent down to see. "If they *are* fingers, each hand would have had seven or eight."

Mr. Hartleton studied them with care. "Most of these are sea lilies."

Darcy laughed at Elizabeth's expression. "Perhaps we should walk on? Miss Burnaby has outpaced us."

They all walked ahead, slowly enough to see what they had come to see, but not so slowly they lost sight of Miss Bingley, Miss Burnaby, Mr. Steele, and Mr. Culpepper, who had gone ahead in search of 'better' fossils.

"Should we not follow more closely?" asked Elizabeth.

Bingley shook his head. "Have you seen their shoes? You, Jane, and Georgiana have worn practical footwear, and could easily climb that hill over there." He gestured towards one that was steep, then at his sister and Miss Burnaby. "But those two did not, and will need to stop and rest soon."

Darcy, smiling, agreed. "We may walk as leisurely as we please."

After observing more fossils than most thought to see in their lifetimes, they stopped to view a waterfall along the rock face, with a swirling pool at the bottom. Assured of Jane's comfort on the dry outcropping, Bingley settled on the edge, his feet dangling.

"Fossils are all well and good, but one day I'd like to see something monumental. I've read about a place near the city of Naples in a southern Italian province, or region—I'm not certain what the various areas are called now. Anyway, a horrific volcanic eruption buried two large cities almost two thousand years ago."[40] He flicked a loose stone into the water. "Do you remember your history, Darcy?"

Darcy too had settled on the edge, seeking loose stones to skip across the water. "I recall the tale, but not the locations."

Bingley tried to catch Mr. Hartleton's eye, but he and Georgiana were intent upon viewing stones he had taken from the water's edge. "I suppose it is of little difference what they're called, but excavations began there many, many years ago, and have continued on and off.[41] Someday, we can all go together, and after seeing those buried cities we could visit ancient ruins." He flipped another stone into the water. "Only yesterday I was reading about the temples at Paestum."

Darcy watched Bingley's stone skip four times. "Not until the conference has ended, if you please."

---

[40] Bingley refers to Mount Vesuvius, which erupted August 24-25, 79 C.E.

[41] The two cities Bingley and Darcy were trying to recall were Herculaneum and Pompeii.

Undaunted, Bingley turned round to face Jane. "We will stay in our villa and stroll through the vineyard in the evenings. In the winter we can sit outdoors while tasting our own wine!"

None of his companions demurred.

An excursion involving exercise should never be attempted without provisions, and at the appointed time the entire party lounged on blankets spread in a clearing at the peak of a hill.

Two large baskets had been filled under the direction of the Burnabys' cook, with tepid tea, ale, or wine to drink, and Deidre played their charming, if giggly, hostess.

Before leaving the dale, it was decided there was still time for a final exploration. While the others were discussing which direction to take, Miss Bingley took firm hold of Mr. Steele's arm.

Deidre observed this with narrowed eyes and eschewed Mr. Culpepper's arm, choosing Mr. Hartleton instead as her escort. For the next half hour she expostulated breathlessly about every rock and tree within sight.

Despite her promise to Mrs. Burnaby, Elizabeth held Darcy back to allow more space between them, discreetly raising her fingertips to her temples.

Georgiana, ever gracious, supported Mr. Culpepper's light-hearted suggestion that they have a contest to find an entirely different fossil from any seen that day. Jane and Charles remained stationary, perfectly content to sit together upon a fallen log while the other couples broke off to search on their own.

At the appointed time they returned, each laughing despite having failed in their quest, and unanimously declared the entire excursion a success.

Deidre clapped her hands with glee. "We must go to Parkhouse Hill next! They say the views are incomparable!"

"A fine idea, if this warm weather holds," said Mr. Steele, standing ready to assist the ladies into the Burnaby carriage. "Perhaps one day this same party could travel to Kent to visit Audley Abbey—my ancestral home—where you may see relics of a different nature."

Miss Bingley placed her lace-gloved hand in his. "An abbey is above all things what I like best to explore. To see an ancient house through the eyes of one whose family has lived there for centuries would be a treat indeed." She took her seat and arranged the fall of her gown. "Perhaps you know I have been acting as a kind of secretary to Mr. Hartleton in his research, and as a result have become interested in history." Her gaze held an element of challenge as Deidre stepped into the carriage. "What are you reading now, my dear? Another novel, I suppose."

Deidre flushed. "As a matter of fact, I *am* reading a novel. It's called *The Wine Cellar*, written anonymously by 'A Lady' but I know who the author is and consider her a dear friend."[42]

"It is hardly necessary to be so clandestine, since everyone knows Mary has been writing those books." Miss Bingley's chin went up. "I have not read any of her novels, for I prefer literature more beneficial to the mind." She waited until Mr. Steele was seated opposite her. "Which do you prefer?"

He took a moment to consider. "In the morning, it is my preference to read for edification, but later in the day I often enjoy a novel."

"And what about you, Archibald?" Miss Bingley eyed Mr. Culpepper as he stepped inside.

His response was a look of confusion and Deidre, her ears perking up at Miss Bingley's use of his first name, said with wide eyes, "Your acquaintanceship is of some duration, I see." She smiled prettily at him. "It is surprising that we never crossed paths in town, especially given how very often my mother and I came across Miss Bingley when we called at Darcy House."

The sound of their voices carried quite well, and it was not only Elizabeth who began to rub her temples.

---

[42] Mary might have been surprised to hear this.

Chapter 21

Hertford-street, London
November 1814

Given her husband's response to Uncle Gardiner's news about the young couple and the very bad Frenchmen, Mary was having trouble concentrating. She therefore placed the feather pen in the silver holder (another gift from Christopher) and rang for her maid.

When Molly entered the bedchamber, Mary was at the window looking out at the back garden, where the muted shades reflected the season. "I've been thinking about Anna. It's quite possible she knows something that could be of use to major and Colonel Fitzwilliam's investigation." She considered the young maid for a moment, no longer naïve and inexperienced, before relaying some of what had happened to the young couple. "It is because of this recent event that I would like you to speak with Anna about her uncle. Anything she can remember could be helpful."

"I'm to meet her in the sewing room shortly." Molly hesitated. "But before I go, perhaps you would like me to freshen your hair?"

Mary grimaced as she sat at the dressing table and caught sight of her reflection. "I do make a mess of it when I'm writing, don't I?"

Molly smiled in response and quickly restored order.

"That's much better, thank you," said Mary, patting her fresh coiffure. "Now I am off to the library. The workmen are asking about the placement of the half-walls."

In the sewing room with Anna, Molly removed a few pins to adjust the hem of Anna's dress while the other maid stood still on the pedestal, hands resting at her sides as instructed.

Following her mother's counsel to always speak plainly, Molly said, "Do you remember telling me your uncle was once a smuggler?"

The younger maid's surprise could be seen through the mirror. "My uncle?"

"The one you mentioned that day we met in the park," prompted Molly.

"Oh, you mean Uncle George! My mum's youngest brother. She thought he was wild, and a fool, because he refused to go into service and was always looking for easy ways to get money. But I liked him. He laughed a lot and gave me sweets."

Molly leaned back on her heels to view the evenness of the hem. "The reason I ask is because there is a maid from Sanditon who was married a couple weeks ago. Her husband took her out on a boat, and they were...one second." She removed a pin to adjust the width, then told the story up to the point when the young couple were frightened and hid in the cave.

"What happened next?" Anna suddenly turned around and Molly motioned for her to face forward again.

"The Frenchmen found them, tied their hands and feet together, and took their boat. Leaving them stranded."

"Did they die?" breathed Anna.

"No. They managed to free themselves and climb out of the cave but weren't found for days." Molly stood up. "We can sew it now." She helped Anna out of the dress and took out needles, thread, and scissors.

While showing the younger maid how to make a knot of the two ends, Molly went on, "Major Ashton is helping to find the men who did this. I thought maybe you can remember something about the time your uncle was smuggling that could help him."

"Oh," said Anna, frowning. "Why did the Frenchmen leave them to die?"

"They might have been smugglers, talking about something really secret they thought those two understood." Molly began to sew the hem. "Small, even stitches," she reminded Anna, who started at the other side, much more slowly.

Anna was frowning as she worked. "Do you think the Frenchmen were smugglers?"

"Maybe, or escaped prisoners, but they haven't been found yet." Molly looked up. "Did you ever hear your uncle talk about such things?"

Anna held her needle above the fabric. "My mum always made me go to bed early when my uncle came to visit, but one night I hid at the top of the stairs after she was asleep. He had brought friends with him, and I remember being disappointed because they were only talking about a funeral." She began to sew again. "They talked about someone's grave... Linus, maybe? I remember thinking it was an odd name."

"You've a good memory." Molly had reached the halfway point and stopped to watch her protégé. "Can you remember anything else? Even the slightest thing."

"It was so long ago now, and I was scared and cold, so it wasn't long before I snuck back into the bed." She bit her lip. "But, just as I left, they started talking about farming."

"Farming?"

"Or maybe it was about horses...I remember wondering why they were so interested in dung." Anna looked at Molly's even stitches and then her own. "Mine aren't nearly as good."

"No one will see," said Molly. "Just keep working on small and even, and you'll get better fast."

Anna stitched quietly for a while. "I'm sorry, Molly, but that's all I can remember right now. I promise to let you know if I think of anything else."

"The major will be pleased you remembered anything at all." She secured her last stitch and cut the thread. "I'll leave you to finish." She smiled encouragingly and went to find her mistress, who was playing fetch with Bonnie in the back garden despite the chill in the air.

After hearing what Anna had said, Mary handed Molly the stick and went to the study, where her husband had gone immediately upon his return from the foreign office. When she entered, she found him peering at a map through a magnifying lens. "What are you looking for?"

"Any place between Brighton and Sanditon where smugglers could hide from the patrols, such as the cave the young couple were exploring."

She bent over the map. "Where is Sanditon?"

"This predates the village, sadly." He ran a finger from Brighton along the shoreline. "But it would be about here."

Mary focused on that point, then on the opposite shore of the Dover Narrows. "Christopher, our new maid Anna recalled something her uncle said that may be inconsequential, but—" she placed her finger on the map "—she heard her uncle speak with his friends about a grave for a person she thought was named Linus, and here is a place called Gravelines!"

Christopher took up a graphite pencil tucked inside a silver sleeve (a gift from his wife) to draw a line from Brighton to Gravelines. "You are a treasure, Mary. Who else would think to find this young maid as you did?" He leaned closer to the map. "It would be riskier to cross at Brighton than at Dover, perhaps, but also less patrolled. Did Anna say anything else?"

"In the same conversation, she thought her uncle talked about farming. Dung, in particular."

"Dung?" Christopher straightened.

"Yes." Mary's cheeks were tinged with pink.

He bent down to consult the map once more, searching the English shoreline first, then the French. "Look at this: Dunkirk! Gravelines and Dunkirk are a short distance apart, relatively speaking...and not the usual places known for smugglers." He went to his desk to pen a note. "If they cross at Dover, it may yet be possible to find those Frenchmen...I'm afraid one of our couriers is in for a long, hard ride." He finished writing and retrieved his jacket from the back of a chair, putting it on as he went to the door. "I'm sorry, but we must delay our walk to Hatchards. Please give my thanks to Molly and Anna."

Mary watched him go, then returned to the garden where Bonnie was lying on the grass, panting.

"Apparently what Anna remembered is useful. The major wants me to thank each of you."

"She will be glad to hear it, madam," said Molly cheerily. "Maybe it's a good thing her uncle retired from the business before now?"

"No doubt." Mary bent down to pet Bonnie. "Does she seem bigger all of a sudden?"

"She does, and I asked Jimmy about it. He said not to worry. She'll have growth spurts until she's about a year and a half."

"She'll be as big as Samson by Christmas at this rate." Mary rubbed her puppy's tummy. "I won't be able to carry you around for much longer."

"Before I forget, madam—" Molly removed a letter from her apron pocket "—this came when you were with the major."

Mary took the neatly folded packet, the perfectly formed script a telltale sign of the sender.

Chapter 22

~a letter from Georgiana Darcy to Mary Ashton~

Pemberley
November 1814

Dear Mary,

There is news from Sanditon. The owner of the villa may in truth be Sir Edward Denham, Lady Denham's nephew by her second marriage!

According to Mr. Parker, Sir Edward is dependent upon an inheritance from his aunt, which she revoked due to his disreputable behaviour. (This was before any connection to smuggling was suspected.) It seems Sir Edward used a false name to purchase the villa, and another for the receiving and selling of smuggled goods (storing them in the cave Elizabeth and I discovered). Sir Edward is not to be found, but the mysterious George has been incarcerated. He is Sir Edward's manservant, who is clever at disguises having once been on the boards. It was he and his cousin, a sometime stable-boy, who Elizabeth and I heard on the day we found those crates.

More pleasantly, the weather has allowed for enjoyable outdoor excursions organized by Deidre, who, I can say without jest has the aptitude for such things. Elizabeth responded to each of those plans with one of her own, so the same party has often been together of late. But now the wind has changed, and outdoor activity may be curtailed.

There are signs that Deidre has her eyes on Mr. Culpepper. I cannot think Caroline likes it, as she enjoys the attention of all three unattached gentlemen.

Whilst searching for works to play on the harpsichord I discovered old treasures. There are some that evoke memories of my mother, which is especially pleasing.

On most evenings we take turns reading to one another. Mr. Hartleton often chooses entries from Mr. Evelyn's diary to entertain us, and there are plenty, as it dates from 1640 to 1706. Mr. H has found none dated later than January of the final year and thinks it is near the time of Evelyn's death, for on that day he wrote about being quite ill. So far, his descriptions of what occurred historically have been so clear it is as if we experienced it ourselves. Included are reports of severe changes in weather, the tremendous loss of life from a terrible plague in 1665, and the state of London following the great fire.[43] Evelyn also wrote at great length about the troubling years during Cromwell's power, his fall, and the reign of King Charles II, with whom Mr. Evelyn was very close at one time (but was ultimately disappointed). In a single entry Evelyn's words will illustrate his despondency about the state of this world, followed by his admiration for gardens he visited (he was a skilled cultivator), and ending with a glowing report of some prodigy's performance. Of particular interest to you may be his great reverence for libraries, and the descriptions of those he visited. Mr. H considers this diary a priceless treasure, and calls it 'an honest account of life in a tumultuous time.'

Jane and Charles will soon return to Beechwood with Mr. Steele and Mr. Culpepper. Caroline will go as well, though it means the end of her assistance to Mr. Hartleton, who will remain with us. We will not be apart for long, as the Burnabys plan to visit Beechwood (their first time) and we are all to enjoy several nights in residence. This is the consequence of entertaining unmarried gentlemen!

My next bit of news is Mr. H has purchased a house! Would you believe it is the first of those we viewed in September—with

---

[43] Georgiana refers to the Great Fire of London, which raged from 2 September – 6 September 1666.

the ballroom, and the fountain we liked so well? I will be sorry to see him go, for I have grown quite fond of his dog—you will recall he has an English Mastiff named Carrick, who he says will have the ballroom to run about and play.

The other day, he described recent experiments in the new field of electrochemistry and, once we are back in Town, has offered to escort us to see what is called a voltaic pile, a remarkable machine that creates an electric current. I do not fully comprehend what this means but think it may be a type of man-made static electricity. Remember the demonstration we saw at the Royal Institute? (Afterwards, we would drag our feet along rugs and give one another shocks.) I also recall how much we enjoyed the demonstration of nitrous oxide, which Cousin Richard took us to see.

I imagine you are curious to hear more about our guests. Mr. Culpepper has proved to be good-natured, and an excellent partner at cards. Elizabeth wonders whether he came to Derbyshire because of Charles or because of Caroline. (She treats him like a discarded trinket, but he does not seem to mind.) Mr. Steele is universal in his attentions and an exceptional rider, but happily not one to speak extensively about horses. Mr. H joins us on our daily rides and is happy to go along with the gentlemen in their other outdoor pursuits (they rode to Lambton only yesterday). He speaks well on any topic and is ever civil, even when deep in research. I can honestly say it has been a pleasure to have them here—even Caroline, for their presence has kept her in good humour and I have never seen her in better looks.

It is now time to dress for our afternoon ride, so I must close.

Yours most affly,
Georgiana

n.b. Here is something unexpected: Mr. H has inexplicably decided to return to town and will not join us at Beechwood.

Chapter 23

Pemberley
November 1814

Dinner at Pemberley the night before the Bingleys and their guests departed was a lively affair, with a good deal of conversation.

Certainly, Aunt Catherine de Bourgh would not approve of the freedom with which her niece spoke with Mr. Hartleton about a Darcy ancestor's escapades, as described in one of the old journals, but Darcy observed the exchange with interest and tolerance.

At the sound of Georgiana's charming laughter, Miss Bingley turned sharply to Mr. Hartleton. "It is just as well you found something of interest, since you depart for London tomorrow."

Apparently Georgiana had not heard this particular news, causing Elizabeth to give her husband a look of appeal.

"You are welcome to return any time, should you wish to continue your research," said Darcy with sincerity.

Bingley lifted his glass. "And to Beechwood."

Mr. Hartleton thanked his respective hosts for their kindness, then Elizabeth directed their attention to the sole, another specialty of Chef Renault's.

Later, Darcy performed his nightly ritual of brushing Elizabeth's hair, a habit formed early in their marriage.

"You are quiet this evening, Fitzwilliam."

The brush went still. "I am a bit concerned about Georgiana."

"I noticed she only played works in a minor key tonight." Elizabeth took the brush from him, placed it on the bedside table, and leaned back against the pillows.

Darcy reached over to snuff the candle and laid back, neatly arranging the bedcovers over them. "I was beginning to think a match between Georgiana and Hartleton might be acceptable. Why does Caroline insist on making trouble?"

Elizabeth nestled closer to him. "He likes Georgiana best—I'm sure of it. There is a good deal of camaraderie between them, they share a genuine interest in history and in music, and they adore dogs. All which bodes well." She closed her eyes, a sudden notion opening them again. "You were not teasing about an engagement?"

"No, given acceptable results of a rigorous investigation."

"I suppose we must be grateful there are two others to keep Caroline's attention divided in the meantime."

Darcy's frown was lost in the darkness. "This sudden decision to return to London is confusing. I thought he had much more reading to do."

*   *   *

The next morning after all their guests departed, Darcy went to his study to attend to neglected letters. It was not long before Simms appeared with a note on a salver. "Mr. Hartleton asked me to bring this to you after he was gone, sir."

Slightly alarmed, Darcy motioned for his butler to remain as he read the single paragraph. With a sigh, he placed the note on his desk. "Will you ask Mrs. Darcy to join me here, at her convenience?"

"Certainly, sir." The butler bowed and departed.

Nearly twenty minutes passed before Elizabeth appeared, a little out of breath. "Gregory is a bit out of sorts after waking so often last night—as am I." She glanced at his unusually cluttered desktop. "I hope it isn't bad news?"

"You may see it as such." He leaned against the desk, arms folded. "Hartleton has written a formal apology for sometimes having been in the library with Georgiana without a proper chaperone. He begged my pardon for not realizing this could endanger her reputation, and credited Miss Bingley for kindly drawing his attention to the oversight. He believes he has insulted both her and her family, and therefore feels his immediate departure was de rigueur."

Elizabeth raised her eyes to the ceiling and released a great sigh. "The situation is almost laughable. Caroline led him to this conclusion, and yet he didn't draw a parallel for being alone with *her*." She began to pace. "What can we do?"

Darcy, also restless, went to stand by the window. "Hartleton is sure to visit Christopher and Mary, who could make him see reason."

She turned to him, her eyes dancing. "It *is* my turn to write. But what will we say to Georgiana?"

"You may say anything you like to me."

Neither of them had seen the object of their discussion enter the room.

Darcy looked at Elizabeth, who said gently, "Come and sit by the fire for a moment."

Georgiana's reaction to the news about Mr. Hartleton was not quite what her brother and sister-in-law expected. Instead of being hurt by his unexpected departure, or vexed by Caroline's interference, she was smiling. "What a relief! I thought it was something *I* had done!" She stood up with renewed energy. "I came to tell you that Deidre wrote. She thinks if we do not go to Beechwood soon we will have to wait for spring, and asks if we might leave on Saturday. The Burnabys would come to us the day before so we can travel as a group."[44]

"I see no reason not to, as long as the weather holds," said Darcy, going to his desk. "I will write to Hartleton to say his fears are groundless, and then to Charles to warn him of our imminent arrival."

"And I will respond to Deidre." As Georgiana left the room, there was a distinct bounce in her step.

---

[44] Ever since Georgiana and Mary were taken prisoner by ne'er-do-wells on the road to Devonham, home of Lord and Lady Matlock (as recorded in *Mary, Mary, Not So Ordinary*), Mrs. Burnaby had been a nervous traveller.

Beechwood Manor, Derbyshire
November 1814

Charles Bingley entered Jane's dressing room waving Darcy's missive. "They'll be here on Saturday, my dear!"

Jane acknowledged her husband's news with a smile as she patted the back of her simple coiffure. "I like this style very well, Harriet. You may go to the kitchen now, if you like."

"Thank you, mum." The young maid curtsied in her unique manner and hurried from the room.

"She wants to be a cook, Charles."

"Harriet? A cook?"

Jane brought a hand mirror over to the long looking-glass to see the back of her hair properly. "It will be hard to replace her, for she is a pleasing girl and has learned a great deal in little time."

"What makes you think she's unhappy with things as they are now?" asked Bingley, not one to welcome change.

"She has never shirked her duties to me, but her preference is clear. It was she who made the dish with anchovies and vermicelli you liked so well at dinner last night."

"Truly?" Bingley tapped his lips. "You know, our cook does not take kindly to the requests I make for the dishes we liked so well on our wedding trip. She claims she can't understand the receipts, which were painstakingly translated for her benefit." Idly, he picked up a jar of scented talcum and sniffed the contents. "Do you think Harriet would like to be our Italian-style cook?"

"She has so far shown not only an aptitude, but an inclination towards those dishes." Jane patiently took the talcum from him and set it on the dressing-table. "I will ask Lizzy's advice on the matter."

"She will know exactly what to do." Bingley held out his hand. "Are you ready for the tour? There is plentiful ripe fruit in the orangery, which is sure to please Caroline and Culpepper. I cannot say the same for Steele, who probably has an enormous greenhouse, living in a former abbey as he does. Monks were avid gardeners and fruit growers, so I understand." He was quiet for a moment. "Do you suppose our guests would enjoy a ride to the apple orchard?"

"To see barren trees in uncomfortably cool air?" Jane looked doubtful. "Caroline might object."

"You're probably right. It's just that the orchardist thinks it might be well to survey the younger trees one last time before the real cold hits."

Chapter 24

Beechwood Manor
November 1814

Dear Molly,

    I am so grateful Mrs. Bingley taught me to read and write. I wish we could teach our mother. Then we wouldn't have to be so careful with our letters to her, knowing Mrs. Perkins will be reading them (and you know how she likes to spread tales).

    I sent the black butter receipt to Mum, with two changes—zest of lemon to brighten the taste, and less sugar unless the apples are very tart.

    When we were at Pemberley last week, Monsieur Renault let me do a bit of cooking (and showed me how to write his name). The other kitchen maids are afraid of him, especially when he gets excited and talks so loud and fast, waving his arms about. They said he does this more often when Miss Bingley is there. You should have heard him go on when he was told she wanted her food made without butter! And, her maid is still one of the meanest I've ever met. Mum always says it comes down from the mistress.

    One day M. Renault showed me how to make a pastry bread (with a good deal of butter inside). When I told him the cook at Beechwood couldn't make the bread Mr. Bingley likes best, with a tough crust and soft inside, he found a receipt in one of his own books and helped me to make it (Mr. Bingley said he liked it very well). And, on the day before we left, M. Renault reminded me to put a pan of water in the oven with the bread while it bakes.

Since we came back here I've been making all the Italian-style dishes because Mrs. Carter threatened to give notice if she had to make them anymore. Luckily, the receipts are written in English so I can read them.

The servants here say they don't like to eat 'strange' things. I tell them I used to think the same way, that all food should taste like English food.

Mrs. Bingley asked if I wanted to work in the kitchen all the time, instead of being her lady's maid. At first, all I could do was stare at the carpet, thinking she was unhappy with me. I've never been able to fix hair, or make dresses like you can, but I didn't think I was doing so very bad. Then she told me she thinks cooking is in my blood, and that I'm very good at it. (Who would think about a maid's feelings like our mistresses do?) Mrs. Bingley also wants me to ask if you know someone who could fill my position. What do you think of Cousin Jennine? Or Cousin Margaret?

For now, I'm happy with the way things are. I'm in the kitchen for part of each day because there are guests here. Miss B is one of them. Today I'm to make potato dumplings in a green herb sauce, different than anything I've tried before.

Your sister,
Harriet

~ ~ ~

~a letter from Georgiana Darcy to Mary Ashton~

November 1814

Dear Mary,

We travelled with the Burnabys to Beechwood, where Mr. Culpepper, Mr. Steele, and Caroline are also in residence. (Mr. Hartleton has returned to London, which you may already know.)

Jane and Charles have made many plans for our entertainment. On the afternoon of our arrival we went to the orangery to partake of fresh fruit. Inside the glass structure it felt like a perfect summer day.

Caroline and Deidre continually vie for the attention of Mr. S and Mr. C (Elizabeth has chosen Mr. C for Deidre). This brings to mind my aunt's ball at Devonham, when we observed (and judged) the gentlemen—including Major Ashton, who enjoyed teasing you so. You found him irritating, yet somehow it seems perfectly reasonable for you to have married him in the end. And just think of Cousin Anne, now married to Mr. Chandler, who you chose for me!

You know I have long seen Mr. H as a friend. But imagine my confusion when I began to experience something close to anger when Caroline would interrupt a conversation between us, or make little of something I said or did whilst in his company, or lead him away from me on some pretext as she did at Anne's wedding dance. I told myself it was not jealousy, but that I have come to value the time I spend in his company. Not only is he a thoughtful gentleman, but a scholar with a profound appreciation for literature and music, along with a formidable knowledge of history and foreign languages. It seems I would never tire of talking with him.

Having witnessed true affection between married couples, I am determined to wed only if I find what you, Jane, and Elizabeth share with your husbands. I now feel Mr. H would suit me. I believe you hoped I would eventually feel this way, and now that it has come to pass I need your help.

When he left us with so little warning I was admittedly hurt, and wondered if he had feelings for Caroline.

But now we know Caroline told him he was endangering my reputation and consequently my chances for a marriage appropriate to my station. Notably, the thought of him marrying her, or anyone else, makes me very unhappy. Also, when Deidre recently confessed to me that she found him too serious I could not speak to her for an hour! You may be surprised, but, rather than being upset with Caroline, I was happy because he chose London over Beechwood, which means he wasn't desperate to spend time with her.

Fitzwilliam has already responded to Mr. Hartleton's apology, and Elizabeth will soon invite him for Christmas. If you would tell him you know how very welcome he is, I think he might respond in the affirmative.

You must help me, Mary, for this time I feel I am in real danger. All my former infatuations were those of a young girl, and I can say in all honesty that I was not influenced by his purchase of a house I loved at first sight, and is also close to yours.

Do send your next letter to Pemberley, for we are returning home soon.

Yours affly,
Georgiana

n.b. As I was blotting this page, Elizabeth came to share some interesting news. Given the fine weather, Mr. Steele has invited us all to his abbey. Caroline and Deidre will go directly from here, accompanied by Mr. and Mrs. Burnaby, with Mr. Culpepper on horseback. Charles and Jane declined, as have Elizabeth and Fitzwilliam. I would enjoy seeing the abbey, but just now I do not care to play the part of the superfluous young lady.

Pemberley
December 1814

Elizabeth stood at the half-open door of the music room until she heard the fallboard close. "Was that a new piece?" she asked, approaching the pianoforte. "It seems to alternate between sadness and some other strong emotion." She peered at the music. "I don't think I could play this, even after a full year of practice."

"I imagine it would take far less time." Georgiana smiled softly. "This is a recent gift from Signor Clementi—Herr Beethoven's twenty-sixth sonata, called *Les Adieux*, which apparently has to do with a dear friend departing Vienna because of Napoleon's invasion. As a whole it is a masterful work, which must belie the cruel rumours about the composer's hearing loss."

Elizabeth tipped her head to the side. "Last night you played a work far different than this."

"It was a set of thirty variations by J.S. Bach. The theme, an aria, is a sarabande."[45] A flush rose to Georgiana's cheeks. "According to Mr. Hartleton. He enjoys hearing new works, but prefers those by the old masters, which has given me a fresh perspective of pieces I have not played in a long time."

"Your diligence shames me. I should be applying myself for Fitzwilliam and Gregory's sake, for who will play for them after you are married?"

This made Georgiana laugh. "May I suggest the sonatas of Scarlatti as a starting point?"

"You may." Elizabeth took her sister-in-law's arm as they started out. "But I completely forgot the reason I came to see you...although Mamma says forgetfulness is part and parcel of having children." She stopped at the door to announce, "Mr. Hartleton has replied to our invitation. He will join us for Christmas!"

Georgiana's pleasure was clear to see. "Then my practice has not been in vain."

---

[45] The work Georgiana played was first published in 1741, later to be called the *Goldberg Variations*.

Chapter 25

Hertford-street, London
December 1814

Christopher Ashton sat up suddenly, having been awakened by a soft voice calling his name.

"I am sorry to wake you." Mary spoke gently as she took the chair opposite him, eyeing the stack of papers on his desk. "Have you had any good news?"

Her husband adjusted his waistcoat and cravat. "In a way, yes. There has been a decision regarding Miss LeBlanc."

"Deportation?" she asked hopefully.

He nodded. "It was due solely to her cooperation of late. Also, the messages to Vienna have passed through our embassy in Paris, but I fear it will be difficult—if not impossible—to convince the delegates that there is good reason to suspect a plot leading to Napoleon's return to France. My superiors here prefer to think the unseated emperor has been successfully vanquished and will remain so forever."

He rested his elbows on the desk, steepling his fingers. "But enough of that. I hope you have pleasant news."

"I do. Firstly, Mr. Hartleton is now in London. Secondly, Georgiana wants us to convince him to return to Pemberley for Christmas."

"And?"

"I thought we could ask him to dinner."

"Any day you wish, my dear."

"Then I shall send the invitation directly after we view the library." She stood, holding her hand out to him. "Come, the architect and workmen are waiting for us."

Sunshine poured through the windows of the finished space as the architect proudly pointed out the fine woodwork, the secluded alcoves, the comfort of the window seats, the practicality of the circular bookstands that doubled as side-tables, and finally, the handsomeness of the wrought iron railing on the circular stairs and the balcony.

"It is perfect! You have transformed an over-large, unused room into something I hardly dared to imagine."

"Thank you, Mrs. Ashton." The architect bowed his head.

At that moment several trays were brought in, filled with savory and sweet items, along with pitchers of ale and cider.

Following a toast to those responsible for creating the library Mary and Christopher left, allowing the architect and the workmen to freely enjoy what had been especially prepared for them below-stairs.

Upon reaching the first floor, the Ashtons came across an unusually disheveled Molly with an oddly shaped bundle in her arms.

"Oh, Madam, Major Ashton! I had hoped not to see anyone! We came across those nasty mute swans in the park, and somehow ended up in the Serpentine." She pulled back a corner of the wet towel she was holding, and Bonnie stuck her nose out. "I just gave her a bath." The embarrassed maid looked down, the flush in her cheeks deepening. "Mr. Fletcher told me to leave my muddy shoes in the washroom." As she said this, their puppy's wagging tail also appeared. "I'd better see she is properly dried."

After her maid hurried away, Mary followed Christopher back into his study. "Is it too soon for us to think about another puppy?"

"You think Bonnie would like a playfellow, now we are settled in this house?"

"Only if you think it is a good idea as well."

"Darcy is expecting another litter. I'll write to him before they are all spoken for." He smiled gently, took her hand, and lifted it to his lips. "Would you care to go for a walk with me? The sun is shining and there is but a light breeze."

"It would be a pleasure. But if you don't mind, I'll write to Mr. Hartleton first." Idly, she aligned his pen and ink stand with the edge of the desk. "Do you wonder how we will ever fill those shelves?"

"As it happens, my father wrote to me about a friend who would like to sell the contents of his library, which are said to be remarkable." He came to her side. "However, he will not part with his books without first vetting the buyer. Shall we undergo the process, keeping in mind he may not choose us?"

She raised her chin. "I am not afraid."

Unexpectedly, Christopher lifted her up and twirled her around. Their laughter was interrupted by Mr. Fletcher, who cleared his throat.

"Excuse me, sir, and madam. Mr. Hartleton is here. Shall I say you are in?"

"We will tell him ourselves," said Christopher.

What began as a courtesy call led to a delightful walk in Hyde Park—bypassing the Serpentine—with Bonnie and Carrick, the latter being retrieved from Mr. Hartleton's carriage, then dinner, and later several games of cards in the library, with the two dogs sleeping near the hearth.

The next morning, Christopher entered the breakfast room waving a note. "Good news, Mary! We've been invited to view the contents of Mr. Mallery's library, who is—" he consulted the trimmed foolscap "—*extremely pleased to show my treasures to you*. Would this afternoon suit?"

"Yes it would. And as soon as may be," said Mary. "Last night, Mr. Hartleton mentioned his desire to have a proper library in his house. He was quite intrigued when you mentioned Mr. Mallery's fine collection."

"I had no idea you were so competitive, my dear."

"In the case of this library, I admit to the charge. What time shall we leave here?"

Christopher silently calculated the time. "No later than half-past noon, I'd say."

She calmly spread peach preserves on a warm crumpet. "My heart is beating faster at the very thought of it."

The intervening hours passed swiftly, and as the library had to be seen once more to count the number of shelves there was less time than normal for Molly to prepare madam's hair. Happily, the gown she had already pressed for the afternoon was ideal for the visit, and the Ashtons stepped out onto the pavement at the arranged time.

Once the carriage began to move, Mary returned to the topic of Mr. Hartleton. "Last night, did you find it odd when he called Georgiana 'Miss Darcy'? When at Pemberley, I recall him bandying her name about freely."

"Bandying?"

She made a face. "Perhaps the word is too strong. But the fact remains that he was used to calling her by her first name. Last night, from the very start, when I said something about her horse, and the possibility of a new puppy from the Pemberley kennels, it was 'Miss Darcy' with him."

"He did seem quite interested in the puppy."

Mary lifted her brows suggestively. "He did seem to be, just as he was with Mr. Mallery's library."

Christopher laughed. "I still wish to know why you think *not* using Georgiana's name is significant."

"Having been charged by Caroline with insulting the Darcys, he does not wish to be seen as taking liberties."

"So, by not bandying her name about—" he could not repress a smile "—we should assume he is thinking seriously about a relationship with the Darcy family?"

"Just so." Mary nodded smartly.

"I have read many novels, and thought I had a good idea of the ways of the world, but this situation I find perplexing."

"As it should be, my dear." She reached for his hand. "At Pemberley, you will have many opportunities to see I am right. And if all goes as it should in the end, Georgiana will be living in a house very near to ours!"

Chapter 26

Hertford-street, London
December 1814

In their shared room, Molly was plaiting Anna's hair in the same manner she did for their mistress most days. "Mrs. Ashton doesn't like to fuss in the morning, so when you're done, just tie it off and add a pretty ribbon, like this."

Anna used the hand mirror to view the reflection in the larger glass. "I always wondered how to make a real braid, but will I ever be able to do it like this?"

"You will, don't worry. It takes a little practice is all." Molly undid the plait and took up the brush. "Now I'll show you how to make what is called a French roll, but it's just a fancy knot. You want to brush the hair first, then lift the top section and brush it backwards, like this." She pulled the brush down twice to tease the hair. "It makes it sit a little higher in the back, like in the magazine plates. Next, I add just a touch of almond paste with rose water—I'll show you how to make it. Just a tiny bit, mind, near the roots. Then put the hair back in place and brush it lightly before pulling both sides back." She worked slowly for the other maid's benefit. "Push a plain comb in at the bottom, with just enough hair to grab it, twist the rest to one side, then tuck it under and pin it in place." She rubbed a little more paste between her hands, then lightly patted Anna's hair all around. "This should help it stay in place. We'll take a good look at the end of the day to see."

Anna looked into the mirror, shaking her head. "You say it's simple, but don't you think it's a little fancy for a maid?"

"No. It's neat and tidy, as it should be." Molly removed the pins in her own hair and began to brush it. "You can practice by plaiting my hair, then let's go down to the stillroom. I can teach you a little about making scents, and fragrance for lotions. Our mistress likes a light citrus."

Anna's eyes were wide. "You can make scents for ladies?"

Molly nodded. "I was taught when Mrs. Ashton was still Miss Bennet."

They exchanged places, and from her seat at the dressing table Molly pointed to the neatly arranged worktable. "Always have everything freshly cleaned and at hand before you go to bed. It takes only a minute or two." She sat straighter and folded her hands in her lap, grinning at Anna through the looking-glass. "Mind you don't pull so hard this time."

Anna was a good student and after two attempts at a plait managed to satisfy her tutor. Just as she was tying a white ribbon at the bottom, the housemaid appeared.

"There's a young man below-stairs. A boy, really, by the look of him. He asked to speak with Miss Annie Clarke."

Anna blushed. "I can't think of anyone who would visit me here."

"He says he's from the house you left before coming to this one," said the maid helpfully.

Molly looked up. "The boots, maybe?"[46]

"Bernie?" Anna shook her head in confusion. "Will you come with me, Molly?"

"I'd be happy to."

They followed the other maid through the baize door, then down to the servants' receiving room where they found the boots from the house on Grosvenor-street.[47]

The boy quickly got to his feet. "Miss Annie! I hardly knew you." He twisted the cap in his hands. "You may not remember me, but it's Bernie Carpenter—from the old house."

---

[46] 'Boots' or 'boot-boy' as Molly is using the term, means the servant responsible for cleaning boots and other footwear in the house.

[47] It was on an errand one day that Molly and Lucy first came across Bernie. The accidental meeting was instrumental in the discovery of strange goings-on in the former house of Lord Harold on Lower Grosvenor-street, as told in *Parlance at Pemberley*.

"I'm very glad to see you again, Bernie." Anna smiled shyly. "I hope you are well?"

He nodded happily. "I have another position now."

Molly stepped forward. "We met once before, at the cobbler shop near Grosvenor-street."

"I remember!" He shook her hand enthusiastically. "You were with another maid, who was very shy, and you said your master wanted to buy a house."

"You've a good memory. My mistress went to see the house you mentioned and later sent me with a basket to Grosvenor-street to thank you for your help. I'm sorry you weren't there."

"That was a nice basket. Luckily, the mistress didn't know about it, or she would've taken it away from us."

"I hope you have a kinder mistress in your new place." Molly motioned to the table. "Why don't you two sit down? I'll see about a tea tray." She stepped out, leaving the door open.

Mrs. Dougherty, the cook, insisted on sending the tray. "I'll have it ready in a trice. You go sit with Anna and the young man."

Back in the receiving room, the other two were talking about the servants at their former house.

"Mr. Williams was our butler," said Bernie for Molly's benefit. "He took a new position with an unmarried gentleman who recently bought a fine house and asked me to go with him. My duties include walking the master's big dog, but mainly I work as a groom...I want to be a jockey someday."

They were interrupted by the arrival of the tray, with small sandwiches and teacup cakes. The maid placed it on the table before handing Anna a letter that looked a bit worse for wear. "This is for you."

Anna barely glanced at it before slipping it into an apron pocket, while Molly poured the tea, adding four lumps of sugar to Bernie's as requested.

He smiled his thanks and turned to Anna. "Mr. Williams wanted to bring a few of us from the old house to work in this new one, so he sent me to the agencies. You were registered at the one last on my list, which is why it took me so long to find you. They wouldn't tell me much, but they did say you were engaged by a Mrs. Ashton." He took a bite from one of the three sandwiches on his plate. "I know the boots from two houses down, who knows one of the footmen here." His glance went from one to the other. "Jimmy?"

"Everyone likes Jimmy." Molly chose a sandwich with salmon paste.

"Everyone has been so kind to me, and Molly is teaching me how to be a lady's maid," said Anna. "You must thank Mr. Williams, but tell him I'm very happy here."

"You can come visit us then. It's but a short walk away. None of us were happy in the old house, were we?" He made a face and turned to Molly. "The old master had a bad temper, and, as it happened, he was a smuggler. Both he and the mistress were involved in the business, and one of the footmen too—a shifty sort. There were certain rooms the servants weren't allowed to enter. If any of us did, it would have cost us our position at the very least." He lowered his voice. "I heard later that they hid French prisoners in those rooms and were helping them escape. They say the master made a fortune doing it."

"Did they take them by boat across the Narrows?" asked Anna, unconsciously resting a hand against her apron pocket.

Bernie shot her an admiring glance. "You always were a sharp one."

"Not sharp enough to know what was going on beneath our noses in that house." Anna was frowning. "Do you know what happened to Sarah?"

"Mr. Williams asked me to look for her too, but she is not to be found." Seeing Anna's expression, Bernie added gently, "It's likely she went back home, but never did say where she was from."

"She just up and left, without a word to any of us." Anna eyed the leaves at the bottom of her cup.

Molly looked up suddenly. "Bernie, what is the name of the man whose house you're in now?"

"Mr. Hartleton, and very fond of books he is. You look funny, Miss Molly. Do you know something of him?"

"Mr. Hartleton is a good friend of our master and mistress!"

A short while later, after promising to watch for them in the park when dog walking, Bernie left and the two maids went to the stillroom as planned.

After being shown where to find all that was necessary to create various scents, Anna asked Molly if she would read her letter. "I'm getting better, thanks to you, but you're so much faster."

Molly, filled with curiosity, took the letter closer to the window and happily obliged.

Dear Anna,

Your mum told me you're finally out of that blackguard Farringdale's house. She said this major you're with now has been good to you, and helped those beer flood people.

I want you to tell him something, but keep my name out of it, for there are those who wouldn't like me blabbing. Here's what I have to say: I know they've been looking for a certain man who owns one of those fancy new houses in Sanditon. I can't risk telling the patrol about this myself, understand, but the man they want is a baron by rights who lately goes by a false name. They say he was cut out of his rich aunt's will and has no money to call his own, so took to smuggling, and worse.

One night at a pub near me, he was in his cups and bragged about how clever he was, using his house to pass smuggled goods with none the wiser. I've seen him before. When he drinks, he gets nasty, and is too free with the barmaids, especially with the daughter of a good friend.

Here's the most important part: this ne'er-do-well is about to scarper off to France. He's going in a three-masted smuggling lugger called the Pegasus, painted green last I saw, and said to go almost twelve knots. It's certain to shove off near Brighton.

That's all I know, but I hope it helps to catch him. Now, work hard, be a good girl, and soak this letter in hot water before tearing it to pieces.

Anna was very quiet as she refolded the paper and tucked it away. "If I tell the major what my uncle says, will he think I'm from a bad family and send me away?"

"No, he won't." Molly was firm. "He'll be glad you told him. If he has questions for you, it will only be to help him decide how to go about things."

The other maid stared blankly at the small bottles arranged on the shelf nearest her. "There were men like this smuggler at the other house...those who think they can say and do anything they please because you're below them. And there's no one to stop them doing it." She bit her lip. "I don't think my uncle would have written unless this baron is very bad. Will you help me tell the major?"

"Since we don't know when he'll be back, we should probably tell Mr. Fletcher you want to see him."

"Won't Mr. Fletcher want to know why?"

"If he asks, we can say you've learned something that might help the major's investigation. Mr. Fletcher's been with him a long time."

Anna nodded, but seemed doubtful as she followed Molly out.

Upon hearing their request, Mr. Fletcher said the master and mistress were expected late. "It can wait until tomorrow."

After a quick glance at Anna, Molly said, "It's about a smuggler who plans to escape to France very soon."

"I see." His tone was no different than if they had said it was raining. "I will inform the master upon his return." He eyed Anna over his spectacles. "Prepare what you wish to say to him in advance, in case he will see you. You want to be as clear as possible. Also, you must remain dressed as you are, no matter how late the hour, and no yawning."

"Yes, Mr. Fletcher," said Anna quietly. "Thank you."

"If what you have to tell Major Ashton is useful, then it is you who will be thanked." He took out his pocket watch. "Now, we would not care to make the others wait for their dinner, would we?"

Chapter 27

In a handsome home near Richmond, the Ashtons took as much pleasure in perusing the contents of the library as the Mallerys did in showing them. It was clear that the collection would exactly suit their guests and Mrs. Mallery suggested Mary might like to see the chapel, thus allowing the gentlemen to discuss business.

"It is the only part left of the original house, dating from the fifteenth century." As they walked down the main corridor together, she added, "The stained glass is still intact, and is quite something."

The two ended the tour in a sitting room connected to the library, where a tea tray was waiting for them. While Mrs. Mallery poured, she said, "I was pleased to hear Christopher had married, for we thought him a confirmed bachelor. And now to know he is not only wed to an authoress, but the very one who wrote *The Turret Room*!" She held up the sugar tongs.

"Just lemon, thank you." Mary leaned forward to take the cup. "I understand you and your husband knew Christopher as a youngster."

"We did, and have enjoyed watching him grow into a fine young man." Mrs. Mallery dropped the lump into her own tea. "He grew to be an observer of society rather than a participant, and shunned those acquaintances he sensed were more interested in his father's position than in his own merit."

"It is a side of him I know well; he told me about his father only after we were married."

Mrs. Mallery laughed, shaking her head. "I look forward to hearing his side of the story at dinner."

When their tea was finished, but still no sign of Mr. Mallery and Christopher, Mrs. Mallery suggested they view the family portraits. "I expect the gentlemen will find us shortly."

The two stopped before a painting of a man dressed in a somber coat with a wide white collar, ruffs at his wrists, and wide-topped boots. "He is an ancestor of Mr. Mallery, sadly found guilty of traitorous exploits against Oliver Cromwell."

While viewing the portrait of the unfortunate man's wife, also in somber garb, Mrs. Mallery said, "I hope you intend to continue writing."

"I do. When Christopher proposed, he said he would very much like to be married to a novelist."

"Good for him! And what are you calling your latest book?"

"*The Bell Tower*." Mary turned to her hostess. "All save one of the novels are drawn from personal experience."

"Truly?"

"Yes, so I cannot take full credit for imagination."

Winding her arm through Mary's, Mrs. Mallery led them past the remaining portraits. "How pleased I am to know you, my dear."

At dinner, Christopher did not encourage many tales from his childhood, but there was never a shortage of topics. As they were saying good-bye, Mrs. Mallery hugged each of them. "You must promise to visit again before we leave."

"And you must come to us once our library shelves are filled," said Christopher with a handsome bow.

Later than planned, the Ashtons' carriage went down the crushed-stone drive, but a waning gibbous moon and the footmen's lanterns enabled them to reach Hertford-street safely. At the house, they were met by Mr. Fletcher, who relayed Anna's request as he took the major's coat.

"Will you stay with me, Mary?" asked Christopher. "She'll likely be more comfortable with you there."

"Of course." Mary handed over her gloves and redingote before picking up Bonnie. "Shall we meet in the garden room? It is the least formal."

Upon receiving the summons Anna and Molly hurried down the stairs, slowing their steps only as they approached the room.

As Mr. Fletcher suggested, they had decided in advance what Anna would say. Without evidence of nerves, the new maid recited the relevant portions of her uncle's letter, just as they had practiced. When finished, she took the letter from her apron pocket. "If you would like to have it, sir."

The major did not immediately take it from her. "I will black out his name and anything else that might indicate who wrote it, or from where it was sent."

"Thank you, sir." Anna curtseyed.

Once the maids had gone, he said to Mary, "I must send a messenger tonight."

"Then I will see you later." She stood on her tiptoes, kissed his cheek, and motioned for Bonnie to follow her out.

Chapter 28

The next afternoon Christopher found Mary in the library, humming absently as she went from one empty section to the next. He leaned against the door frame, arms crossed, observing as she stopped frequently to write in her notebook.

Finally, he tapped lightly on the wood and stepped inside.

She started. "Christopher! I had no idea you were back. Any news of the baron smuggler?"

"The riding officers near Brighton and Sanditon should have been alerted by now, and the search begun."

"If only they could find him, so many questions might be answered. Do you think he was with those Frenchmen who left the maid and her husband to perish?"

"It's possible those men are still waiting for a boat, maybe even the Pegasus mentioned by Anna's uncle."

"I hope this can be resolved without violence." She took hold of his hand and pulled him to the center of the room. "Perhaps I can turn your thoughts to something more pleasant." She pointed upwards. "Do you think it best to begin placing the collection on the balcony or the main level?"

Christopher took time to consider the question. "You may decide to organize the books by what you want most accessible, with science, history, and the like in one area, poetry and novels in another."

"That appeals to me. When will the books be delivered?"

"In a fortnight, if all goes as planned."

"In which case, the project may need to wait until our return from Derbyshire." She folded her arms. "Do you think we could convince Georgiana to come back with us? She would be a great help to me."

"You need only ask her." Christopher reached out to move a stray lock of hair from her cheek. "Especially if she knows you asked for Hartleton's assistance as well."

Mary smiled mischievously. "I will write to each of them this afternoon."

"When you've finished, would you care to take Bonnie for a walk in the park? It's a fine day—something I fear is soon to be an exception."

"I would love to."

As they walked out of the library, a maid appeared with a note. "It's from Hartleton," said Christopher. "His new dining table has arrived, and he would like us to come to dinner this evening."

"What perfect timing!" Excessively pleased, Mary watched her husband write the response.

The lamp lighters had already been by when the Ashtons stepped down from their carriage. Pausing on the wide pavement to admire the white-brick building's façade, Christopher said quietly, "Hartleton *must* be thinking of marriage and a family."

Mary leaned her head back, but the light from the street lamps did not reach the top floor. "Georgiana thought the nursery was too small, and I found the furnishings a little oppressive." She tapped his arm. "Wait until you see the ballroom."

The two stepped up to the door, which was opened by their host just as Christopher was reaching for the lion head knocker.

"I saw your carriage and was too impatient to wait." Mr. Hartleton smiled and waved them inside. "Welcome!"

The butler took their outer garments, then Mr. Hartleton led his guests to a nearby sitting room, offering sherry, port, and madeira. "Or would you prefer something else?"

Mary and Christopher gave their preferences and he went to the sideboard to pour the drinks himself. "I'm unaccustomed to being served every little thing. All this—" he made a sweeping motion "—is an adjustment for me, just as my ways are for the servants, who are used to a more...shall I say conventional master?" He brought the three glasses on a tray, then took a seat across the low table. "Each was hand-picked by Williams, the butler. He is from the house on lower Grosvenor-street, the former home of those smugglers you caught last month." At Christopher's sharp glance, he added, "I find him trustworthy."

After hearing about their host's inability to decide upon furnishings, Mary and Christopher expressed their interest in a tour and soon the three were passing from one elaborately adorned room to another, ultimately going out to view the back garden where hanging lanterns gave off little light amongst the shadows.

"It grows dark so early now," said Mr. Hartleton.

"Before long, we'll all have gas lamps to light our back gardens," said Christopher as he approached the fountain with spouting metal fish. "You mentioned this feature particularly, Mary."

"I've seen finches stop to drink from it," said Mr. Hartleton proudly. "But it is chilly out here. Shall we go back inside?"

"How does Carrick like the ballroom?" asked Mary as they re-entered the house.

"She treats it as her own—you will see."

They ascended the stairs to the galleried landing, waking Hartleton's dog from a nap when they passed through the set of tall, ornate doors.

"Do you think I should keep this as it is?" asked Mr. Hartleton, scratching Carrick's head when she came to his side.

"It is beautifully done, and not over-large," observed Mary. "I would hesitate before making any changes just yet."

"I agree," said Christopher, moving to the line of windows facing out on the street. "Should you choose to wed, which I can highly recommend—" he caught Mary's eye "—your wife may have very definite ideas."

Their host was apparently not opposed to the thought. "Lord Exeter expressed an interest in visiting when back in town, and said he hoped to bring his bride with him. I'd like to host a dinner for them and would like you to be here." There was a slight hesitation. "Perhaps Miss Darcy could also join the party, if she is in London."

Mary avoided Christopher's gaze, apparently fascinated by some scrollwork on a pillar. "We were introduced to Mrs. Beasely at the race-ball in York. She is a charming lady and I would very much like to know her better." Turning away from the pillar, she added casually, "Only today, I wrote to Georgiana about returning with us after Christmas to help organize the library."

Just then the dinner bell rang, and Mr. Hartleton made a slight motion for Carrick to walk beside him as they left the ballroom.

"We must tell you about the contents of the Mallery library," said Christopher. "Choosing where to place so many books will be a monumental task, and we could use your help as well."

"It would be a pleasure, I assure you. I am curious to see the treasures you've acquired." Mr. Hartleton paused at the top of the stairs. "And envious."

Three places were set at the end of the highly polished dining table, nearest the fire, with Mr. Hartleton between Mary and Christopher.

At the onset of the first course, their host mentioned a concert being held the next evening at St. George's, Hanover Square. "The program includes operatic works of Niccolò Piccinni, and his flute concerto. Will you be my guests?"

The Ashtons smiled at one another across the table.

"We would be delighted," said Christopher. "In turn, would you be our guest next week to hear the *Christmas Oratorio*? "[48]

"Yes, thank you. I appreciate any opportunity to hear music from bygone eras. Many great composers are sadly neglected of late." Mr. Hartleton tried the soup, appeared satisfied, and his guests followed suit. Shortly afterwards, he asked, "When do you leave for Pemberley?"

"On the fifteenth, if the weather holds," said Christopher.

---

[48] Christopher is referring to a work by J.S. Bach, comprised of six single cantatas historically performed over the same number of days during the season. In this case, the performance of all six would last three hours or more.

"Winter does have a way of surprising us," said Mr. Hartleton. "One has only to recall last February, when another frost fair was held on the Thames."

"With a thick fog over London beforehand," said Christopher. "Did you read the account of the Maidenhead coach getting lost in it, and ultimately overturning?"

"I did, and also the accounts of various coachmen forced to lead their horses on foot through the streets of London. I am not sorry to have missed it."

Mary shivered. "I hope this year will be different."

"Evelyn commonly made notes about the weather during the seventeenth century. Throughout the sixty-six years of his diary, he described extreme drought, flood, frosts, extraordinarily cold and warm winters, and more than once wrote about the Thames freezing." He took a sip of wine. "I just read an entry which described in detail one of the fairs held atop the ice, but don't recall the exact dates."[49]

"I hope the family chooses to publish this diary one day, for I would very much like to read it." Just then, Mary perceived a large dog sitting patiently at her side. Shaking her head with regret, she did not offer anything from the table to Carrick, given recent restrictions about doing the same with Bonnie.

"I too hope they agree to it," said Mr. Hartleton. "His words must bear true witness to the era, as he apparently was free to describe events exactly as he saw them."

"Was Evelyn not one of a group of physicians and natural philosophers who founded the Royal Society?" asked Christopher, ignoring Mary's surprised glance.

"Indeed he was. I believe certain diary entries might be of use to our scientists today and hope to broach the topic with his family when next I am in Sussex." Mr. Hartleton then said to Mary, "I plan to suggest publication, but daresay they will want careful editing, should they agree."

---

[49] The entry, which Mr. Hartleton later found, was written 24 January 1684. In it, Evelyn describes the Frost Fair as "...a bacchanalian triumph, or carnival on the [frozen] water." The 9 January 1684 entry reads: "I went across the Thames on the ice, now become so thick as to bear...streets of booths, in which they roasted meat, and had divers shops of wares...as in a town...."

During the dessert course, consisting of nutmeats, stewed fruit, and aniseed biscuits, Mary broached a topic of particular interest to her. "Miss Darcy wrote to me about seeing a new electrical device, which you offered to show her when she comes to town."

For a moment Mr. Hartleton seemed confused. "Oh, yes. You refer to the voltaic pile—a recent invention that produces an electric current."

"Such as what Mr. Benjamin Franklin thought to capture from lightning strikes?" asked Christopher.

"Nothing so powerful, but it is man-made and offers many possibilities for the future. Mr. Humphrey Davy, a fellow of the royal society, has told me I might bring whomever I wish to see it. Does the subject interest you?"

"I enjoy learning anything about science," replied Mary. "Miss Darcy and I once attended a lecture on static electricity and found it fascinating."

"Then I will arrange a private showing when Miss Darcy is expected in town."

After dinner they adjourned to the sitting room for port and tea. Comfortably seated, Christopher lifted his glass. "You have a fine cook, Hartleton."

Mary took advantage of their quiet toast to broach another topic of great interest to her. "Mr. Hartleton, it occurs to me that I've never heard anyone call you by your first name."

"Nor I," said her husband.

Mr. Hartleton set his glass down. "It requires explanation, I'm afraid. My parents were both historians and when it came time, after much deliberation, they chose Perceval." He noted their reactions and spelled it. "The name derives from a twelfth-century romance, in verse form, by Chrétien de Troyes, who wrote the earliest known account of King Arthur's knights and the quest for the grail. Perceval was one of the knights, known for his child-like innocence, which was proof against worldly evils."

"How charming," said Mary. "Do you think we know one another well enough now to make use of it?"

The two men looked at one another with mock seriousness for a moment before Christopher broke the silence. "What plans have you for your ballroom, Perceval?"

"Honestly, I think it would make an ideal music room, one which could accommodate a good number of guests and musicians...Christopher." Perceval was smiling when he turned to Mary. "Yesterday I visited Muzio Clementi's shop—as suggested by Miss Darcy—to purchase a pianoforte. Do you think I should have a harpsichord as well?"

Mary took a slow breath. "I believe Georgiana takes great pleasure in playing music by the elder Bach and his contemporaries on the one at Pemberley." She included Christopher in her glance. "But before I forget, might we host a light dinner prior to the Piccinni concert? If I'm hungry I will begin looking at the programme to see how much longer the music will continue."

"I never like to feel hungry during a performance," agreed Christopher solemnly. "We should allow enough time for a proper look at our empty library."

"I look forward to it," replied Mr. Hartleton. "But as you've convinced me to leave the ballroom as it is, I now need to choose where to place my own library. There are two sizeable rooms on the ground floor, one facing the back garden."

"Windows are highly desirable in a library," said Mary as she petted Carrick beside her. "And from our garden room Bonnie has the freedom to go outdoors without a lead."

Her husband took a sip of port. "Since being married, I've learned the location of rooms where one spends a great deal of time is important to a wife."

Mr. Hartleton observed his guests closely. "My parents enjoyed a harmonious marriage, even when working together on a research project. Not many I know are so fortunate...aside from the three Bennet sisters and their husbands." He hesitated. "I had never thought to be so lucky, but there is one...a pearl beyond price. She could wed a duke, or a prince, or simply decide never to marry. She is a refined musician, a dedicated scholar, and as far above me as any I can name. If I had even the smallest chance of succeeding, I would have every room in this house done over exactly to her specifications."

It was the most the Ashtons had ever heard him say at once, and a little time passed before either could respond.

*　*　*

Later, travelling the short distance between houses, Christopher took Mary's hand in his. "You should be well-pleased."

Mary was unconsciously biting her lip. "About anything in particular?"

"We learned two important things this evening."

"Let me see...you must be referring to Perceval."

"Yes. If he is to be part of the family, we can't always be addressing him by his surname, can we?"

"And *I'm* the one with match-making tendencies," she teased. "What of the second important thing?" Her tone betrayed an element of anxiety.

"Can there be any question who is the 'pearl beyond price'?"

"I think not, but what if I'm wrong? There are *two* wealthy, independent ladies who play and sing well, and who spent a good deal of time in the Pemberley library with our friend Perceval." She spoke quietly, as if giving voice to the thought might adversely affect the fate of her dearest friend. "One was Miss Caroline Bingley."

"Caroline? Never!" Had there been light enough to see, Christopher's expression alone should have convinced her. "Hartleton is a man of sense. He knows the difference between a real scholar and a spurious one. No, it is without doubt Georgiana. You can rest easy, my dear." Silence followed his declaration, save the clopping of horses' hooves, until he added, "I've been meaning to say how well you look in your new hat."

Mary entwined her gloved fingers through his. "It is only new trimming, done by Anna."

"She did very well." He paused. "I wonder...with the library almost complete, would you care to start thinking about a water feature for our back garden, such as Perceval has?"

Chapter 29

Hertford-street, London
December 1814

Mary had responded to Lydia's request[50] for monetary aid by sending the funds directly to Mr. Bennet in York to distribute at his will.

Since her father rarely wrote letters and Lydia only did so when she wanted something, the unexpected appearance of one from the former had her glancing across the table at Christopher, who was at the moment hidden behind the morning edition of *The Times*.

With a look of pleased anticipation, she broke the seal.

~a letter from Mr. Bennet to Mary Ashton~

York, November 1814

Dear Mary,

Your mamma wishes me to say how much we are enjoying our stay in your house. She also wants me to say she has an idea about the curtains, but I have told her she must write to you herself.

I find this town ideal for a somewhat retiring man accustomed to country life. The location of the house allows me to step out at will, and to visit the bookseller next door each day,

---

[50] 'Demand' was the word Elizabeth used in her letter.

no matter the weather. Your mamma and I have seen a good number of the churches already, and go frequently to the magnificent minster, where we have heard the most beautiful music.

Your sister Kitty keeps more and more to her chamber as her time approaches, craving the same foods your mamma did in the weeks before each of you were born. She would wake me in the wee hours to ask for odd things, most often India pickle and brown bread. In those days I would go to the kitchen myself to forage rather than wake the servants, though I cannot imagine Mr. Darnell doing the same.

I have given only one quarter of the money you sent to Lydia, for she must learn to curb her expenses. We have yet to hear any word about Wickham, and she claims to know nothing about his whereabouts. She has grown bored here and nearly convinced me to escort her and your mamma to an assembly, but when Kitty heard about the plan she cried all one night and into the next day. Some say this sort of thing can lead to sadness in the child, and I have made it plain there will be no assemblies until the Darnells can be included in the party.

There is something more pressing, however. I would like to ask Christopher to make inquiries about a Mr. Milton, who was amongst those passengers on the ship sailing from the West Indies that was taken prisoner by the Americans. Apparently, this man formed an acquaintanceship with Lydia during the voyage, claiming to be friends with Wickham when they served together in Newcastle. This person has called twice at least at Garden Place, and yesterday I found Lydia alone with him in the sitting room when Mr. Darnell was at his place of business and your mamma was with Kitty. Knowing well what she might do if I absolutely forbade her to see him again, I have told the servants she is not to be at home to him unless your mamma, myself, or Mr. Darnell are with her. She stamped her feet and pretended to cry, as expected, but I daresay she will do as I decreed for a short time at least.

Fondly,
Your Papa

By the time Mary finished reading, Christopher had set aside his newspaper. "Is there bad news?"

"No, it is only Lydia." She slid the letter towards him. "Papa wants you to investigate a man who visits her at Kitty's house. He was aboard the ship when the Americans took the passengers prisoner."

"How interesting."

"And worrisome. It seems the only way to control her is through her allowance."

Christopher read the pertinent section. "The name Milton is not familiar to me, but I will make inquiries."

"Thank you." Mary took up a second letter. "Georgiana wrote as well. Do you mind if I read it now? There is much to be done before Perceval comes this afternoon."

"Not at all. I'll write to a man I've engaged in the past. If anyone can learn something about this Milton fellow, he can."

~a letter from Georgiana Darcy to Mary Ashton~

Pemberley
December 1814

Dear Mary,

It is so quiet here now that I can see the benefits of occasionally hosting a large party.

Elizabeth has begun to plan for Christmas, and, as Mr. Hartleton has a preference for Herr Haydn, I am practicing his last three sonatas for pianoforte, composed during his London years. (By the bye, have you called on Mr. H at the new house? I wonder if the previous owner's furnishings are still in place, and what he will do with the ballroom.) But back to music: I recently found a book of harpsichord pieces my mother used to play. They are delightful, but the dogs tend to howl with the harpsichord, which, as you know, can be very loud. Or perhaps it is the action of the keys. There are also three Night Songs composed by Mr.

Field,[51] and the recently published Sonata in E Minor) by Herr Beethoven. The last is a singular work, the opening themes almost like a spirited conversation between parties, and I am convinced those who say he has lost his hearing cannot be right. Having read about Napoleon's invasions of Vienna, I believe the consequences of war weigh heavily upon this great composer, and he expresses this through his music.

Caroline, Deidre, and Mr. and Mrs. Burnaby are now at Audley Abbey in Kent. According to C's letter, it is replete with hidden passageways, narrow stone chambers, enormous fireplaces, a balustraded parapet, and a belfry. Sadly, she did not write about ghostly sounds or apparitions. They have been to Tunbridge Wells to visit the shops along the Parade, formerly known as the Pantiles. Apparently, Tunbridge is not the fashionable watering place it once was, when the likes of Richardson, Johnson, and Garrick visited,[52] yet she says it has ageless charm, and claims the water is more healthful than in Bath. (Notably, she now refers to Mr. S and Mr. C by their first names. I do hope the Burnabys are not distracted chaperones.)

During our time at Beechwood, Molly's sister Harriet made several Italian-style dishes requested by Charles, which pleased him no end. One evening, Mr. Steele had so much difficulty with the long vermicelli that he could not eat it, whilst Mr. Culpepper, who mastered the twirling fork, said aloud that he preferred English cooking! I recall Mr. H was always happy to try new foods.

I hope your return to Pemberley will not be delayed by weather, and should you still wish it I would very much like to return to London with you and Christopher.

Affly,
Georgiana

n.b. You might tell Mr. H that he is bound to be called upon to play duets. Also, does Molly have another sister or cousin she can recommend for the position of lady's maid?

---

[51] These works were later referred to as nocturnes; Field is often called the inventor of the genre.
[52] The three named are, respectively, author, dictionary writer, and actor/playwright.

Chapter 30

Hertford-street, London
same day

Before going to her dressing room, preparatory to Mr. Hartleton's arrival, Mary told Christopher about Georgiana's hopes of coming to London in January.

"Then all the characters will be in place, and we need only sit back and wait to see how things come to pass."

"You sound like a novelist."

"Or perhaps a husband with a novelist-wife?".

"Not for much longer, I fear." Mary sighed. "Miss Hutton insists I use my pen to improve the state of the world, but I feel inadequate to the task."

"Miss Hutton's advice, unsolicited as it was, could have hit upon an inner desire of your own. If you give yourself time and think not of what she or the publisher wants, it will come to you."

She rested her head against his chest. "Thank you."

Seated at the dressing table, Mary looked through the mirror at Molly. "Have you heard from Harriet?"

"Yes. She told me Mrs. Bingley asked if she would prefer to work solely in the kitchen."

"And what does Harriet think?"

"She is happy with her current situation, and afraid of such a change."

Mary thought for a moment. "You and she share that feeling, I believe. She about cooking, and you with dressmaking."

Molly frowned as she continued with the complicated coiffure. "Anna needs more training, and I'm happy to keep things as they are for now."

"To be quite honest, it is a relief to hear you say it." Mary smiled. "But, just in case Harriet chooses the kitchen, do you happen to have another sister?"

"Not a sister, but I do have a cousin just outside Lambton who might be a fair replacement." Molly took a dab of almond paste to dab the hair, then gave her mistress a hand mirror. "Will this do?"

Mary turned her head back and forth. "It's lovely." She set the mirror down and went to the dressing screen.

"Anna prepared the silk and the embroidered muslin for you," said Molly proudly.

Arms folded, Mary considered each. "She must be getting better at ironing."

"She is, but I don't dare leave her alone yet."

"The silk for tonight, I think. Those big halls can be drafty."

Later, as Mary and Christopher approached the library, she gave voice to a nagging thought. "Some might say my desire to match our two friends is self-serving, for if they marry I will have Georgiana living much closer to me than I could have dreamed. With any other man, she could move far away, perhaps to a distant island, or even Cornwall."

Christopher laughed. "We would benefit by their proximity, surely, but who would blame us for wishing for it?" He took a moment to study her gown. "Is this new?"

"I have worn it but once." Mary turned in a circle so he could see it properly. "It may seem new because Molly continues to make modifications to my dresses."

"It suits you very well." He smiled and looked about the room. "Were we not to host a literary evening when the library was finished?"

"I sent a note to Mrs. Penrose to say I wished to wait until the books were on the shelves. When we return home, Georgiana can help me plan the event."

"And what of Miss Hutton? I thought she was particularly interested in visiting."

"She has caught a chill and sent a note to say she must regrettably postpone. I had cook prepare a basket and sent it along with various ladies' magazines, though I had to explain why certain pages were missing, as Molly had cut out many of the fashion plates." Given his bewildered look, Mary explained, "Miss Hutton expressed an interest in those magazines." She wore a mischievous smile. "She sent a note to thank me, stating her wish to discuss the contents when we return home."

"I do like to hear you say 'home' when referring to this house."

"Not, perhaps, as much as I like to say it. But back to Miss Hutton. She is nearing sixty, when any little illness leads to weeks in bed. She claims she does not mind as there is much work to do on her father's autobiography. When we spoke at Mrs. Penrose's party, she told me he once walked the entire length of Hadrian's Wall, and suggested I read the personal account in his book, *The History of the Roman Wall*."[53]

"He's an ambitious man. The wall is seventy-three miles long, 'from sea to sea'—" Christopher grinned "—another bit of information passed on by a tutor."

"Which makes the feat even more remarkable, for Mr. Hutton completed this walk at nearly eighty years of age. *Then* he wrote the book."[54]

"He may be the only person in history, or in the future, to walk its length. I think it would be wise to have his book in our library, before Miss Hutton's visit if possible."

Just as Mary was about to reply, Mr. Hartleton was announced.

* * *

December 1814

On the morning following the concert, Molly brought a breakfast tray to her mistress much later than usual, placing it on the dressing room desk as requested.

---

[53] Also known as Hadrian's Wall (Latin: *Vallum Hadriana*), and Picts' Wall.
[54] Mr. Hutton had been heard to say that the word 'bank' was a better descriptor than 'wall' given its construction.

Mary yawned and stretched her arms before putting on the soft dressing gown Molly had placed on the edge of the bed. "Mr. Hartleton came home with us last night after the concert. I slept later than intended and would like to get a letter in the next post, so I'll wait to dress."

Molly nodded and slipped out quietly, for the master had informed her of the long concert, followed by a late night with their guest.

In the dressing room, Mary poured a cup of coffee from the silver pot, took a sip, and picked up her feather pen. Following a description of the music the night before, the attending audience, and the colder temperatures, she addressed her friend's questions singly. First was the intended date of their departure for Hertfordshire.

Originally, we planned to leave on the fifteenth, but Christopher now thinks we should leave on or before the thirteenth, thus giving Sunday travel a wide berth.

The next topic was Mr. Hartleton's house, furnishings, and the like.

I did not care to recommend changes, even when asked, but Christopher and I agreed about keeping the ballroom as it is, for it is beautifully done and a perfect size for so many things—plays, music, and throwing the ball for Carrick (which is an amusing thing to watch). As for the nursery, I did mention the possibility of expansion.

She then addressed the question about a new maid for Jane.

Since Anna came to us, Molly has time for dressmaking but still retains certain duties she does not wish to surrender. There is a cousin who may do (I'll add the address at the bottom), but if Harriet is like her sister, she may not be ready to surrender her position altogether. In which case, Jane could engage the cousin to lighten Harriet's duties.

With a sigh, she wrote the latest news from the Gardiners.

We have seen them only once since they returned to London, after which they have had to decline all invitations, including to roast dinner, for the children are passing an illness to one another—in order of age strangely enough—and now the physician recommends quarantine, which means it is unlikely that they will go to Pemberley for Christmas. My aunt thinks the cause of the illness may be the London fogs, which I suspect will eventually lead to their permanent residence in Sanditon.

Mr. H will happily arrange a demonstration of the voltaic pile for us when you are in town. Yesterday I lent him some of the duets you and I have played together, which he promises to practice diligently (on his handsome new pianoforte). He and Christopher plan to prepare works for violin and pianoforte as well.

Next week we are attending a performance of the Christmas Oratorio, with Mr. H as our guest. Then it will be time to prepare for our journey to Derbyshire, the thought of which gives me great pleasure.

About to write the address on the back of the sheet, she thought of something else. Not overly fond of cross-written letters, she added on the side, in the smallest possible script:

Mr. H hopes to speak with your kennel master about a spaniel puppy (he would like a second dog, but his valet threatened to leave if he chooses another mastiff).

Before folding the packet, Mary included a brief note to Elizabeth stating her concern about their youngest sister's actions as described by Mr. Bennet.

"Foolish, foolish Lydia," she whispered.

Chapter 31

In the little study at the Ashtons' house in York, Mr. Bennet's normally clear brow was marred by a deep furrow. He was reading his son-in-law's letter, sent by special messenger, regarding the man who had befriended Lydia on the ship captured by the Americans.

> *His name is not Milton, but Blanchard. When stationed in Newcastle, he and Wickham were frequently together, each known for unscrupulous, scandalous behaviour, and reckless gambling. Each was infamously slow in paying debts to merchants and to their fellows in the Regulars. The two escaped their creditors by emigrating to the West Indies. Why Blanchard has returned to England is in question, for he risks debtors' prison. My agent was quite clear: this man is untrustworthy, and without doubt an undesirable acquaintance.*

Mr. Bennet leaned back, fingers steepled. He sat there for a while, deep in thought, before going to find Mrs. Bennet, who was in the kitchen with the cook-housekeeper. The two were seated near the fire, each with a cup of tea in hand, laughing.

"Mr. Bennet!" His wife dabbed at her eyes with an embroidered handkerchief. "You cannot imagine what I thought Mrs. Shaw said she was making for our dinner! After all these weeks, I still do not understand the language here!"

He eyed the two with amusement. "I *had* thought it was English, Mrs. Bennet."

"Dear me, yes. But it is *how* they speak it."

He cleared his throat. "I must see Edward on a matter of business."

"Then I will go with you, and sit with Kitty, poor dear." Mrs. Bennet rose with unusual alacrity. "It has been a pleasure, Mrs. Shaw."

Leading the way up the steep, narrow stairs, Mrs. Bennet kept a firm grip on the handrail. At the landing she turned to say, "It will take no time at all for me to change, so don't get too comfortable, my dear."

"I will remain close by, Mrs. Bennet." Mr. Bennet's glance was teasing. "I do find a small house to be a great benefit when time is of the essence."

Mrs. Bennet looked uncomprehending as she stepped into their chamber, after which her husband of more than four and twenty years went to the study to retrieve a book from the shelf (Mrs. Bennet insisted the house was too small to leave anything lying about). He settled into the chair by the window, and forty minutes later his wife appeared, freshly dressed and bonneted.

"You see, Mr. Bennet? I am as good as my word."

"You are indeed, my dear." He rose and made a gallant bow. "Shall we?"

With the help of the housemaid, the Bennets donned their heavy outer things, but once outside Mr. Bennet pulled his wool scarf more tightly round his neck. "If you don't care to walk in this weather, Mrs. Bennet, I will ask one of the servants to fetch sedan chairs."

Mrs. Bennet turned her head side to side as if to gauge the wind. "It is not so bad today." She took firm hold of his arm and tested the stone with the toe of one of her practical boots. "Nor is it slippery. Today we will walk, Mr. Bennet, for the exercise is healthful."

As they walked on, she was seemingly unaware of his bemusement.

Upon reaching their son-in-law's house in Garden-place, the Bennets were told by the maid that Mrs. Darnell was resting and shown into the sitting room.

Standing near the fire to warm his hands, Mr. Bennet said he would like to speak with Mr. Darnell without delay.

"The master is at his place of business, sir."

"And Mrs. Wickham?"

"She had a visitor, sir, and has gone out walking."

"Out walking? Lydia?" Mrs. Bennet turned to her husband with astonishment. "In this weather?"

Mr. Bennet addressed the maid once more. "Can you name this visitor?"

The maid, her face flushed, answered weakly, "Mr. Milton, sir."

At this admission, Mr. Bennet's jaw clenched. "Please see to Kitty, Mrs. Bennet, for it seems she's been abandoned. I must speak with Edward without further delay."

*　　*　　*

Mr. Edward Darnell, the fourth Bennet son-in-law by wedding date and by order of daughters, sent his clerk to ask Mr. Bennet if he would please take a seat.

The clerk apologized for the delay. "Mr. Darnell will be with you shortly, and asks if you would care to accompany him to a nearby pub, renowned for its fish pie."

Though impatient to address the issue of Lydia's caller, Mr. Bennet assented, and in a reasonable time the two men were stepping out of the building.

As they strolled down the narrow pavement, Mr. Bennet relayed the contents of Christopher's letter. "It is a matter of some urgency that you forbid this man entry into your home, while I forbid Lydia to see him again."

"These are extreme measures," said Mr. Darnell. "Mr. Milton has always behaved with decorum in my house, and seems only sympathetic to Lydia, as befits her husband's good friend."

Mr. Bennet hurried to keep up with him as they crossed the narrow cobblestone street. "Wickham was the same in Meryton—charming and cheating all those he met. Not until he had run away with Lydia did we know his true nature. But for the sake of my family, I would have seen the scoundrel put in irons.

Therefore, when Christopher says there is reason to question this man's intentions, I believe him."

They had reached the pub and he struck his walking-stick against the pavement for emphasis.

The strength of his father-in-law's words, a clear chastisement, brought a spot of color to Mr. Darnell's normally pale cheeks as they went inside.

They took a quiet table at the back and ordered brown porter ale from the barmaid. Removing his coat, for the pub was almost too warm inside, Mr. Darnell said, "I think it best for you, as Lydia's father, to deal with Milton. I will instruct my maid to refuse him entry should the need arise, but I am often away from home and don't see how a servant girl can prevent Lydia from slipping out on her own to meet him."

"I see you have come to know her," said Mr. Bennet wryly as he sampled the ale with an approving look. "We will try it your way. I will write to Mr. Milton and speak firmly with Lydia. She has always been headstrong and foolish, and I daresay will object to any restrictions. Should she refuse to end the acquaintance, I will cut off her allowance and send her back to Jamaica."

With the business settled the two men attended to the fish pie, worthy of its reputation, and afterwards set off to Garden Place.

Immediately upon stepping inside the white-washed house Mr. Bennet inquired after Lydia, who had only recently returned from her constitutional with Mr. Milton, though that gentleman had already left.

She entered the sitting room meekly enough, until hearing what Christopher's agent had divulged.

"What does he know about it? He has never met him!" She stamped her foot and marched to the window facing the street, chin trembling. "Mr. Milton has been nothing but kind to me since that horrid American ship attacked ours." She swung round to face her father, having produced a tear or two. "There is nothing here to amuse me! Kitty never leaves her room and is always complaining. Mamma speaks only of babies, and how she longs for me to give her a grandchild. It is too much, I tell you!" Again she stamped, her hands forming little fists.

"Lydia, you will agree never to see that man again, or you will be put aboard a ship and sent back to your husband." Her father's tone alone should have subdued her.

"Husband? Wickham is unworthy of the word!" At this, actual tears began to flow and she ran from the room.

Mr. Bennet, preferring calm to storm when dealing with the female members of his family, rang the bell to ask for a glass of port. "And please ask Mr. Darnell to join me," he said to the wide-eyed maid, who had witnessed Mrs. Wickham's exit.

~a letter from Mr. Bennet to Christopher Ashton~

Grape-street, York, December 1814

Dear Christopher,

Thank you for the information about Mr. Milton. Both Edward and I have instructed our servants never to allow the man inside the house, and Lydia has promised (after a good deal of crying) not to see him. She cannot be trusted, but if she misbehaves there will be no allowance for her. Additionally, I have sent a very strong letter forbidding him to see my daughter again, and spoke with a local constable about the matter.

Aside from this, Lydia has finally admitted to some trouble with Wickham, which might explain her solitary journey across the sea, but she would give no details and refuses to say more on the subject. Therefore, I write with yet another request for information. Is it possible for you to learn something about George Wickham's situation in Jamaica? How I wish we had never met the man!

Regarding Kitty, Mrs. Bennet believes the child will arrive within the next fortnight and anticipates a difficult birth. She has ever been more fearful for Kitty than the other girls in the way of health and strength, but I know better than to suggest my wife coddle less and challenge more. We shall see.

Sincerely,
R. Bennet

Having sent the letter, Mr. Bennet remained in his study until it was time for dinner, wondering just how to convince his wife to approach Lydia regarding the topic of Wickham.

It was not until after they had partaken of the leek soup and shepherd's pie that he decided on a strategy, and waited until later, when they were tucked under the covers of the bed, the curtains drawn round the frame. Fluffing his pillow, he sat back in a posture to welcome conversation.

"You wish to say something, Mr. Bennet?" Mrs. Bennet's head, covered by a flannel nightcap, remained firmly on her pillow.

"I do, my dear." He took a deep breath. "It is about Lydia and Wickham. There has been no letter from him and she rarely mentions his name. I have begun to wonder if there is a serious breach."

"A serious breach, Mr. Bennet?" Mrs. Bennet leaned up on an elbow. "Why would you think there has been a breach between them?"

"He has sent nothing for her support, and when I spoke to her today about Mr. Milton, she stamped her foot and said Wickham was no husband to her." Mr. Bennet was quiet for a few seconds. "You must admit it is an unusual situation."

"It is, but did not we, in our early days together especially, experience difficult times?"

Mr. Bennet wisely took a moment to consider his response. "Those times were rare and short-lived, as I recall. I would never have wished you so far away from me as those two are from one another, no matter the cause of the discord."

"When you put it in such a way, I must admit to wondering myself what might have happened. They were always so happy."

Mr. Bennet pressed his point in a near-whisper. "I fear she will not willingly speak to me about the matter." He let a few moments pass. "She must be terribly worried by now. Do you not think she would naturally turn to you for solace?"

"It is too bad Christopher had to spoil her friendship with Mr. Milton. I thought him a charming man, and a suitable companion for her at a time when there is little to entertain her. I too enjoyed his company, especially after sitting with Kitty so long in the afternoons, when she tends to be the most irritable."

"Yes, it is too bad." He maintained an even tone. "However, his absence may cause her to think more about Wickham."

"I suppose so." Mrs. Bennet sounded doubtful. "But what can I do?"

"If we are to help them, I believe we must know what happened before she left Jamaica."

Mrs. Bennet sighed. "I will try my best, but Lydia can be more stubborn than her four sisters combined, as you well know."

"She can. But I have every faith in your ability to get her to confide in you." He leaned over to kiss his wife's cheek. "Good night, my dear."

"Good night, Mr. Bennet." Mrs. Bennet moved a little closer to him. "I am grateful you and I were never parted."

The next day Mrs. Bennet went to spend some time with Kitty, afterwards taking Lydia aside for a private conversation.

"She is very angry with Wickham," reported Mrs. Bennet to her husband later. "Apparently, he lost everything in what she calls a stupid venture. Lydia has left him forever…unless he returns from the war with America with a fortune in prize money."

"Wickham is a soldier again?"

"Yes, on a ship!" Mrs. Bennet leaned forward in her chair. "Once Lydia began to tell the tale, it was as a flood. She only learned about Wickham's misfortune when the merchants no longer allowed her credit in the shops. And you know how she likes to look her best."

Mr. Bennet huffed. "What did Wickham have to say for himself?"

"Since he is no longer welcome in England or in Jamaica, his plan was for her to sail to England while he sought his fortune, promising to send money for her passage to the Canadas once the war ended." Mrs. Bennet stopped to think. "I remember a novel we read aloud at Longbourn—this was after Lydia married Wickham—it was about a beautiful young heroine, much prone to fainting, who was kidnapped by a very wicked man she had steadfastly refused to marry." She clicked her tongue. "Do you recall the book? That awful man dragged her into the wilds of Canada and left her to perish!"

"I do recall the book. It was long, sometimes ridiculous, and the title was misleading."[55] Mr. Bennet reached over to pat her hand. "It was but a work of fiction, my dear. You need not be concerned about anything of the kind happening to Lydia."

---

[55] Mr. Bennet's opinion of Mary Brunton's *Self-Control* (published in 1811) is his own.

Chapter 32

Christopher Ashton had news for his father-in-law but did not start his letter immediately, instead holding the quill pen suspended as he decided upon the salutation. Even after more than five months of marriage he was intimidated by Mr. Bennet and did not feel comfortable addressing him as papa or father. In the end, he chose the usual way, no doubt hoping it would go unnoticed, or that Mr. Bennet would assume it was done unconsciously.

~*a letter from Christopher Ashton to Mr. Bennet*~

Hertford-street, London
December 1814

Dear Mr. Bennet,

As it happens, tales of George Wickham have reached members of my regiment, who confirm that he lost all his holdings in the West Indies on a risky venture and was forced to flee the country.

Due to the defeat of Napoleon there is growing hope of victory in the war with the American states, and our navy has been taking on additional men without a great deal of scrutiny, which would explain how Wickham managed to get aboard a warship.

According to my sources, the ship Wickham was assigned to was destined for battle weeks ago, which means there would have been little choice other than to put Lydia on a ship bound for England.[56]

The whereabouts of Wickham's ship are unknown, but it means nothing given the chaos of war. I will write to you without delay should I receive any other information.

Mary and I look forward to hearing the good news of a healthy mother and child. Please give our best to Kitty and Edward.

Sincerely,
C. Ashton

n.b. We leave for Pemberley tomorrow.

*   *   *

Locking the final travelling trunk, Molly threaded a long ribbon through the bow of the key and tied it round her neck.

"Now, what have I forgotten to tell you?" Hands on her hips, she surveyed the room while Anna continued with the dusting. "Mrs. Chadwick knows you'll be working in the sewing room, and that you need to practice ironing. You'll want to take a little time to study the plates in ladies' magazines, and each day practice plaiting hair—ask for volunteers below-stairs." She went to straighten a window curtain. "Why are you laughing?"

"Because you've said all this before, Molly." Anna set her feather duster aside. "And, you wrote a list and made me read it to you so you could be sure I knew the words."

"Well, it's the first time you'll be doing all this without me, isn't it?" Molly's dimples showed as she took a muslin furniture cover from the top of the stack and motioned for Anna to take the opposite end. As they worked, she remembered little things for

---

[56] Interestingly, at the time Christopher wrote this letter, delegates and commissioners from the two warring countries were at the time meeting in Belgium to discuss peace terms. This led to the signing of the Treaty of Ghent on 24 December 1814, officially ending the war (before Wickham's ship would join the fight). However, hostilities did not end until after the Battle of New Orleans, 8 January 1815, fought after the signing because word of the treaty had not reached all armies in the field.

the younger maid to remember to do while the Ashtons were away, and by the time they finished covering the furniture, Anna claimed she could repeat the entire list from memory.

"Don't you worry, Molly. I'll make certain Mrs. Ashton's things are aired, practice everything you've been teaching me, and keep trying to read from that big book by the lady who knows how to do all things the right way."[57]

Molly gave her a quick hug, then pulled a small brown-paper package from her apron pocket. "Don't open this until Christmas."

Before either could say more, there was a light knock and the housemaid stepped inside to tell them they had a visitor. "It's the one who came before, called Bernie...he brought a girl named Sarah with him," she added, clearly curious to know why.

"Sarah?" Anna's shocked eyes were on Molly. "She's the maid who left without any word."

"We'd better go see them." Molly gave one last tweak to a cover before following the housemaid out.

When they entered the receiving room, they saw a disheveled young woman. She moved toward Anna but stopped when she saw the other maid's expression.

"You left without a single word, Sarah," said Anna in a tight, hurt voice. "We were so worried, and you never even wrote to say you were safe."

Sarah's blush rose all the way to the roots of the auburn hair visible beneath her drab bonnet. "I'm so sorry."

"I found her this morning on my way to the blacksmith," said Bernie. "She was, er...well, I bought her an eel pie, and she told me how things were." He twisted the cap in his hands. "I might have done wrong, but I knew the lady of this house helped Anna and thought maybe she could help Sarah too."

Anna faced Molly. "This is Sarah Miller—one of the maids from our last house." She turned to eye their visitor narrowly. "Where did you go?"

Sarah seemed at a complete loss, perhaps about to cry, and Molly motioned to the table. "Let's sit down."

---

[57] Anna refers to *The Experienced English Housekeeper*, by Elizabeth Raffald, a book Mary gave to Molly when they resided at Darcy House, which Molly had used to practice reading and writing but now used for reference.

Half an hour later, much disturbed by what she had just been told, Molly went to speak with her mistress, approaching her with trepidation. "I'm sorry to interrupt your writing, madam."

Molly's halting manner was so unusual that Mary stood instantly and motioned to the upholstered chairs near the fire. "Come sit, take a breath, and tell me what has so obviously upset you."

Molly sat down, but remained perched at the edge of the chair as she relayed pertinent details about Anna's visitors, still waiting below-stairs.

"This girl Sarah is in a bad way, madam. There's a baby, and she's not married, and might have to go out on the street—" Molly stopped suddenly, her face several shades of red.

Mary nodded, asking gently, "Did she name the father?"

"No, madam. She would only say he is—or was—a gentleman. She's prettier than most, I'd say, and caught his attention when visiting a friend in service where Lord Harold lived."

Mary inhaled sharply. "You're certain about the house?"

"Yes, madam. She knows all about the secret passages because that's where she went the day she disappeared."

"Oh my." Mary rose and began to pace. "Did she say the age of the child?"

"Nearly two years, madam."

Mary stopped in her tracks. "Two...where does she live now?"

"She was turned out from her lodgings this very morning because she couldn't pay what was owed. She'd been living there since the baby was born, and stayed even after the gentleman stopped coming to see her. He always sent her money, but not for weeks now and she has only a few pence left to her name."

"It seems your friend Bernie may have rescued her and the child from a terrible fate." Mary rubbed her forehead. "I need to speak with the major about this. Meanwhile, please offer your guests tea, and, if you would, try to learn more about the baby's father."

"Yes, madam." Molly was in a brown study as she left the room.

*   *   *

"This maid, Sarah, was clear about the father being a gentleman at Harry's house?" Christopher folded his arms across his chest, then shook his head firmly. "For all we know, she could have been taken in by a footman. Did she offer a description of this man, or have you a guess as to his identity?"

"I shouldn't admit to my own thoughts, and she refused to say anything else about him."

"I have a person in mind. No man of sense would allow a friend or associate to keep a mistress in his house, but Harry could certainly do so. It would answer many questions, such as why his uncle disinherited him."

"But what are we to do about the poor girl?"

Christopher thought for a moment. "The situation begs for charity, but there is also a very good reason to befriend her, for she lived in two houses of particular interest to the foreign office."

His words made her sit straighter. "I hadn't thought of that. But where can she go?"

"There is a good chance our housekeeper may know a kind soul willing to take in a young widow and her child."

She smiled slowly. "You have thought of a story to protect Sarah's reputation?"

He bowed his head in acknowledgement. "Perhaps we should embellish a bit...there are many young widows seeking a new home, what with the two wars."

"Perhaps her husband could have been on a ship. A chaplain, or a curate, with little fortune." Mary drummed her fingers. "One hears a good deal about yellow fever."

"Sadly enough." Christopher rose and adjusted his waistcoat. "I'll speak with Mrs. Chadwick now. With any luck, we'll have a solution to this little problem in short order."

"And we might still leave tomorrow?"

"Definitely."

As it turned out, Christopher's confidence in Mrs. Chadwick was well-founded, and arrangements for Sarah and her son were in place well before the dinner bell rang.

In the end, it was Molly who learned the father's identity. When asked how she accomplished this, she shrugged her shoulders. "I told her the major is a very good man, madam, and that it was he and Colonel Fitzwilliam who arrested her former master and mistress. She was miserable in that house, more so than any of the other servants. In the end, she told me the father is Lord Harold and said he was always very kind to her."

"Until he left her to a terrible fate," said Mary.

Again, Molly shrugged. "She won't hear anything against him."

*   *   *

By the time the Ashton carriage crossed the Thames, the early morning fog was lifting and it seemed an ideal day for travel. Deeper in the countryside, however, heavy rain had led to deep ruts in the road and the Ashtons occasionally stepped out to walk while the coachman maneuvered through them.

Mary preferred being outside the carriage when there were difficulties, especially following an accident months earlier, in which the carriage she was in overturned.[58]

"This is quite an adventure," she said brightly, holding tight to Bonnie's lead. "Something I can use in my next novel."[59]

Christopher had experienced difficult conditions throughout his military career, and warned her that there might be many more delays before reaching Pemberley.

"Mr. Hartleton—pardon me, Perceval—did mention the unpredictability of winter travel." Just then, Mary stepped directly into a puddle and looked down at her mud-soaked boots. "Molly will not be happy about this."

With each new impassable stretch of road it seemed less likely they would reach their first-night destination, but conditions

---

[58] This occurred during the adventures described in *Mary, Mary, How Extraordinary*.

[59] Being dressed in a fur-lined cloak, her husband's ability to lift her over patches of wet ground, and a warming foot-box waiting for them once they were back inside the carriage might all have had something to do with her frame of mind.

improved and the final set of horses were fresh, allowing them to reach the gravel courtyard of the inn by the onset of dusk.

Inside the coaching inn, modest but reasonably clean, they were led up narrow stairs to their room by one of the innkeeper's three daughters. Molly had come ahead with the luggage and fresh sheets, and though Mary had asked her not to fuss ("one must anticipate discomfort after all"), she was in truth quite pleased to find her travelling bag unpacked, with a clean dress laid out upon the bed.

When Molly came with hot water, Mary apologized for the state of her clothes. "We walked a little today, as you can probably guess." She indicated her boots, which she had placed near the fire. "And I may have ruined those. Did you have any trouble along the way?"

"Very little, madam." Molly held up a dressing gown she had warmed by the fire. "Maybe the weight of the luggage helped."

Mary, sitting down in the only chair, was too tired to think about weight or mud. "There was a good deal of swaying, which made it difficult to read or sleep." She lifted a hand to cover a yawn. "If I weren't so hungry, I would go right to bed. I hope you will do the same once you've had your dinner."

"After I've put your things up to dry, madam, I promise I will." Molly held the hairbrush aloft. "Do you think I could take a tray to my room?"

"I'm certain they will oblige. Give the bell a pull, won't you?"

The same daughter responded to the summons. "I can bring your dinner just as soon as you like," she said to Molly. "It's only stew, bread, and cheese. But there's spiced cake."

Simply dressed in the warm travelling gown she would wear the next day, Mary joined Christopher in the small dining room. It was occupied by one other couple, a clergyman and his wife, on a journey to Wiltshire where their daughter was expecting their first grandchild.

They shared a table, conversing easily about the weather and the difficulties one should anticipate in December. The meal was simple, possibly made more appealing by candlelight, the cake especially good.

Back in their chamber, Christopher assisted with Mary's buttons, who then quickly donned her nightdress and slipped under the bed covers, for the wind was making itself felt through the thick stone walls.

After the candle was snuffed and he was beside her, she whispered, "Do you know what I wish for?"

"Other than another puppy?"

"I believe that wish will be granted." She turned to face him, threading her fingers through his. "But just now my wish is to know the truth about Harry...to close the chapter, so to speak."

"It is a wish I share but cannot say will be granted." For a short while they were quiet, until he said, "Do you prefer a male or female companion for Bonnie?"

"A girl. It is the way of my family, you know."

"So I have noticed."

"Although Elizabeth has a male child," said Mary reflectively.

"She and Darcy seem perfectly happy with him."

"When the time comes, I am determined to have one as well. Men have so much more freedom than women."

"Please do nothing specially for my sake. If we have daughters, they will be independent souls, just like their mother. I sometimes enjoy picturing our seven little Marys practicing pugilism, playing duets with their Aunt Georgiana, or perusing our library for books and pamphlets that challenge the world order."

"Did you say seven?" she whispered.

"Yes, but any number will do. And I will teach each of them to fence."

It was, perhaps, just as well that the wind muted the sound of their laughter.

Chapter 33

The coachman brought the carriage to a stop under the porte-cochère, as the cold rain that had plagued the Ashtons during the final portion of their journey continued unabated. The Darcys stepped out to greet their guests but ushered them inside without delay.

Georgiana examined Mary's cloak. "You're soaked through!"

"Not completely." Mary slipped out of the waterlogged pelisse. "We were obliged to walk at several points along the way."

"You must both get into dry clothes before you catch a chill," said Elizabeth. "Then we can sit by a warming fire and hear everything that has happened in the last few weeks." Smiling and full of plans, she led her sisters up the staircase.

Christopher, happily relinquishing his greatcoat to a waiting footman, turned to Darcy. "I feel redundant."

His brother-in-law nodded. "It may be hours before we're asked to join them. Shall we meet in my study after you change? I can provide spiced claret and a good fire while we look at the latest ciphered message from Richard. I was just beginning to translate it when you arrived."

Not much later, sitting with his feet upon the fender, a mug of warm wine in his hand, Christopher was reading the latest report from Vienna, his eyebrows raised. "So, Harry has been charged with high treason."

"He did leave a French novel with code-breaking information within its pages to be discovered by an enemy agent," said Darcy. "But isn't it possible he was under orders to do so from someone in our own government? After all, you were ordered to glean information from Caroline regarding Mr. Petersham."

Christopher frowned at the mention of the abhorrent man who was now living quite well in America. "If that is the case, any involvement will be denied and Harry forsaken."

"What will happen to him if he's found guilty?"

"Normally, he would go before the judge advocate general, but this could fall under the jurisdiction of the Vienna police. If so, we should be prepared for the worst, because of the Viennese agent who was found dead at the opening of the conference. They could easily decide it was Harry who did it."

"All this during a meeting of allied countries hoping for lasting peace." Darcy's lips formed a thin line. "I wish it was over and done."

The two lifted their mugs in a silent toast.

"There's more." Christopher leaned forward. "I believe we've discovered why Harry's uncle disinherited him." He told the tale of the serving maid who named Lord Harold as the father of her child.

"I did wonder if something like this was the cause of his uncle's actions." Darcy paused, frowning. "Where is this maid now?"

"I've placed her with a trustworthy couple who have been engaged in the past."

"Do you think the uncle knew this maid was dependent upon Harry when he disinherited him?"

"I can't say, but I'd rather think he didn't."

Darcy went to the sideboard and brought back the pitcher to refill their mugs. "Have you any *good* news?"

"Yes, but there's more of the bad, I'm afraid. Have you heard from Papa Bennet about Wickham?"

Darcy let go a great sigh, as he did when hearing any news of the man who had been a bane to his existence for years. "I did, very recently. We can compare notes, but I assume you were told, as was I, that he had to leave Jamaica for financial reasons, and no one can say exactly where he is now."

"I've started an inquiry with a naval officer I know well. If Wickham means to be found, we can find him. If not—" Christopher lifted his hands, palms upwards. "But let us move on to pleasanter things." He moved his feet to a cooler spot on the fender. "Hartleton chose a very good house, but it's too large for only a man and his dog."

"Carrick is a very *large* dog." Darcy grinned.

"Indeed." Christopher smiled in return. "Hartleton's given name is Perceval, by-the-bye. Both his parents were historians who enjoyed a companionable marriage. He hopes for the same, and recently admitted to having feelings for a young lady, one superior to him in rank, whom he is hesitant to approach."

"So, Elizabeth was right." Darcy rubbed his chin. "Did he name this fortunate lady?"

"Not exactly. He said only that she is a dedicated scholar and musician. Mary is half-fearful it is Caroline, who also plays well and assisted him in the library."

"Caroline?" Darcy harrumphed. "No. It is Georgiana."

Christopher nodded. "Just as I said to Mary."

"And, as I can find nothing to object to in Hartleton as a brother-in-law—which is all I will say about it now or you will accuse me of matchmaking—I think we should make certain he has a number of opportunities to propose." He rose, stretching. "After three days in a carriage you must be wanting exercise. Does a bout of fencing appeal to you? This weather makes riding impossible."

"It does." Christopher followed him out, waiting until he was sure they were alone in the corridor before sharing more news. "I had word from the waterguard about Lady Denham's nephew, Sir Edward, who we now know for certain is a smuggler and the former owner of the house you rented in Sanditon."

"Former?" Darcy stopped dead in his tracks. "Has the house been sold?"

"Seized by the bank for non-payment. Sir Edward was positively identified as one who boarded a boat late one night near Brighton. He was with a group of men, presumably French. Unfortunately, it is a very fast vessel, which outran the water guard."

"And the crates in the cave, was the nephew responsible?"

"Yes. His manservant is in custody and being very communicative. Denham is not only wanted for smuggling. He left gambling debts behind in at least four different watering places, including Brighton."

Darcy resumed his pace. "I cannot help but think the rent I paid for that house may have funded his escape, and other nefarious activities." He held the door to the fencing room open. "All we need do now is decide how much of this can be shared with Elizabeth and Georgiana."

Whilst Darcy and Christopher were discussing the misconduct of three men, one unfortunately their brother-in-law, Mary and Georgiana were with Elizabeth in her sitting room, talking of less serious things, including Mr. Hartleton's first name.

Mary, wrapped in the heavy blanket Elizabeth insisted upon, described Perceval's house, mostly for Elizabeth's benefit, along with the small changes he had made, and those he was considering.

"I hope he leaves the ballroom as it is," said Georgiana blithely. "Carrick will benefit from it in the winter months, as will her new companion, for Delilah has had her pups! Five of them, all healthy. Three females and two males, four of which are black and white."

"And the fifth?" asked Mary.

"Black, white, and tan."

"And which have you chosen for Perceval?"

"Georgiana and I think the tan would complement Carrick's coat," answered Elizabeth. "But he may need to decide soon, for there are others who wish to have a puppy from this litter, including Mr. Burnaby."

"Mr. Burnaby?" Mary shoved the blanket aside, making as if to rise. "Christopher and I had hoped—"

Elizabeth waved away her fears. "You and Christopher are to have first choice; the kennel master has been informed."

Much pleased, Mary replaced the blanket and patted her lap for Bonnie to come up. "Did you hear? You are to have a little sister!"

A sudden gust of rain and wind against the windows made Elizabeth shudder. "I wonder if we are to have a repetition of last winter's extreme cold?"

"Lucy's father believes it will be a warmer winter, but a cold spring," said Georgiana. "She tells me a green Christmas means a white Easter."

"I've heard that said before," said Elizabeth. "But it doesn't always come true," she added with false confidence. "Mamma used to sing an old song—do you remember it, Mary? *If Candlemas be fair and bright, come winter, have another flight—*"

"*If Candlemas brings clouds and rain, go winter,*" recited Mary, "*and come not again.*"

*   *   *

The Ashtons happened to reach their apartment at the same time, after she had gone with Georgiana to the kennels and he had been fencing with Darcy.

Mary's mind was still on the baby spaniels. "The pups are tiny, but their eyes are open and they've begun to walk. The kennel master allowed us to hold them, and said it is important at this stage to do so." She looked down at her dress and frowned. "Will you come with me to see them now? I could wait to change until we're back."

"I was hoping you would ask." He grinned. "I can be ready in a few minutes."

"You look quite handsome in your suit," she noted, flicking an imaginary speck from his sleeve.

Christopher pulled down on the snug fencing jacket. "You are most kind, but I don't think 'suit' is the right word."

"Perhaps I should say you look handsome in your white ensemble."

With a smirk he stepped inside his dressing room and Mary went to sit down, taking up the single volume of Mary Russell Mitford's *Narrative Poems on the Female Character.*

In a relatively short time Christopher stepped back into their chamber, buttoning his waistcoat.

"You were very fast."

"Benton already had the pitcher and basin on the washstand, and my clothes laid out." He glanced at the book in her hand. "Are you enjoying that?"

Mary sighed and marked the page before setting the volume aside. "She is a progressive thinker, but I cannot agree with her stance on Napoleon."

"Do you mind?" Christopher, having dismissed his valet, stood ready for her to tie his cravat, a skill Molly taught her.

As she formed the complicated arrangement of the neckcloth, she wondered aloud if they should ask the kennel master which puppy he thought most compatible with Bonnie.

"A fine idea," he said, lifting his chin higher as requested.

Mary finished and gently patted his chest. "Now you are presentable."

Chapter 34

Two days later, Elizabeth found Darcy seated behind the imposing desk made for his paternal grandfather. "What has you so distracted, Fitzwilliam?"

"Lizzy! I was just thinking about you." He refolded the letter in his hand and placed it aside. "Only a little matter of business...but you look as if you might have received bad news. Are Charles and Jane delayed?"

"No, I expect them any time now. Aunt Gardiner wrote to say they will not be coming to Derbyshire at all this winter, and Mamma's letter is full of increasing concern for Kitty."

"It must be a comfort to your sister to have your mother so close."

"I sincerely hope so." Elizabeth took the chair across from him. "But worry can't change the future, only the present." Her smile was determined.

"Then we shall move on to another topic." Darcy leaned back. "I wonder if we should plan anything special for Mr. Hartleton's arrival?"

"Perceval, you mean?"

He smiled in return. "'Tis an interesting name. Why didn't we consider it for our son?"

"We never went beyond the letter 'G' if I recall."

A light knock at the door interrupted them, followed by the Pemberley butler.

"You asked to be told when Mr. Bingley's carriage was seen by the gatekeeper, sir."

"Thank you, Simms. We'll be in the hall directly."

Darcy rose and came to Elizabeth's side. "Shall we?"

She was on her feet in an instant. "Do you know, I rather like hosting Christmas at Pemberley. There is an intangible quality to the atmosphere...anticipatory, in a kind of happy, hold your breath way. Do you feel it as well?"

Darcy stopped at the door to bring her hand to his lips. "I do, and have done since the day you crossed the threshold as my wife."

As usual, there was a cacophony of excited chatter when the Bingleys arrived, increased by the happy squeals of two children— one a bit unsteady on her feet, hand clasped firmly in her mother's, the other squirming in Darcy's arms.

Bingley handed his coat to a waiting footman, then blew on his hands. "It feels like snow."

"It is colder than yesterday, certainly," said Jane, eyeing her daughter, whose face wore a peculiar look. "I believe Eliza could do with a change."

Elizabeth immediately suggested they take the two young cousins to the nursery straightaway. "Georgiana, Mary, and Christopher are in the music room; we can meet there before dinner."

The two men nodded and watched their wives walk away at a pace faster than usual.

"Want to meet in the billiard room?" asked Darcy.

"Prepare yourself. I've been practicing." Bingley grinned and headed towards the east wing.

Later, in the dining room, Darcy waited until each of his guests had a cup of wassail before making a toast to the season.

Jane sipped the spiced cider before asking, "Who is to arrive next?"

"Hartleton," he responded.

"We are to call him by his first name now," Elizabeth reminded him with a smile.

Charles shook his head. "I never knew it until today. At school he was either Hartleton or Percy."

"I like Percy," she said. "He should be here in the next few days, and we have yet to hear from Louisa or Caroline."

"The last time Louisa wrote—and I must say she can be annoyingly vague—they were planning to remain in Bath for the healthful waters until spring."

"And Caroline?" asked Georgiana in a quiet voice.

"She, like her sister, does not like to divulge her plans," said Bingley with chagrin. "As much as one can gather from her letters, she remains in the abbey in company with the Burnabys."

Darcy was frowning. "Charles, what do you know about Neville Steele?"

"He has good manners, rides well, and has an abbey." Bingley thought for a moment. "But dancing is not his forte, and I think he may have offended Deidre Burnaby at Almack's because of it."

Elizabeth, seated at the opposite end of the table from Darcy, lifted a single brow at him before turning to Christopher. "Mary said you also visited the kennels today. Have you two made a choice?"

Christopher nodded. "The kennel master took the dam for a run, leaving us alone with the pups. Beforehand, he instructed us to take small backward steps away from them, and the female with the yellow ribbon went directly to Mary."

"She chose us," said his wife, beaming.

The remainder of dinner passed pleasantly, and when the dessert was brought in Bingley cleared his throat. "Tomorrow we are to have a special treat prepared by Jane's maid, who has taken a fancy to cookery. Our kind hosts in Milan shared the ingredients, but the portions and method are a closely kept secret. It is a sweet bread that has for hundreds of years been served at Christmas throughout the Italian states, perhaps as far back as the Roman Empire. There are many legends about how it came to be. If you wish to hear it, I can tell you the one relayed by our hosts." He paused, eyeing the others at the table, who appeared dazed. With a pleased look, he continued.

"There was a great banquet held hundreds of years ago on the eve of Christmas, given by a powerful man in Milan. Each course contained countless exquisite dishes, with no expense spared. A spectacular dessert was planned as *il miglior dolce di sempre*—" he beamed at Jane "—and it would have been a triumph had it not been for the pastry chef's overwhelming affection for a certain signorina. Imprudently, the chef stepped away from his ovens to meet her outside and the dessert was burned to a crisp. After such a feast, there was nothing left in the kitchen save a bit of fermenting dough, orange peelings, raisins, and sugar. Interestingly, it wasn't the pastry chef who prevailed, but a kitchen scullion named Toni, who quickly mixed those ingredients together, formed a loaf, and placed it in the oven. When presented, the new dessert was highly praised by the guests and the duke summoned the pastry chef. When asked what it was called, of course the chef did not know, so he said, '*Pane di Antonio*.' Eventually it was simply called *panettone*."

With that, Bingley grinned and made a flamboyant bow.

Following a single glass of port, Darcy, Bingley, and Christopher joined the ladies in the music room. Darcy, who had remained standing, said he would like to make an announcement.

A speech by Bingley was surprising enough, but one by Darcy even more so, and he had their full attention. "The sixteenth of this month marked the second-year anniversary of the happiest day of my life, and that of Charles. To mark the occasion we planned a skating party, knowing how well our wives enjoy the activity. Sadly, it has not been cold enough to freeze the pond, shallow as it is, and so we abandoned the plan for another, which will be revealed to you tomorrow afternoon."

"Mrs. Reynolds is certain the weather will turn much colder," said Elizabeth, "so we will undoubtedly be skating before long." She turned to Georgiana. "You mentioned finding a book with instructions for performing spins and jumps. It might be entertaining, and useful when the pond does freeze."[60]

Georgiana nodded. "The author included a piece called 'The Skater's March.' It's hideous." She grinned at Mary.

Darcy, sitting down, could not prevent a yawn. "It must be the change in weather," he said apologetically.

---

[60] Georgiana refers to *A Treatise on Skating* by Robert Jones, first published in 1772. (The Pemberley library contains the 1780 edition.)

"Or Gregory not sleeping through the night," suggested his wife kindly. "When are we to see your surprise?"

"I would like us to assemble in the main hall at one o'clock tomorrow, dressed for an outdoor excursion."

After discussing outerwear, especially what would be appropriate in the way of boots, they dispersed.

Upon reaching their chamber Elizabeth said, "There is a mysterious side to you, Fitzwilliam."

"Indeed."

Chapter 35

At one o'clock precisely, Elizabeth and Jane's secretive husbands stood before them in the hall, ready to reveal their plan.

"A few weeks ago," began Darcy, "I came across an article in the *Times* about an inventor who created artificial ice. Later, when it looked as if the pond wouldn't freeze in time, I wrote to him."

Bingley was smiling broadly. "He's been here for the last few days working on the pond, and now it is perfectly safe for skating!" He motioned towards the open door, from which could be seen a carriage and three horses standing at the ready. As expected there were questions, but the two men insisted they delay no longer.

The lane to the pond was hardened by the overnight frost, making it possible for them to move along at an even pace and they were soon at their destination. Placed along the edge was a large tent with rug-covered benches, skating shoes with attachable blades (single or double depending on skill), and a warming coal-filled brazier.

As they sat down on the benches and began to remove their boots, Darcy said the ice would be considered safe only that day. "The inventor can promise no more, as the process is still experimental."

Christopher had his own skates on by then and was helping Mary. "How was it done?"

By the application of chemical compounds to water, we were told," said Darcy. "Later sprinkled with talc to make the ice smoother."

"The formula is secret," said Bingley with a shake of his head, "but it wouldn't matter to me since I didn't understand a word of it."

"I thought it was snow on top," mused Elizabeth as her husband tied the laces on her skates.

He double checked the knots. "Are you pleased?"

"Very much so." She smiled, took his hand, and together they made their way slowly to the ice. "Has it been tested?"

Darcy nodded proudly. "Our steward is a skating enthusiast and has deemed it perfectly safe."

Jane and Bingley soon followed, well-matched for skill, both pink-cheeked and smiling as they moved along slowly to get familiar with the somewhat unusual surface.

Mary, unlike her sisters, had never taken to skating, and as such took firm hold of Christopher's arm. "If I fall, you must promise to bring me back to the tent—discreetly if possible."

"I promise." He moved carefully onto the ice, one arm round her waist. "Try not to look at your feet."

Just then, Georgiana, who had already skated to the far side of the pond, gracefully pushed off with one foot and spun in a circle three times.

Mary watched in wonder. "Oh my."

The skating party came to an end only by threat of darkness and as they changed back into their boots a good-natured contest ensued.

No one was surprised that it was Mary who had fallen most often, but she took it in good stead. "Had it not been for Christopher the number would be higher, though having done so with such great frequency I am no longer afraid of falling." Laughing, Bingley took second place, though he claimed most his falls were made while daring to imitate Georgiana. Jane, Elizabeth, Darcy, and Christopher each suffered a few falls but brushed themselves off and began again. Georgiana, who was voted the best and most daring, graciously credited the treatise.

There was more than an hour before the dinner bell when they returned to the house, and Georgiana used the opportunity to ask Mary if they could speak privately.

Upon reaching her apartment, she began without preamble. "Thanks to Caroline's recent efforts I fear Mr. Hartleton thinks me too far above him in station. Therefore, I have decided that some encouragement will be necessary if ever he is to approach me with a proposal of marriage."

Mary's expression was similar to her mother's upon learning that Mr. Darcy had proposed to Elizabeth. "You are serious?"

"I have never been more so in my life." Georgiana went to straighten a painting above the mantel, then faced her friend. "After so many childish infatuations, I now know what I want. I want what you, Jane, and Elizabeth have. A friend, a confidante, and a true companion for life. I want a husband whose company I will enjoy for all the years to come and who enjoys mine." Taking the chair across from Mary, her expression was earnest. "I am willing to fight for it."

Mary had to smile. "You suspect Caroline might return, unannounced, to continue her mischief-making?"

"She seems to do so with great regularity."

"Then we had best make plans now," said Mary, tapping her lip, "and I may have an idea."

Georgiana visibly relaxed. "What do you suggest?"

"It stems from how Jane and Charles finally came together— but I think a bit of history would be helpful." Mary shifted in her chair. "Elizabeth never faltered in her belief that Charles was madly in love with Jane from the very beginning of their acquaintance, and only his sisters' relentless interference made him question how Jane felt about *him*, and because of it he ultimately left Hertfordshire. Luckily, something made him think he might be wrong, and after months of absence from Netherfield he and your brother returned, ostensibly for the hunting, and together they called at Longbourn. My mother was unreserved in her welcome to Charles but hardly greeted your brother, for a reason we knew not at the time."

"But you know now?"

Mary nodded. "He said, in my mother's hearing, that he did not care to dance with Elizabeth at a Meryton assembly."

Georgiana nodded sagely. "Fitzwilliam admitted to behaving poorly when first meeting your family...this confession was during what I think of as the dark months, when he realized he had feelings for Elizabeth and no hope of reciprocation."

Despite the attraction of hearing another side to the story, Mary continued her tale. "I can picture us in the sitting room with the two wealthy gentlemen we thought would never return: Jane, Elizabeth, Kitty, Mamma, and me. Thankfully, Lydia had gone with Mr. Wickham to Newcastle, or it would have been even more uncomfortable. I offered to play, but Mamma said no, and so we sat there." She shook her head. "Kitty's unfortunate giggling resulted in the hiccups. Luckily, Charles seemed not to notice. Instead, he responded politely to my mother's unending questions whilst sneaking glances at Jane, who was unable to act contrary to her nature and only smiled shyly in return.

"Eventually, the visit came to an end, but Mamma insisted the two men come to dinner the next day...an invitation they could hardly refuse, but as it came to pass it was a pleasant evening, with only a few friends." She blinked. "But I have gone back too far."

Georgiana shook her head fiercely. "It is a good story."

"Well, that evening, Jane and Charles talked with each other companionably, with much smiling, as they always did prior to his departure from Netherfield so many months earlier." Mary stared blankly at the wall. "But there was something else I was thinking of...oh yes, an incident I witnessed, when, during coffee, Elizabeth made a notable effort to speak to Mr. Darcy—a man we all thought she reviled."

"And?"

"Charles called on his own the next morning. It was really too early for visitors, and I was the only one dressed. When I offered to go downstairs, Mamma absolutely forbade it and took the maid to Jane's room. I suppose Papa entertained Mr. Bingley for the twenty minutes or so it took the others to make themselves presentable and we went down together.

"Papa excused himself and Mamma talked a good deal about the dinner the evening before, until without warning she said it was the time I regularly practice on the pianoforte. It wasn't, but

I felt it wise not to argue and left the room." Mary paused. "From here, all my information is secondhand."

"It is perfectly acceptable," said Georgiana, leaning forward.

"After I left, Mamma reportedly made an excuse for Kitty to leave the room as well, but Kitty did not comprehend her meaning and said something foolish. Ignoring her, Mamma soon stepped out on a flimsy pretext and within seconds re-opened the door to tell Kitty she was needed elsewhere. Elizabeth was next to be summoned and departed with reluctance, leaving Jane and Charles alone." Mary looked up with a smile. "Jane refused to tell all of what happened in our absence, but Charles admitted his feelings for her and asked her to be his bride. She accepted, and he went to speak with Papa!"

"I have heard a similar tale from Elizabeth, but how nice to gain your perspective." Georgiana studied her friend. "I gather you think Mr. Hartleton could be encouraged if something of the kind is orchestrated here?"

"Yes, and I may know the perfect stage." Mary leaned forward to whisper her plan.

Chapter 36

In the wake of an uncommonly restful night's sleep, Darcy opened his eyes to find a note from Elizabeth on the empty pillow next to his. He read the few lines, leaned back with a contented sigh, and after a few minutes of silent contemplation rang for his valet.

A short while later he found the breakfast room empty, save for a footman with a silver tray containing a single letter.

"Has everyone breakfasted?" asked Darcy.

The footman nodded. "Mrs. Darcy asked me to say you could find her either in her morning room or the nursery, sir."

"Thank you, John," said Darcy, going to the sideboard to fill a plate.

A short while later he entered the morning room. "Lizzy, I have here a letter from Cousin Anne, who has news you will want to hear." He glanced at her desk. "But I am interrupting."

"Not at all." Elizabeth placed her pen in the stand and rolled a blotter over the recent lines. "I was writing to Aunt Gardiner to ask after the children. What has Anne to say?"

He sat in the chair beside her writing desk. "She has legally signed half her allowance over to Richard!"

"Can you repeat that?"

With a smile Darcy did so. "*And* she asked Aunt Catherine to name him as the heir to Rosings."

"My word! And what did your aunt say?"

"She will agree to the proposal only if she can choose his wife." He caught Elizabeth's eye. "My aunt has attempted interference of this kind before."

"I recall it well, *and* that she failed miserably."

He took her hand and lifted it to his lips. "It seems yours is not the only family with a propensity for matchmaking; Anne's mission is now to prove Miss Diana Leigh—conveniently also their guest in Scotland—worthy of the role."

"I like Diana enormously. She has all the qualities I could desire for Richard, but for Anne to sacrifice so much—"

"Since she married Chandler her true nature has blossomed, and to her this is simply the right thing to do." Darcy rubbed his chin. "My aunt cannot be blind to the advantages of having the heir to Rosings in residence, whereas Scotland is now Anne's home."

"Where will they hold the wedding, I wonder?" Elizabeth's eyes were dancing. "I have never been to Scotland."

The twenty-second of December brought colder temperatures, heavy snow, and Mr. Hartleton to Pemberley.

Darcy and Elizabeth met their guest in the great hall, where he was apologizing to the footman for the snow-covered state of his greatcoat and winter accoutrement.

After greeting his hosts, he explained, "I travelled on horseback and was forced to stop late yesterday afternoon at a nearby coaching inn, where Lord Exeter and Mrs. Beasely had also taken refuge." He reached into his waistcoat pocket. "I have a message from him."

Darcy read quickly, then said to Elizabeth, "Their coach is damaged, and it is unsafe for them to continue on to Brighton, where they planned to be married."

"Married?" Elizabeth's eyes were wide. "Is it safe to send a carriage or sledge to bring them here?"

Mr. Hartleton nodded. "With an experienced driver, certainly. It would be a great kindness to them; the inn is not at all comfortable. Last night's wind cut through the outer walls. Once the fire in my chamber was reduced to embers, no amount of blankets could keep me warm."

"I will see to the matter now," said Darcy, who strode down the corridor leading to his steward's office.

Watching him go, Elizabeth took Mr. Hartleton's arm. "I hope you come prepared to play for us this evening."

"I've been practicing, but would prefer a duet at first. I can take the secondo part—nothing too fast or difficult, such as the pieces Miss Bingley plays."

"I hope you will not be too disappointed." Had Elizabeth allowed it, her expression might have contained guile. "It seems Miss Bingley does not plan to join us."

Judging by his obvious relief, Mr. Hartleton did not mind at all. "Where are the Ashtons, and Miss Darcy?"

"In the music room. Just as you arrived, Christopher was playing something to help calm Gregory, who slept poorly last night."[61] She stopped at the bottom of the stairs. "Please join them when you're ready. I need to speak with Mrs. Reynolds about Lord Exeter and Mrs. Beasely, whom I have never had the pleasure of meeting."

"She is a charming lady, Mrs. Darcy."

"Elizabeth, please."

"Elizabeth." He smiled. "Then you must call me Percy."

*   *   *

Without doubt, Georgiana was in her best looks that evening. Gold threads woven into her gown and the ribbons entwined in her swept-up hair glinted almost magically in the candlelight.

At dinner, there was never a moment without general conversation amongst them, beginning with Darcy's request for more information about Mr. Hartleton's house.

"Certainly," he said, "but I would ask Miss Darcy and Mrs. Ashton to share their impressions as well, for when we saw it together they showed a greater appreciation for detail."

Georgiana and Mary happily obliged, laughing when their memories failed them in regard to the location of rooms or the furnishings therein.

When it seemed the topic was exhausted, Mr. Hartleton, seated by Elizabeth's design at Georgiana's side, said quietly,

---

[61] Christopher played the Telemann violin fantasias, which he knew his wife liked very well. Not long after he began, Gregory, cradled in his father's arms, had fallen into a deep sleep. (It is possible Darcy's eyes were closed as well.)

"When you are next in town I hope you will assist me in making decisions about what to change and what to keep."

Mary, seated on his left, could not help overhearing but made no sign of it other than a slight lifting of the brows when she caught Christopher's eye.

After-dinner port was a custom generally dismissed by Darcy, but with the addition of Bingley and Hartleton the gentlemen remained in the dining room for a short while after the ladies departed.

When they entered the music room Georgiana was at the pianoforte and they sat down to listen, Mr. Hartleton never taking his eyes from her.

"Was that an arrangement from *The Magic Flute*?" asked Christopher when the final chord faded away.

"It is a sonata by Maestro Clementi, but he once told me Herr Mozart borrowed something from it for his opera, which he took as a compliment."[62]

When asked what they would like to hear next, Elizabeth suggested a duet composed by Herr Haydn, and as Mary had lent her score to Mr. Hartleton it was he who joined Georgiana at the keyboard. After the first few measures they forgot any nervousness and played to the end without pause, each taking a bow at the insistence of the others.

When Elizabeth asked Georgiana and Mr. Hartleton if they would care to prepare another duet for the following day, he suggested Miss Darcy assist him in the selection, and while the couple started going through the contents of the music cabinet the three Bennet sisters shared a secretive glance which they mistakenly thought their husbands did not see.

Quite pleased with herself, Elizabeth approached Christopher. "Would you care to oblige us?"

"I would be happy to, if Mary would accompany me."

His wife looked doubtful. "I haven't practiced much this week, so must beg your forbearance."

---

[62] The piece Georgiana played was the first movement of Clementi's Sonata in B-flat, Op. 24 no. 2.

Christopher found the music in a stack he had been adding to since their arrival and brought it to Mary at the keyboard. The two soon agreed upon a tempo and she began to play the introduction.

When the movement came to an end, there was a moment of silence before the others applauded. "I should like to hear something you *did* rehearse, for I cannot imagine it sounding any better," said Jane.

"Christopher is remarkably easy to follow," insisted Mary.

Jane and Charles were asked to perform next, choosing a well-known carol, after which Elizabeth joined her at the keyboard for a second one. Bingley sang the melody and Darcy the harmony, and when the piece ended with a faster tempo than at the beginning, they were all laughing.

The next of Elizabeth's plans was a game of whist, and they proceeded to the two tables. Seated at one were the Darcys and Bingleys; at the other the Ashtons, Georgiana, and Mr. Hartleton.

By mutual agreement, talk during the shuffle and deal was to be allowed, and after taking the final trick in the first hand, Mr. Hartleton returned to the topic of Aunt Matlock's letters from Vienna, which had been touched upon at dinner. "Given the number of composers active there, a concert could be held nearly every night."

Georgiana, as dealer, began to shuffle. "Aunt Matlock has twice had the pleasure of seeing Beethoven's works performed. Once, when the composer himself conducted." She dealt the cards face down, turning up the last.

Mary peeked over her cards to see it. "Molly would say we will have something to celebrate." She used her head to indicate the upturned card. "She claims the ten of hearts is good luck."

"I could use it myself," commented Elizabeth from the other table as she rearranged her cards.

During the next hand Georgiana spoke again. "I envy those who visit faraway places, not only to see statues and buildings, but the people who live so differently than we do here. What an education it would be."

"It's the aim of the grand tour," said Christopher.

"My father always hoped I would go, and take Georgiana with me," said Darcy.

Elizabeth sent him a teasing glance. "You approve of women touring the continent?"

"In the company of a husband or brother." He smiled at her.

"It is a fancy of mine to follow Evelyn's path on the tour," said Mr. Hartleton, looking up from his cards. "But not until it is truly safe."

"Charles hopes to return to the Italian states soon." Jane frowned ever so slightly as Elizabeth placed a trump over her card.

"I agree with Percy," said Christopher with a touch of apology. "It is best to wait until order on the continent is restored."

"If you don't mind," said Bingley good-naturedly, "we have but two hands left, and Jane and I need the points."

Collectively, their attention returned to the game. At the close of the match the number of mother-of-pearl counters was compared and the Darcy and Hartleton teams declared winners.

"Am I the only one who is hungry?" asked Elizabeth. "I keep thinking of the dessert tray; none of us did justice to Harriet's panettone."

"It is the fault of your chef," said Bingley, resting a hand on the center of his waistcoat. "Jane's maid has also learned to make ricciarelli quite well, and struffoli. I had to bribe the cook at our villa to make them."

"She did not care much for foreigners," remarked Jane.

"Darcy," said Bingley, "why not ring for a tray?"

Their host bowed his head, rose without a word, and went to the bellpull. "While we wait, would anyone care for port or sherry?"

While Darcy and Bingley went to the sideboard, Elizabeth led the others to the sitting area. "Percy, as a student of history, do you think there are signs of another severe winter?"

"I cannot foresee the weather, but I sincerely hope there is never another ice fair," he answered. "Last winter was so cold that even with the advent of unexpected warm spells no one thought the ice on the Thames would melt so suddenly, but carriages, horses, and people fell through it. Such a disaster also happened in Evelyn's time."

"As my tutors so often warned," said Christopher, "the lessons of history are too often ignored."

"This is serious talk before bedtime," declared Bingley. "I would much rather talk of skating." He faced Elizabeth. "Tell us, what have you planned for tomorrow?"

"Perhaps you could each make a suggestion," she answered, just as the dessert tray was brought in. Various ideas were put forth, but they eventually decided to wait and see what the morrow would bring.

As they were leaving the room, Mary held Georgiana back until the others were out of hearing. "Shall we go forward with our plan tomorrow?"

Georgiana did not hesitate. "Yes."

Chapter 37

Prior to retiring the night before, it was Mary who suggested they meet again for breakfast, and while snow and wind beat against the windows, the Ashtons, Bingleys, Darcys, Georgiana, and Mr. Hartleton enjoyed the comfort of a warming fire and food kept warm in chafing dishes on the sideboard.

Darcy noted his wife's concern as she looked outside. "Our coachman will not take undo risk, Lizzy. Exeter and Mrs. Beasely will arrive safely, even if the exact day is yet uncertain."

Near the end of breakfast Georgiana and Mary made plans to visit the kennels. "Though we'll need to change our shoes and get a warm shawl first," said the latter, turning to Mr. Hartleton. "Would you care to join us?"

"I would like to but have a bit of business before I will be free." He thought for a moment. "If delayed too long, I will meet you there."

That plan made, Mary caught Christopher's eye. "Will you be joining us?"

"I hope so," replied her husband, "but have a matter of business to attend to."

"We may go on ahead, if you don't mind," said Mary.

"Not at all," said Christopher, setting his napkin aside. "I'll see to the business now."

The three of them made their excuses and left the room.

Mr. Hartleton waited a full minute before approaching Darcy at the coffee service to ask if he might speak with him privately.

His host nodded, glancing over at Elizabeth, who was so immersed in her conversation with Jane (regarding a possible wedding service at Pemberley before Christmas). As he did not care to interrupt, he tipped his head to the side and led the way out.

Nearly a quarter-hour passed before Bingley, absorbed in an older edition of the newspaper, became aware that he was the only gentleman remaining. "Where has Darcy gone?"

The two sisters had moved on to the subject of Kitty and Lydia, and Elizabeth answered with some surprise. "He is not here?"

"No, and neither are Ashton and Hartleton." Bingley pulled at his waistcoat and left the room in what might have been a huff.

*   *   *

Mr. Hartleton was dressed to go outside when Georgiana and Mary came across him on their way to the west entrance. Together they stepped outside, where new snow was falling on the recently swept walkway, and Mr. Hartleton offered an arm to each of them. "Remind me again, Mrs. Ashton—Mary—which pup have you chosen?"

"She is black and white, with a yellow ribbon. Do you have a preference for male or female?"

"The kennel master wants to observe how Carrick behaves near the pups before making his recommendation, but any would do." Mr. Hartleton turned to Georgiana. "Which have you chosen to remain at Pemberley, Miss Darcy?"

Georgiana had been given that privilege by Darcy at her own request. "It will be easier after you choose." She smiled softly.

They had reached the building and were soon in the whelping room, on their knees in the clean straw, arms spread wide.

After watching a great many antics performed by the little spaniels, Mary stood and brushed off her skirt. "If you don't mind, I'll see what's keeping Christopher."

Seemingly unaware that they had been left alone, Mr. Hartleton carefully handed the female with the green ribbon to Georgiana, who lowered her head and held the pup close to her chest.

About the same time Georgiana, Mary, and Mr. Hartleton went out together, Darcy re-entered the breakfast room to find only Elizabeth and Jane still there. "Where is Charles?"

"He asked the same of you earlier." Elizabeth studied his face. "Has something happened? You look...bemused." She tipped her head to the side. "No, not bemused, but perhaps secretly pleased about something."

"Nothing has happened yet, Mrs. Darcy."

"Yet," she repeated, her gaze suspicious. She turned to her sister. "Jane, shall we go and find your husband?"

The three set off, and after being directed to the library found Bingley standing before a section of shelves on the east wall, discarded volumes on the floor nearby. He had just read the spine of another book and was setting it atop the pile. "Ah, there you are," he said, as if expecting them.

Darcy was perplexed. "Why are you in the library?"

"I'm looking for a book, of course." Bingley took another volume from the shelf. "One recommended by Hartleton. He said it was funny. And very popular."

"What is the title?" asked Jane.

"*The Miseries of Human Life*."

"It doesn't sound funny." Darcy went to a different section. "Do you know the author's name?"

"Bradford?" Bingley thought. "Or was it Bentley?"[63]

Elizabeth pointed to the gallery above. "I believe authors beginning with 'B' are up there."

"Are you looking for another skating treatise?" asked Mary cheekily, having just entered the room along with Christopher.

"Charles is hoping to find a humorous book recommended by Percy." Elizabeth peered at her sister and brother-in-law. "Where have you two been?"

"With the puppies," said Mary, all innocence. "May I help?"

After being given the name of the author, she and Elizabeth ascended the spiral stairs and found the work without difficulty.

---

[63] The name Mr. Bingley is trying to remember is Beresford (James).

Bingley accepted the two volumes with gratitude.[64] "Hartleton and I thought it would be fun to read together."

"You found *The Miseries of Human Life*?"

All those in the library turned at the sound of Mr. Hartleton's voice. To their astonishment, Georgiana was standing within a hair's breadth of him, her hand clasped in his.

"Georgiana?" Elizabeth was staring at her sister-in-law, who was beaming.

"Percy and I are to be married!"

Hugs and hand clasps followed the announcement, after which Elizabeth insisted that the newly engaged couple tell how it came about. "The last I knew we were all at breakfast."

"Which is when Percy asked if we could speak privately," admitted Darcy. "We went to my study, where he asked for my blessing." He smiled fondly at his sister. "It wasn't a complete surprise, for there was some idea of your mutual affection. I gave my permission to ask for your hand in marriage without reserve and believed you would accept him." He paused. "But I could not have guessed it would happen within the hour."

"It was the puppy," said Georgiana, still smiling. "Mr. Hartleton realized how fond I was of the one destined to be his, and said he could not bear to take it from me." She turned to her fiancé. "Then he said he wished he and I would never have to part."

Jane was first to ask a question on many minds. "When do you want to have the wedding?"

"I had hoped to take Miss Darcy to Sussex in the spring," said Percy, adding boldly, "as my wife."

"But I think we must wait until Aunt Catherine returns from Scotland," said Georgiana shyly.

"Must we?" Elizabeth stepped forward to embrace the two of them. "What a Christmas this is going to be!"

A cough at the door preceded Simms, who entered with a tray. Mary was so confident of her plan's outcome that she had asked Christopher to speak with the butler about a proper way to celebrate.

---

[64] The first edition was published as one volume in 1806; the second edition was in two volumes later that same year.

While the others were engaged in talk about future events, Simms took the opportunity to quietly inform Darcy that the Pemberley sledge had returned.

"Lord Exeter and Mrs. Beasely have arrived?"

"Excuse me, sir, but it is Miss Bingley and her maid who have come. Fearing a chill, Mrs. Reynolds had Miss Bingley taken to her apartment with orders to be put to bed."

"Thank you, Simms." While talking with his butler, Darcy had kept his back to the party.

Concerned, Elizabeth came to his side. "Has something happened with the sledge, Fitzwilliam?"

Darcy repeated what Simms had told him.

"But what of Lord Exeter and Mrs. Beasely?"

"What has happened, Lizzy?" Jane too had come to see if anything was amiss.

After Elizabeth whispered the news, Jane motioned to her husband to join them, then told him what little they knew. "Charles, you must speak with Caroline."

"I'll see her now." He gave Darcy a telling look and went on his errand.

*　*　*

Charles Bingley was a man of even temper, except of late when his sister Caroline was involved. Her very recent bids for the attention of Hartleton, Steele, and even Culpepper had not gone unnoticed by him, and with grim determination he knocked on the door of her chamber inside the opulent apartment she was given when a guest at Pemberley.

"Oh, Charles," she said wanly, quilts tucked up to her chin. "How kind of you to see me. You've no idea what I suffered."

Experience had taught him not to be affected by her apparently weakened state. "Caroline, how did you come to be in the sledge Darcy sent for Exeter and his future bride?" He stood at the end of the bed, hands on hips. "What have you done?"

"I have done nothing!" Tears would not come, but she managed a quivering lip. "It is something about which I can never speak, except to say I was dreadfully mistaken, and cleverly manipulated!" She hid her face in one of the down pillows, her shoulders shaking.

Bingley drew a chair closer to her and sat, his countenance reflecting his skepticism. "Caroline, you must tell me something about what has occurred, especially in regard to Lord Exeter. I will not leave until then."

"You would treat me so, after the peril I faced?"

"I would." He crossed his arms. "Tell me."

Pouting, she sat up a little, keeping firm hold of the quilt. "There, on the table—" she indicated the location "—you will find a letter to Darcy, which will, I imagine, satisfy your curiosity." Her chin quivered. "As I am weary beyond imagination, I will say nothing other than Mr. Steele and Mr. Culpeper are never to be mentioned in my presence again!" With that, she flipped over and pulled the blankets over her head.

Bingley's eyes narrowed, but he no doubt knew any further effort would be wasted. Therefore, after saying he hoped a rest would revive her spirits, he took the letter and left the room.

Back in the library, he repeated what Caroline had said to him. "I can't imagine what Steele or Culpepper could have done."

Jane suggested she might need only a little time to pass before confessing what had upset her.

"I have no patience for waiting," said Elizabeth. "Might there be something helpful in the letter?" She eyed the folded packet in Darcy's hand.

~a letter from R. Exeter to F. Darcy~

the George
23 December 1814

Dear Darcy,

I write in haste to thank you for your kind invitation and the use of your sledge.

Mrs. Beasely and I were poised to leave this place less than half an hour ago when to our great shock Miss Bingley stumbled down from the mail coach that had just arrived. Her nerves were in a terrible state and we felt compelled to offer her a place in your sledge. We had already done the same for another stranded traveller, the Reverend Mr. Collins, who reminded me he is Mrs. Darcy's cousin and heir to her father's estate. However, Miss Bingley believes that her condition makes travelling with anyone other than her maid a risk to her health, and she will be the one to deliver this note (your kind coachman is at this moment waiting for me to finish writing).

There is no other conveyance here and the accommodation is some of the worst I have experienced. Might we impose upon you further by asking you to send the sledge back for us?

Needless to say, I am in your debt.

Gratefully,

R.E.

n.b. Mr. Collins learned about our thwarted plans to marry in Brighton and has offered to perform the service, though he insists upon it being held at Pemberley!

Darcy observed Jane patting Elizabeth's hand, as if to calm her. "Lizzy, would you care to write a brief response to Exeter and Mrs. Beasely?"

Elizabeth rose instantly and went to a nearby table with writing materials. "It will take but a minute."

"Then I'll see to arrangements for the sledge. I think we can expect the Exeter party sometime tomorrow afternoon." He bowed to the newly engaged couple. "My sincere congratulations to you both."

"Percy," said Christopher after Darcy had gone, "as you are soon to be our brother-in-law, it is best we get to know your game. Shall we have a go at billiards?"

The three gentlemen eyed their ladies to see if there was any objection, but there was not.

"One second," said Elizabeth, signing her note with a flourish. "Would you bring this to Darcy straightaway?"

"Certainly. Darcy can make a fourth, but we'd best make haste." Bingley grinned, pocketed the note, motioned for the others to follow, and on the way out grabbed both volumes of *The Miseries of Human Life*.

Elizabeth rubbed her forehead. "How many will be at dinner this evening?"

Jane counted on her fingers. "Nine, unless Caroline decides to take a tray in her room."

"Tomorrow there will be five more if Mrs. Annesley and Mrs. Halifax arrive as planned," said Elizabeth, smiling at Jane and Mary while pointing discreetly towards the young Miss Darcy, who was standing before the poetry section, humming as she ran her fingers along the spines.

"It's time I was in the nursery," said Jane quietly.

"I'll go with you," said Elizabeth, "But first I need to speak with Mrs. Reynolds."

Their departure roused Georgiana, who finally chose Scott's *The Lady of the Lake*. Joining Mary at the window, she said, "The snow seems to be lightening."

"It does," said Mary, turning to face her dear friend. "And it also appears that my plan was a complete success."

"It happened so naturally." Georgiana's face was radiant. "And now I have begun to think of a wedding, which I dared not do before...might I ask Molly if she would like to design the gown?"

"Let's go now. She and Lucy will be in the sewing room— they're making something special for Gregory and Eliza to wear on Christmas morning."

Chapter 38

On Christmas Eve morning all but one of the guests joined their hosts in the large dining room for breakfast. The scent of fresh pine boughs and burning cedar logs filled the room, while red holly berries and shining silver caught the eye.

At each place setting was a goblet for the moscato wine Bingley had brought from the Beechwood House cellar. "My acquirer tells me it is a tradition in some Italian states at Christmastime, no matter the hour," he said proudly as the wine was poured.

Just as he was about to make a toast there was sudden silence, for Miss Bingley had entered the room. Her presence was a surprise to all, since she had purportedly been too ill to leave her bed the day before. At that moment, however, she looked perfectly healthy, dressed in a flattering velvet gown with long sleeves and lace edging.

Bingley waited only until she was seated at the table and her goblet filled before lifting his own to wish the betrothed couple joy.

Her lips forming a thin line, Miss Bingley demanded, "What has happened?"

"Hartleton—er, Percy—and Georgiana are to be married," said Bingley, a sudden flush rising from his neck upwards.

"I see." Miss Bingley's joy at the news was restrained at best. "And when is the wedding to be? And where are you to reside?" Her demure glance rested upon Mr. Hartleton.

Her happiness impossible to diminish, Georgiana said with a smile, "Percy has a house in town, close to Mary and Christopher, and to Darcy House."

"How fortunate," murmured Miss Bingley and sipped her wine.

"Caroline," said Jane carefully, "we expect Lord Exeter today." She glanced out the window to see lightly falling snow. "He brings with him his future bride."

"Bride?" Miss Bingley's face froze. "Do you refer to Mrs. Beasely?"

"The very one," said Mary. "We met her briefly in York."

"And I in Bath," responded Caroline coolly.

At that moment Simms entered, approaching Darcy with a salver upon which lay a gentleman's calling card.

The master of Pemberley turned the card over with a slight frown. "Charles, there is someone here who wishes to speak with us privately."

The two made their excuses, and Darcy said nothing more until they were far enough away to avoid being overheard. "Culpepper is here."

"Culpepper? Do you think he—"

"Has come to propose?" interrupted Darcy, shrugging. "I can think of no other explanation."

Bingley huffed. "Unless Steele has sent him to recover the ancestral pearls Caroline stole from his abbey."

The two shared a glance, but all signs of amusement were gone when they reached the sitting room closest to the main hall.

Inside, they found Mr. Culpepper still in his greatcoat, pacing, hands behind his back. Wasting no time, he said Mr. Steele had sent him, but not because of missing pearls. "He was thrown by his horse and is badly injured."

"Will he recover?" asked Bingley, genuinely concerned.

"The physician is optimistic. In fact, Neville is expected to be up and around again in little time, which is extremely lucky," said Mr. Culpepper. "He was planning to ask Miss Bingley to be his wife, but something he said—and I am not party to it—caused her to fly from him. He wishes her to return, if she will do so willingly, and thought to use this accident as impetus."

"You wish us to exaggerate his condition?" asked Bingley.

"If any exaggeration is necessary, it will fall to me," said Culpepper. "Also, should you fear impropriety, I have brought with me Steele's former nanny—an elderly retainer, who is with Darcy's housekeeper while we wait."

"It seems Steele expected his plan to succeed," remarked Bingley with a touch of irony. "I'll speak with Caroline now and will return with her answer."

The two men left their visitor, one to speak with his sister, the other to approach a servant about hot tea for his guest.

Bingley duly went to relay the tale to his sister in the breakfast room, who cried out in dismay. "Dear, dear Neville! I must go to him!" She rose with quiet grace, lifting a delicate handkerchief to her eyes. "Charles, please tell Mr. Culpepper I will be with him directly."

When the door was closed behind her, Elizabeth mused aloud, "What could possibly have made Caroline run away from the abbey, and in such weather?"

"Maybe Steele took her by the elbows, just as Exeter did," said Bingley drily.

"Charles!" exclaimed Jane.

"One never knows with Caroline, does one?" Smiling jauntily, he went to the door. "I must tell Culpepper she will join him on the return journey."

"I hesitate to suggest it," said Jane, "but should you not accompany her?"

"No. I've had Culpepper and Steele investigated—a brother's prerogative—and there was nothing objectionable about either, should they wish to tie themselves to my sister. Also, Culpepper brought Steele's former nanny for propriety's sake, but, as Caroline is forever reminding me, she is of age with a fortune and a mind of her own." As there was no arguing this, he went on his errand.

A short interval passed before Simms entered once more with the salver, this time approaching Elizabeth who looked a little fearful as she opened the note. "It's from Mrs. Annesley. She and Mrs. Halifax are at the inn at Beckville, where a fellow guest is having difficulty with a birth." She squinted at the page. "They will remain there until the mother and baby are safe."

"How fortunate Mrs. Halifax was there," said Georgiana.

Jane nodded. "She was an ideal midwife for Gregory's birth. The mother could not be in better hands."

"Even Mamma was impressed." Elizabeth eyed the mantel clock. "I should speak with Mrs. Reynolds about a basket for Caroline's journey, and about Mrs. Annesley and her sister—I'm sure she would want to send something to Beckville for them."

Shortly after Elizabeth left on her errand, Bingley brought Mr. Culpepper back with him.

"I must apologize for interrupting your meal," said the latter, "and for the element of subterfuge in this affair. Neville thought it might be the only way to convince Miss Bingley to come to him."

"An effective measure," replied Darcy, motioning towards an empty place at the table. "Though I must admit to some curiosity as to the reason for Miss Bingley's flight from the abbey."

"I know very little, I'm afraid. The night before it happened, Miss Burnaby was at the pianoforte. Neville was partnering Miss Bingley in whist, and Mrs. Burnaby and I played against them. Mr. Burnaby had his pipe near the fire." Mr. Culpepper used his knife to crack the top of an egg. "It was a late night, and I didn't come down until after noon the next day. By then Neville had gone after Miss Bingley but had to be brought back after being thrown by his horse." He looked up. "That is when he asked me to go after her."

The others looked at Mr. Bingley, who shrugged. "They must have had a quarrel before retiring, though about what?"

Mr. Culpepper shook his head. "Everything seemed perfectly civil to me."

At this point Jane, Mary, and Georgiana looked at one another with some amount of skepticism.

Had anyone doubted Miss Bingley's affection for the suffering Mr. Steele, they would have been convinced of it when she appeared in the main hall after only half an hour had gone by, looking very stylish in her fur-lined pelisse.

"I will write from the abbey." Her eyes were bright with unshed tears as she bid the others farewell. "I hope it is with good news."

"As do I," said her brother and shook Culpepper's hand firmly. "Safe journey."

Chapter 39

The Darcys' butler appeared with a special delivery letter addressed to Mrs. Darcy just as she was leaving the housekeeper's sitting room.

"Thank you, Simms." Elizabeth glanced at the script on the outside, easily recognized as her mother's. "Has Miss Bingley come down yet?"

"Miss Bingley and the gentleman were impatient to go, madam. She could not wait for the other guests, but Mr. Darcy and Mr. Bingley were there to wish them farewell."

Excused from that duty, Elizabeth went happily on her way. The distance from Mrs. Reynold's room below-stairs to the sewing room two floors above made for an invigorating walk, and by the time she entered the sewing room her sisters and Georgiana were comparing elements in the dress designs Molly had laid out for them.

Georgiana had three different artist renderings in hand when she caught sight of her sister-in-law. "I don't know how I will ever choose."

"It is a pretty problem," said Elizabeth, studying them in turn.

"Molly can create a unique gown using any of the features you choose," said Mary, who was taking a second look at one she found particularly eye-catching.

Jane was looking over her shoulder. "The fur trimming would be lovely at a winter wedding."

Elizabeth listened to them talk about the possibility, a soft smile playing about her lips as she went near the window to read her letter.

~~~~~

~a letter from Mrs. Bennet to Elizabeth Darcy~

Garden Place, York

Dear Lizzy,

I write with good news! Kitty is safely delivered of a son, with a shock of red hair, and a set of lungs Mr. Bennet says puts him in mind of each of his daughters. Indeed, when this child cries, it is difficult to find a place in the house where he cannot be heard. Kitty was certain the baby was going to be a girl; consequently, she and Edward have not yet agreed upon a name.

The weather has become severe. It is not unusual this far north, your papa likes to remind me, but it makes it difficult to walk safely outdoors. Sedan chairs are no better, for the attendants don't always keep their feet, with terrible consequences for those inside the box. I have taken to shuffling along the cobbles, hands out in front of me, when we venture out, and have asked Mr. Bennet to do the same. (He does take care, even if he won't follow my example in this.)

I must thank you for sending the lovely fur-lined pelisses and boots. Lydia looks charming, as will Kitty when she is up and about. For now, she has the beautiful garment resting on a chair in her chamber where she can admire it.

Now I must get back to her, for the baby is crying again.

Your mamma,
C. Bennet

n.b. There is news of Mr. Wickham, which I will leave for your father. His note is enclosed. Also, have you any news from the Lucases? I do not like to be away from Longbourn, as you know, and worry that in our absence Mr. and Mrs. Collins will bother our servants, as they have in the past.

~ ~ ~

~a letter from Mr. Bennet to F. Darcy~

Grape-street, York

Dear Fitzwilliam,

Mrs. Bennet had the pleasure of telling Kitty and Edward's good news, so it falls to me to share the latest about Wickham.

We have been informed that Wickham's ship departing from the West Indies was attacked by an American frigate soon after it sailed. All aboard were taken prisoner except Wickham and one other sailor, who jumped into the sea to escape capture. Amazingly, they were rescued by a British ship sailing to Upper Canada to join the fight.

Apparently, Wickham suffered injuries during the escape, as well as deleterious effects from the immersion and is reportedly under the care of a navy surgeon.

When I informed her of the situation, Lydia grew hysterical and insisted she must go to him without delay. That Wickham was aboard a ship at war made no impression upon her, nor did the impossibility of being given a berth on any ship sailing to the Americas at this time. She simply will not listen to reason. You know as well as I how headstrong she is, and the only recourse is to keep any money out of her reach.

Therefore, when she writes to ask her sisters for help, which she will assuredly do, her pleas must be ignored and requests for funds refused absolutely. Be especially clear to Charles about this, for Jane has always been the most soft-hearted of my daughters.

Wishing you all the best of the season,
R. Bennet

Darcy was thoughtful as he tucked the letter inside his waistcoat pocket. Before seeking Elizabeth and the others to share the news, however, he used a letter-knife to open a packet from his London bank. As he perused the contents, a look of pleasure erased the deep frown formed when reading the latest news about Wickham.

Chapter 40

Mid-afternoon on Christmas Eve, the Pemberley coachman brought the sledge to a gentle stop under the west portico. Darcy and Elizabeth were waiting at the open door to greet their guests but only Lord Exeter and Mrs. Beasely stepped down from the vehicle, with no sign of Mr. Collins.

Once inside, fur coats and winter accoutrement taken away, Lord Exeter answered the unspoken question. "The good reverend received a letter yesterday from his father-in-law, Sir Lucas, with an urgent request for him to return to Hertfordshire immediately. As the wheel to his carriage was by then repaired, he was free to go."

"Did Mr. Collins give you the reason for the urgency?" Elizabeth's eyes met Darcy's. "Charlotte is expecting."

Lord Exeter shook his head. "I believe he was too unsettled to think clearly." He took Mrs. Beasely's hand. "But, before he left he insisted upon holding the marriage ceremony at the inn. 'So as not to darken the doors of Pemberley' is how he put it, if I remember correctly." Sheer happiness was evident in his smile. "May I present my wife, Lady Exeter?"

After offering sincere congratulations to the newlyweds, Elizabeth, with buoyant spirits, asked if Lord and Lady Exeter would like to join them for the lighting of the Yule-log. "And if so, what is your pleasure before then?"

"Do call us Amelia and Reggie," insisted Lady Exeter. "And a change of clothes is all we desire."

An hour or so later all were assembled in the main hall to watch Darcy place the charred remains of the previous year's log amidst the glowing kindling, and after persistent application of a bellows the new log was alight.

From there they went to the ballroom, for Elizabeth had made plans to entertain the children as well as the adults. Upon entry they saw the new litter at play inside a makeshift enclosure. The ladies knelt upon the straw-covered floor, disregarding their finery, and no one prevented young master Darcy from crawling about, squealing with pleasure, dressed as he was in the waistcoat specially made to match his father's. Nor did they stop young Eliza Bingley, adorned in a miniature version of her mother's gown, from following him.

Standing at the edge of the enclosure with Darcy, Lord Exeter watched as his wife held a puppy lovingly to her chest. "Are they all spoken for?"

"Only two of the females." Just then one tired pup plumped down upon the tip of Darcy's shoe and he bent low to pick it up. "Should you like to have one, the siblings could meet when in town...a vision I find quite pleasing."

Lord Exeter's gratitude was clear. "And what may I give in return? I will not accept so great a prize without recompense."

Darcy gently placed the pup on the straw, then faced his guest. "Something in the way of information, perhaps, regarding a titled gentleman who has acted shamelessly and is said to frequent the seaside."

"I will do what I can." Lord Exeter managed to hide his curiosity as the two shook hands.

*   *   *

Later, after a pleasant interval in the music room, with duets on various instruments, along with the singing of carols, Bingley took Lord Exeter aside. "I would like to know how you came to offer the sledge to my sister Caroline, an extremely generous gesture, since it meant you had to spend another night at the George." He looked pointedly at the other. "I was forced to stay there once myself."

"She was too upset to explain anything, though we were shocked and very concerned to see her step down from a mail coach, and at the George of all places. She could have switched coaches and stopped at Lambton, where it would have been a relatively simple matter for you to collect her." Lord Exeter took a sip of mulled wine. "I managed to speak with the coachman. Apparently, your sister had not enough funds to go even as far as the George, where the driver was obliged to force her and the maid to disembark."

"You paid their fare." Bingley instinctively reached into his waistcoat pocket. "I have nothing on me either at this moment," he said with good humor, "but I must insist upon reimbursing you."

Lord Exeter shook his head vehemently, his attention momentarily on his wife, who was laughing with Elizabeth and Jane. "Please don't. I should never have allowed your sister to get the impression—"

"Caroline has a long habit of assuming things," said Bingley firmly. "I can only hope she has found what she is looking for in Mr. Steele."

The two men solemnly clinked their mugs and went to join the others.

*   *   *

Sitting on the edge of their bed, with only light from the fire to see, Darcy was brushing Elizabeth's hair. "I have something for you, Lizzy." He set aside the brush and took a small wooden box adorned by an imperfectly tied ribbon from his dressing-gown pocket. "I was planning to give this to you tomorrow, but find I cannot wait."

He watched as she pulled the ribbon, opened the box, and removed the folded sheet inside. She adjusted the angle to the dim light and read what had earlier given her husband great pleasure.

"You have purchased the villa in Sanditon?"

"I have. And in your name."

*   *   *

Meanwhile, Mary and Christopher were already in their bed.

"Did you enjoy the day?" he whispered.

"It was magical. Kitty and the baby are safe. Georgiana and Percy are so very happy, and you can clearly see that Amelia and Reggie are as well. Dinner was excellent, with good conversation, and lanterns outside the windows so we could see the snow falling." She rested her head against his chest. "And the music! I never laughed so hard as when you and Reggie played the violin duet. It was a perfect day."

"It was, but I did wonder if its perfection was aided by the absence of a certain cousin."

"It may have helped. Plus, we might assume Mr. Steele and Caroline will come to an agreement, but no one thought to ask Mr. Culpepper about Deidre."

"We'll know more when the Burnabys visit."

"If Deidre *is* engaged, she will tell us before she crosses the threshold."

Just then the first chime of the great long-clock echoed through the corridors and up the stairway, and the two silently counted to the last one.

"It is our first Christmas together," whispered Mary's husband.

Epilogue

Christmas morning brought a fresh coating of snow, making pleasant views from every window at Pemberley and enhancing the festive atmosphere.

In the afternoon a host of letters were delivered, having been delayed by various causes (not only the weather). As most of the contents were of interest to the Darcys and to their guests, they gathered in the family sitting room to hear the news from various quarters. One letter in particular was read over many times and discussed at length.

~~~

~a letter from Lady Matlock to Georgiana Darcy~

Vienna
30 November 1814

Dearest Georgiana,

We hear many reports of seized mail, so I cannot guess how many days or weeks will pass before you read this.

Recently, your uncle and I were abed with a virulent influenza that spread in Vienna like a wildfire during the whole of November. Thankfully, we recovered in time to attend a performance of Beethoven's works, including an orchestral piece he himself conducted. (This concert was originally to occur earlier in the month but was postponed because of the influenza.)

The composer's state of mind is a recurrent topic; his dress and manner is sadly often compared to that of an inebriate. Not only this, but last night we saw good reason to suspect the poor man suffers from an extreme loss of hearing, something we had thought to be only a cruel rumour spread by his critics (of which there are many), for one could see he was not always in time with the orchestra.

The concert began with a work written to celebrate Wellington's victory in Spain (the Battle of Vitoria), replete with drumrolls, trumpet fanfares, and even cannon fire (your uncle and I nearly jumped out of our seats). Woven into the music were familiar tunes, which seemed to please the audience, but the orchestra was quite loud at times and to me the experience was a bit unnerving. His seventh symphony, by comparison, was mesmerizing. Despite the stature of the composer, there was a disappointingly small representation of the English in attendance by way of protest of something or other. Even music cannot be free from politics, it seems.

Another person of interest in Vienna, to you and to Mary especially, is Herr Jacob Grimm, one of the writers of the Kinder- und Hausmärchen.[65] He is here to represent the landgraviate of Hesse-Cassel and is often seen in cafés, quill-pen in hand.

There is news about one of our friends, which I did not wish for you to learn from another source. Lady Castlereagh broke the news to me last evening in the most clandestine manner (society here is plagued with spies and false friends). Sadly, it is a question of involvement with enemy spies. I do not like to cast aspersions on one of our own acquaintance, but my belief in his innocence is diminishing. I have seen him with a duchess on his arm one evening, utterly captivated, a countess on the second, and a princess on the third. To make matters even worse, he reportedly visits the niece of one of the French representatives. What may happen in the end we cannot say, but we must all be strong.

Your uncle does not know when we can return to England, for the business of this Congress takes second place to extravagant dinners, musical evenings, and outings that include hundreds. It seems political pacts are made as frequently—perhaps more—in social situations as they are in official

---

[65] Lady Matlock refers to the collection of fairy tales written by Jacob and Wilhelm Grimm. When teaching their maids to read, Mary and Georgiana often read the stories aloud to them. Later, Molly and Lucy read them to one another to practice their lessons, and also to an eager audience below-stairs.

meetings. Therefore, we follow a strict regimen of attending a round of weekly salons (Lady Castlereagh's is held each Tuesday). I have come to see that diplomacy is not a game for the weak-minded.

By-the-bye, amongst other events for the opening week of the Congress was a concert conducted by Signor Salieri, the Hofkapellmeister in Vienna. Sadly, the audience was not long in the anteroom prior to the concert before an interesting tale began to spread: the kapellmeister himself is supposed to have poisoned the young Herr Mozart! Apparently, there was speculation about this at the time of his death, and there are still those who maintain there was a murder.

No doubt it is all nonsense, since Salieri continues to hold prominence in the Viennese court, and even more especially because Mozart's widow engaged him to teach their son. I will say, however, that after hearing various works by Beethoven, those of Salieri pale by comparison.

I will write again when there is more to tell.

Your loving,
Aunt M

~~~~~

~a ciphered letter from Colonel Fitzwilliam to Major Ashton~

Vienna, 8 December 1814

After weeks of trying to convince Lord C and our allies, I have achieved nothing. No one wants to believe there is danger of N's escape or of his raising an army. They are drunk with victory and want no talk of the possibility of another war.

Of note: the codes we discovered in the book H brought to the café were ours. It is still possible he was acting on orders by our government; if not, he is a fool. As of yesterday, he is imprisoned and allowed no visitors.

There is little for me to do here any longer, except escort countesses from countries other than my own to dull events and even duller soirées, all of which last until dawn. I've asked Lord C to approve my return to England and feel confident he will.

Tell Darcy I will go first to visit our cousin Anne in Scotland. There is a young lady residing with her that I have finally decided to ask to be my wife, despite the limits of my fortune.

I hope you have better luck finding someone in England who will consider the evidence we've collected and who can do something to prevent the return of the Monster.

R. F.

~⌣~⌣~

~a letter from Caroline Bingley to her brother Charles~

Christmas Day
Audley Abbey, Kent

Dearest Charles,

You cannot imagine how fearful I was on the return journey to the abbey. I had to force myself to stay awake, thinking if I did so, it would keep Steele alive until I reached him.

The coachman was fearless, and we reached Kent before dark. Not taking the time to remove my pelisse, I ordered the footman to take me to his chamber, where the physician was in attendance.

How shocking it was to see Steele in his weakened state! His countenance was almost grey. I ordered tea immediately, and made as if to remain with him, when the physician (odious and autocratic) insisted I was only to greet him in a soft voice and take my leave without fuss. He also told me not to allow dear Steele to see my tears, which I know would have revived him.

Luckily, I was able to sleep through the night, for otherwise I would not have had the fortitude to face the next day. Late in the morning, after taking a tray in my rooms, I was allowed to see the patient.

When I entered his chamber, a handsomely decorated, comfortable room with a good fire, he was sitting up, and smiled the instant he perceived me (I made certain the physician was made aware of this). In the three following visits I have seen him begin to walk, and we are to take a turn indoors tomorrow. (The physician maintains that his near-miraculous recovery was expected and refuses to credit my return to the abbey.)

I expect to write with far more interesting news in the very near future.

Yours,
Caroline

~a letter from Mr. Bennet to his sons-in-law~

Grape-street, York

Dear Fitzwilliam, Charles, and Christopher,

There is time only to write to you about the latest of Lydia's foolish actions. On the very eve of the day I wrote to say not to send her any money for fear she would use it to attempt to reach Wickham, she was seen entering a carriage with the blinds drawn, driven by a man of the same stature as Mr. Blanchard, his features cleverly disguised, as reported by one of Darnell's maids. Fearing the worst, I alerted the authorities, and need not describe the hysterics Mrs. Bennet suffered.

Luck was with us, for the coach was stopped on the road outside York, and it was indeed Mr. Blanchard in the driver's box, now in the hands of the authorities and awaiting charges for unpaid debts, etc.

Lydia insists that he only desired to help her get to her husband, but his motive had to be money, for he had knowledge about Darcy's wealth from Wickham. The man is a scoundrel, but I am grateful for one thing at least. He had a female companion inside the carriage with Lydia (he claimed this was for propriety's sake), and as he was understood to be the driver, attempting to escape his creditors, I believe we are not going to be the subject of gossip.

Meanwhile, my foolish daughter is back with Kitty and Edward. She seems contrite and promises not to act foolishly in the future, but I don't trust her. Should she apply to you, send her no money or anything she can sell.

Fondly,
E. Bennet

⌒⌣⌢

~a ciphered letter from Paul Hilliard to Colonel Fitzwilliam~

December 1814

I write this in near-darkness, hoping you recognize the cipher as one you and I used recently.

As you know, I am suspected of serious misdeeds, but am guilty of one only. A child of mine was born out of wedlock. The mother was in service, a young maid named Sarah Miller, who I shamefully used to gain information about her employer, a smuggler whose house was down from my own on Grosvenor-street (I was charged with reporting his movements at the time).

I grew to love Sarah and spoke with my uncle about offering marriage. He threatened to disinherit me and I allowed him to convince me of the folly, then disinherited me anyway.

I've always found a way to support Sarah and the child, and found a decent place for her to live, but since leaving for Vienna I've heard nothing from the woman I engaged to watch over her, and fear the money I sent was never received. I beg you to see that Sarah is safe and in funds, for in my current situation I can do nothing to help her. I enclose a letter to my banker, who is in my confidence. Please arrange the mother and child's continued support through him. If ever I am allowed to return to England, I will do right by her, I swear. Knowing you think ill of me, as will those I call friends, is painful, but I make no excuses.

Another accusation I face is spying for the French. This was done under the orders of one who is very high in our government. All my actions were sanctioned by this man, whom we both know quite well. He cannot admit as much, which I knew when I took the assignment. I trust you will share this secret inside the family circle in the hopes it may bring some peace of mind, especially to your mother, who has always been so kind to me.

I can't say where I am going, only that I escaped with the help of another, whose name I cannot reveal. But, should any letters come from Mr. Paul Hilliard in future, you will know they are from your friend H.

~~~

~a ciphered dispatch from Captain Wensford,
Preventative Waterguard, to Major Ashton~

23 December 1814

To Major Ashton:
The smuggling lugger, Pegasus, was found near the halfway
point in the channel along a direct line to Gravelines in France.
There are no signs of those who were aboard, but it does seem
an attempt was made to scuttle the boat. They may have met
another, which took the men aboard and continued to France,
but there is no evidence.
Pursuit of the Frenchmen and the titled smuggler has been
discontinued until we have more information.
Compliments of the season to you and your family,
D. Wensford

⌒◡◡⌒

~a note from Elizabeth Darcy to Anne and James Chandler~

Pemberley
24 December 1814

Dear Anne and James,

We have happy news: Georgiana is to marry Mr. Hartleton, or Percy, as we now call him. They are a perfect match.

The question of when the wedding might take place was raised, as you can imagine, but the necessity of Aunt Catherine's presence was put forward as something of a barrier.

Therefore, I write to you with a proposal, without the knowledge of anyone else, mind, which is that we come to you in Scotland as soon as the weather allows, where we suspect another happy couple will be announcing their engagement. I am very fond of double weddings, as you know, but will be satisfied with the one if necessary.

Should you think this a good plan, I would have you propose it in a letter to my darling sister-in-law and her fiancé. This would make it their choice, and they would not feel obliged because the idea was mine. You are, I believe, not a fan of long engagements, and might agree with me that it would be cruel to delay this happy couple's union unnecessarily.

I look forward to your response, and wish you all the joys of the season.

Affectionately,
E. Darcy

The adventures will continue...

ACKNOWLEDGEMENTS

Without the works of Jane Austen, any book of this kind would not be possible. I am deeply indebted to her. I also owe a big thank you to all those who enjoy my books and look forward to the next, and especially to those who write such nice things about them.

Very Special - I rarely give five stars, but IMO this variation is deserving of the highest rating. Number four of the excellent "Mary, Mary" series, combines mystery, romance, and relationships for a very satisfying read. New and old characters, an evil plot, and persons and places of historic interest mesh together for a book that I could not put down. I hope the author will soon publish Volume Two!

Excellent story - I love this series- Lots of action, clean, and funny. If you like Mary Bennet, as I do, this is a must read.
Looking forward to volume 2.

Couldn't put it down!! - I love this series, one of my favorites.

Fun interesting read - The author continues to write intriguing books about Mary Bennet and her adventures with Georgiana Darcy. Almost all of the wonderful characters from Austen's P&P are included.

Delightful Read - The adventures of the new and improved Mary Bennet continue. Well written with a light playful tone and lots of regency era detail both fashion and historical.

Mayhem, mystery, murder, and Mary Bennet Ashton - What a fitting sequel to the other Mary Bennet stories.... This one was great.

Great Regency Details - ...the author really hit her stride with this one! The plot is involved and engaging...relationship between the servants is rich and complex also...a good read with a cup of tea.

"5.0 out of 5 stars Dear SM Klassen, Thank You! My sister discovered this book series and we have both fallen in love with the characters adapted from P&P! We were so excited to see the new book finally released and I look forward to more! There's such a sweetness in reading how domestic our favorite couples are and I love how the author incorporates history into the story. My classical musical tastes have grown thanks to the author!"

"5.0 out of 5 stars Great read with historical embellishments. I am so looking forward to sequels!
She has brought life to these characters. I hope she plans on several more books."

"5.0 out of 5 stars Excellent Regency period research and a whopping good story! I just finished binge-reading all six of S. M. Klassen's *Adventures of Miss Mary Bennet*, and I'm sorry I only have the prequel, *What Really Happened Before Mr. Darcy's Wedding* left to read. Klassen has promised the adventure will continue, so I will try to wait patiently. I read these books on Kindle Unlimited, but I plan to purchase them. I wish there was a box set."

"The books were like being immersed in the Regency period with our favorite *Pride and Prejudice* characters and some great new ones Klassen created. The author's research into the period was phenomenal. I only started reading the footnotes in volume 5 so will now go back and read the footnotes in the first four volumes. They are a treat not to be missed. I went on several exploratory rabbit trails from things mentioned in the footnotes.
For example, if you wonder how well Georgiana Darcy played the piano, listen on You Tube to the piece mentioned in footnote 70 in *Villainy in Vienna*...Clementi's *Piano Sonata Opus 24, No. 2*.
Or look up the fascinating account of the Horse Shoe Brewery Flood in London in October, 1814. Or download the actual diary of John Evelyn mentioned several times in the last two books of the series.
In my opinion, these books are must reads for those who love reading well-researched fiction set in the regency period and/or want to read a delightful imagining of what happens to Jane Austen's characters after *Pride and Prejudice* ends."

"I enjoyed reading this story, the latest in the series. As with all the previous ones, the range of characters and their lives has been very interesting, and, to my mind, fit very nicely as a follow on to *Pride and Prejudice*. Can't say the same for any others I have read! Look forward to the next one."

Readers' Reviews for *Spies, Lies, & Shoo-Fly Pie*
A Jamey Knight Mystery, by Shelly Mcdunn

"This is a fun and engaging read with surprising plot twists. There are real people portrayed here that maneuver through dangerous circumstances acting honorably or despicably, but with actual behavioral expectations. No cartoonish excess here."

"The locations are beautifully depicted...the Mennonite community shines through with love and warmth."

"Ms. McDunn has created a wonderful first installment on hopefully a series that will develop the stories of these very interesting characters. We will want to know where they are going."

"Just finished reading *Spies, Lies & Shoo-fly Pie*. What a wonderfully refreshing read. This book is fast paced and exciting. Very difficult to put down. Interesting tie in from Philadelphia to The Florida Keys to PA Dutch Amish Country. I am so looking forward to the next Jamey Knight Mystery. Congratulations to Shelly McDunn on her very successful Jamey mystery. Simply, a most enjoyable read."

"I want to know lots more about these characters. For a job well done, congrats Ms. McDunn."

"Great read!! Kept my attention from the start until the end. Looking forward to this author's next book. Would definitely recommend this."

About *City of Dread*, a 1919 New Orleans Mystery
by Shelly McDunn (aka S.M. Klassen)

New Orleans, March 1919:

An axe murderer terrorized the populace.

While excursion boats alive with jazz music floated up and down
the Mississippi River, ships returned wounded and traumatized soldiers
from the Great War.

Tens of millions had died from a pandemic flu.

Prohibition was on the horizon.

Mardi Gras was cancelled for the second year running.

Reviews for Shelly McDunn's *City of Dread*:

"Ms McDunn, in her compelling saga of early twentieth century New
Orleans, brings the colorful and complicated city to life.
Her thorough research enhances the dark ambience, and the characters
are vividly drawn. It is my first novel by Ms McDunn and I am
anxiously awaiting her next."

"A great New Orleans story: murder, music, disease, and
vivid historical setting!"

A continuation of *City of Dread*, by Shelly McDunn

Detective Jimmy O'Connor and Lillette Montague are embroiled in another mystery, this time on the shore of Lake Superior in northern Wisconsin, where the vagaries of nature and of an enormous lake are not the only threat.

The two first met in the Spring of 1919 in Shelly McDunn's historical mystery *City of Dread*, where an axe murderer terrorized New Orleans during the pandemic flu's second wave and Jimmy was investigating a French Quarter murder.

It is now March 1950 and World War II is in the rearview mirror. Optimistic Americans are buying new houses, new cars, and new appliances, though television sets are a luxury few can afford. Radio is still king and stations are broadcasting a new style of music— soon to be widely known as rock 'n' roll—popular with a growing young audience.

Meanwhile, Sinatra's fifth solo album just came out, Hitchcock's *Stage Fright* with Marlene Dietrich was released, and Elvis is on the horizon.

www.ingramcontent.com/pod-product-compliance
Lightning Source LLC
Chambersburg PA
CBHW031716170626
46808CB00005B/1766